PASKAGANKEE

ALLAN LEVERONE

Prologue

November 16, 1691

Stephen Ames shivered in the gathering darkness, a bone-chilling cold seeping into his body as he awaited the girl's arrival.

The wind whispered and moaned through the bare trees like a restless spirit, and he wondered for the hundredth time whether the bronzed young Abnaki woman would come as she had promised. And if she did, whether she would bring the child—*his* child—whose existence he had discovered just yesterday, to meet him for the first time.

Stephen was a member of a small group of missionaries traveling up and down the eastern seaboard of this strange, wild country. Their mission was to convert the native savages to Christianity and thus save their souls. It was a difficult and dangerous life, nearly impossible at times, but it could also be incredibly rewarding on those all-too-rare occasions when they were able to make a positive impact and save a savage from eternal damnation.

It was also a lonely job. The dedicated band of missionaries numbered roughly a dozen, though the exact total was constantly in flux. Men joined the group as others dropped out, unable to handle the stressful life, difficult travel and unrelenting physical danger.

The last time the missionaries had passed through this remote area, working with a tribe located in a small village hard by the Penobscot River, Stephen had met a Native girl, roughly his own age of twenty-two. He had taken refuge in her arms in a temporary respite from the constant, crushing loneliness.

That was two years ago. The missionary group spent a couple of months working with the savages and then moved on, converting no one but making what they felt were potential inroads with a small number of the tribe's more influential members. Unfortunately, the chief, an older savage with a deeply lined face and decades-old battle scars crisscrossing his body, had been unreceptive to the well-intentioned band of young men. He had eventually dropped all pretense of civility and forced the missionaries to move on under threat of violence.

Now back in the area, the group had decided to pay another visit to the village to see if the situation with the tribe had changed. Perhaps the old chief had died and a new warrior had taken his place, one more receptive to the missionaries' soul-saving message.

It was during this visit two days ago that Stephen spied the Native girl walking through the village and signaled her. She had run to him, recognizing him immediately, and in a curious combination of English, French, and the strange Abnaki native tongue, the two had worked out a time and place to meet the following night. She seemed nervous and anxious, glancing around furtively as if fearful of being observed. After finalizing their plans, the girl had turned and disappeared, melting into the bustle of activity in the village.

During their meeting last night, Stephen received the shock of his young life when he learned he was the father of a now eighteen-month-old baby girl. The Native woman had become pregnant by him and given birth long after the band of missionaries had been forced to move on.

She related to Stephen how the tribal elders had nearly sacrificed her when they learned she was with child, but that she had been spared due to her age and the fact that the baby's father had left the area, never to return. The child would be raised as a Native in the customs and traditions of the Abnaki.

Shocked by this development, Stephen had known immediately he could never allow his child to be raised as an Abnaki. The heathen savages continued to refuse Christianity's saving grace, and Stephen was well aware of what that meant for his child: an eternity spent burning in the fires of hell. Although he had never met his baby, although he had only known for twenty-four hours that he even *had* a baby, Stephen realized he must do something to give his little daughter the opportunity to experience eternal salvation.

So he had begged the Native girl for a chance to meet the infant, to see his child if only once, and she reluctantly agreed. Her acceptance of his request came as a surprise to Stephen, as she was clearly experiencing tremendous pressure from the village elders. The savages had never expected to see the band of traveling missionaries again, and it was obvious the Native girl was worried that either she or her baby would suffer some horrible fate thanks to their return.

All the more reason, Stephen thought, *to rescue my child from this primitive land, to give her a chance at a real life back in England.*

His parents would be shocked by the baby's arrival, but he knew they could provide proper care for her until Stephen could return home following his missionary calling. Once home, he would raise her himself.

Now it was the night of the promised meeting and the young mother was late. He feared she'd changed her mind about allowing him to see his baby. Perhaps the elders had somehow learned of the meeting and were even now holding her captive, preventing her from leaving the village.

He hoped not. Such an occurrence would make a bad situation even worse.

But at last the girl padded down the narrow hunting path. She moved silently, gliding through the forest as did all the Natives, moving in a way the missionaries could not match, even years after their arrival in the Great North Woods.

The girl had fastened a sling made of thick animal fur onto her back, and buried deep inside it, swaddled in still more fur to ensure warmth, was Stephen's child. The baby was fast asleep. The Native girl was reluctant to lift her out of the sling due to the cold, but through the top of all that fur Stephen glimpsed a luxurious mane of jet-black hair.

The Native girl's body was shaking, but Stephen knew it was not due to the temperature. If there was one thing the missionaries had learned about the savages in this strange land, it was that they were experts at keeping warm in the winter. They survived in this harsh and unforgiving climate by utilizing skills perfected over the course of centuries.

No, this was something else. The girl was clearly terrified. Stephen was glad he had decided to rescue his child from the clutches of these primitive savages; it seemed obvious to him that something was very wrong.

As he admired the baby—or at least the top of her head— the remainder of the close-knit band of traveling missionaries appeared as planned. They stepped out from behind trees, bushes and rocks and surrounded Stephen and the Native girl.

The baby's mother turned a full three hundred sixty degrees. She looked from face to face in terror, understanding instantly that she had been tricked, that this late-night meeting was much more than she had agreed to.

Stephen hated having to ambush the frightened Native girl, but he could think of no other way to wrest his baby away from clutches of the Abnaki savages.

After discovering he was a father, he had requested council with the rest of the group. The men were unanimously shocked to learn Stephen had lain with the savage two years ago, but they agreed action must be taken to remove the innocent child from the heathens, that she be provided the opportunity to grow to adulthood in civilized society.

In a strategy session lasting deep into the night, a plan had been hastily devised. Stephen would meet the Native girl as agreed upon, and the remainder of the missionaries would reveal themselves upon her arrival. The resulting show of force, they reasoned, would be sufficient to intimidate the frightened girl into handing over the baby.

After that meeting had broken up, however, Stephen had learned from his closest friend that the missionary leaders convened a second session, one to which Stephen Ames had not been invited. The leaders suspected separating the child from her mother might not be so easy and they knew a second, more forceful plan might be required in the event the young savage resisted.

That was all the information Stephen had been able to pry out of his associate but was more than enough to cause him grave concern.

Now, as Stephen watched with his heart in his throat, the young girl turned on her heel and began hurrying as quickly as she was able with a sleeping baby on her back down the narrow hunting path. She found her passage blocked almost immediately by two of the missionaries. They approached her with their hands held out, palms up, in identical gestures of supplication, speaking to her calmly, telling her she had nothing to fear. Stephen knew she did not understand and could see things were going quickly downhill.

He rushed up from behind, hoping to avert disaster. But as he did the rest of the group closed in on her as well. Now she had nowhere to go, nowhere to run.

The young mother tried to shoulder past the man nearest her as Stephen reached for her elbow and missed. The missionary shoved her roughly, and she tumbled into the forest ringing the path.

Stephen shouted and the man grabbed for the baby and that was when everything spiraled out of control.

*   *   *

Abnaki war cries pierced the air as savages materialized seemingly out of nowhere, rushing to protect their tribal member. They moved quickly, within seconds fully surrounding the missionaries.

One warrior struck the man who had pushed the girl, hitting him in the face with his fist. Blood spurted and bone cracked and the man fell to the ground with an anguished cry.

This seemed to panic the interlopers, and one of them pulled a strange-looking silver cylindrical device from the pocket of his long overcoat. He pointed it at the Abnaki warrior who had rushed to the girl's defense. Fire erupted from the end of the cylinder and a frighteningly loud boom shook the woods as the side of the warrior's face disappeared in a pink and grey stew of blood, bone and tissue.

The warrior dropped to the ground and lay still.

Immediately Abnaki bows were drawn and arrows launched, and knives and hatchets brandished.

More cylinders were drawn out of more of the white men's pockets, belching more fire; the awful booming noises crashed through the forest and men on both sides of the conflict fell and lay still.

* * *

Stephen screamed and tumbled to the ground as he was struck in the shoulder by a hatchet thrown from he knew not where. He had known the missionary group would be armed; it was a necessary defense when dealing with savages, but they had never before been forced to use them against this particular tribe.

His left arm felt numb and his hand tingled violently. He knew he was badly injured. Blood covered his shoulder and ran down his chest in a great wave.

He looked for the Native girl, the mother of his child, but could not find her. Smoke from the missionaries' guns hung thickly in the air, obscuring the moonlight and casting the scene in a nightmarish hue.

Screams rent the night, whether from missionaries or tribesmen Stephen could not tell.

His vision began to narrow and he found himself peering down a long tunnel. Soon the black edges of that tunnel began squeezing his vision into a steadily shrinking circle.

The screaming and the cries of anguish now seemed to originate from a point much farther away than they had previously, although Stephen knew that was not possible. He was lying in the middle of the battle zone. He guessed he was dying and wished he could hold his baby daughter just once.

Then nothing.

* * *

Stephen Ames opened his eyes. He was still lying on the frozen November North Woods ground. He felt incredibly, bone-chillingly cold, colder than he ever had. He was surprised he was not dead and wondered how long he had been lying unconscious in the forest.

He attempted to stand and only then realized he could not move. Stephen knew that unless someone helped him he was going to die. He was surprised to discover the prospect didn't frighten him.

Stephen's neck seemed to be the only part of his body he could convince to work properly, so he scanned as much of the area as he could see. Bodies littered the forest, some of them Abnaki tribal warriors and some of them missionaries. A few moaned softly, but most lay unspeaking and unmoving. He suspected the majority of them were dead. Blood was everywhere, congealing on every surface, more blood than he would ever have imagined possible.

His most pressing thought—his only clear thought, really— was for his baby. Was she still near?

He didn't think so. None of the bodies he could see on the ground appeared to be those of women; although he knew he could not see all of the dead. He hoped fervently that the Native girl and his child had somehow escaped the carnage, as unlikely as that seemed.

Motion in his peripheral vision caused Stephen to peer down the hunting path. The smoke from the gunfire had by now cleared, and the moon shone brightly in the frigid November sky.

Struggling up the path was an elderly Abnaki tribesman. Stephen had never before seen the man and that was strange. Until now he thought he had met everyone in the small tribal village at least once.

The man looked older than anyone Stephen had ever seen— ancient, even. Lines etched his face, which was haggard and drawn. Tears rolled down his cheeks. He walked in slow, measured steps and remained utterly silent as he reached the scene of the bloody conflict.

The old warrior's arms were laden with strange-looking items, things like roots and cloth sacks filled with what Stephen could not imagine. At last the man reached a point roughly in the center of the carnage and set all his accoutrements on the ground in a neat pile. He still had not spoken as far as Stephen could tell.

Stephen thought briefly about crying out and alerting the ancient Native to his presence. He knew that by doing so, he would probably seal his fate. The man would certainly kill him after what had been done to his fellow Abnaki tribal members. Stephen didn't care if the man killed him. He would welcome death after this tragic night had gone so horribly wrong, but he was curious as to what the old man was doing all by himself in the middle of the night in this place that reeked of death and destruction and treachery.

He remained quiet and watched the scene unfold. The elderly Abnaki sat cross-legged on the cold, hard ground, arranging his materials in a tight semicircle. It appeared to Stephen that the man was chanting under his breath. His lips were moving but Stephen could hear nothing.

Stephen knew enough about the customs of the Abnaki and about Natives in general to know the elderly man was performing some sacred ritual. He was a tribal medicine man, an individual possessed of incredible power and mysticism.

His voice was now intelligible to Stephen, strengthening in volume as he continued to chant. He mixed ingredients into a great bowl he had placed on the ground in front of him. The man added water to the mixture and stirred slowly for a long time, staring into the distance and chanting. Tendrils of steam rose lazily from the bowl despite the fact there was no fire beneath it. They were clearly apparent in the bright moonlight.

Eventually the elderly Native stood, moving ever so slowly, and walked among the bodies littering the forest floor. He stopped at each of the Abnaki dead, smearing some of the mixture on the foreheads of the men.

He ignored the missionary dead.

Stephen's vision began to waver and he knew he would soon be joining his fellow missionaries in whatever awaited them in the wake of this disaster. He hoped God understood he had not planned this slaughter and prayed he would still be permitted entrance into heaven. He prayed also that his daughter, the baby he had met just once, was alive; although he knew that was unlikely in the extreme.

As the ancient Abnaki medicine man padded silently among

the Native bodies, performing his mysterious ritual, Stephen Ames slipped into unconsciousness for the last time.

The freezing cold vanished and the world went black and there was no pain, and for that Stephen was grateful.

1

Present Day

George Hooper was lost.

He was also hungry and wet, thus completing what he had come to think of as his own personal trifecta of misery. A steady drizzle fell from the slate-grey skies, making George shiver and long for the warmth and comfort of his living room. He tried to take his mind off the chill by picturing himself sitting in front of a roaring fire, three fingers of bourbon warming his insides as he sat in a rocking chair doing nothing in particular, maybe watching a Yankees game on TV or reading a good book.

George didn't own a rocking chair, nor did he have a fireplace in the living room of his small home in Teaneck, New Jersey. He didn't even like to read all that much. But he didn't care. He figured, *What the hell, it's my daydream, I might as well enjoy it.*

He knew he should not have come hunting alone in the dank, desolate woods of Northern Maine in late November, but none of his buddies could make it this weekend, and George was damned if he was going to let his five-day break from the job at the paper mill pass by without getting out and enjoying some fresh air and solitude.

Going off by himself in the woods was a piss-poor idea— George knew that like he knew his own name—but he had hiked and hunted his entire life in some of the most remote and rugged areas this country had to offer, so it wasn't like he lacked outdoor experience. Besides, with his trusty hand-held GPS, how bad could things get?

Pretty bad indeed, George decided with the benefit of hindsight.

The goddamned GPS had crapped out on him two days ago for no particular reason that George could determine. It simply made the decision, somewhere inside its freakin' soulless solid-state electronic guts, to cease operations.

That in itself wasn't a particularly big deal. As long as George had his trusty map book, he didn't really *need* the GPS anyway.

Then he lost his trusty map book. It washed away during a river crossing, and just like that, George was more or less totally screwed.

He unzipped the right front pocket of his insulated hunting jacket and pulled out his cell phone for what he guessed might be about the two hundredth time in the last two days. He knew what he would see when he powered it up but tried anyway.

The device clicked and whirred, eventually awakening from its slumber and informing George that, so sorry, there was still no cell coverage in this part of the God-forsaken northern Maine woods, and that furthermore, its battery was getting dangerously low, so if he wished to make a call, this might be a good goddamned time to do it.

He cursed under his breath. The damn thing was about as useful to him as the broken GPS. Two worthless electronic paperweights.

His hands were shaking as he shoved the cell phone back into his pocket and re-zipped it. He had only removed his gloves for a couple of minutes, and his fingers were already stiffening and losing feeling. Dammit, it was cold!

George stopped in a small clearing and tried to get his bearings, knowing it was pointless but not having the faintest clue what else to do. The lowering sky was dark grey, almost black, the sun a distant memory even though it was still midday. Orienting himself direction-wise was a no go.

The drizzle, which had fallen constantly since—incredibly—just about the exact moment his GPS had given up the ghost was now increasing in intensity from a soft mist to a steady, slanting rain. The temperature was falling, too, and George knew he needed to find shelter and hole up until the weather cleared.

He had been walking nonstop for almost two days now and exhaustion hung on him like a cloak. Conventional outdoor wisdom dictated that when someone got lost they should stay in one place and wait for help, but George knew while that was good advice for a twelve-year-old who had become disoriented during a Boy Scout hike, it would do nothing to help him in his present situation. No one knew he had come here, and as far as George could remember from his map book before it decided to go for a swim and never return, there was only one small town within twenty miles in any direction, so the chances of some random hiker or hunter stumbling upon him and helping him out of this mess were pretty slim. Almost nonexistent, when it came right down to brass tacks.

That being the case, George figured he might just as well keep moving. Maybe he would get lucky and stumble upon the little hamlet. And if he didn't, well, he would be no worse off walking when the sun finally came out than he would have been had he stayed in one place.

Either way, if he didn't find that town, he was going to have some serious hiking to do once he was able to determine which way was south.

Now though, hungry, tired, depressed and drenched, with a steadily lowering body temperature as an added bonus, George Hooper decided his number one priority had to be to seek shelter and wait out the rest of the storm.

But where?

Most of the trees in this thickly forested area were towering pines, their branches sagging from the weight of all the water collecting on their needles the past two days. Perhaps he could burrow under the branches toward the middle of one of the mammoth firs in the hopes of finding some dry ground.

George glanced again up at the dark sky, at the clouds roiling high above the treetops. His breath caught in his throat as his brain at first refused to believe what his eyes were telling him. He stared without moving for a good sixty seconds at a thin column of smoke rising above the forest and disappearing into the rain and mist.

A fire!

Whether the smoke was coming from a fireplace or a campfire or a cook stove, George had no way of knowing, but one thing he *did* know was that someone was near, and if someone was near then that meant food and warmth and directions out of here and maybe even a ride back to civilization if he got really lucky.

He couldn't believe his incredible good fortune. He almost laughed out loud at the thought that he had been seconds away from crawling on his belly through the mud under a tree where he would have spent the next twenty-four hours or more cold and miserable, and now, because he just happened to look skyward at the right time, he might just be on his way home with a full belly and warm, dry clothes within hours.

Hefting his pack, which had started out heavy but was now even more so thanks to the water soaking the canvas, George angled in the general direction of the smoke. He zigzagged through the trees, ducking under branches and putting up with ice-cold water dripping down his neck. He kept his eyes on the prize: that thin column of nearly invisible wispy smoke, fearing that if he lost sight of it he might never relocate it.

After roughly twenty minutes of struggling, he trudged through a particularly thick line of trees into a large clearing and stopped dead in his tracks. Spread out before him was what had once been a tiny village, clearly abandoned years ago, probably decades ago. Hell, maybe even centuries ago.

The remnants of about a half-dozen small granite foundations lined each side of a narrow, rutted dirt trail. The trail was barely wide enough to accommodate a car, not that any car would be able to navigate this rough terrain. Even a four-wheel drive vehicle would probably get stuck trying to make it out here.

In addition to the ancient stone foundations, which George assumed had at one time held houses, a couple of similar but larger foundations—perhaps a general store and maybe a police station or jail?—sat in disrepair at the far end of the clearing. Weeds and scrub grass and even large trees sprouted out, around and through the foundations, giving the area a look of utter abandonment.

The forest had nearly completed its reclamation of the lonely and isolated village that had been hacked out of it at some point in the distant past.

In his shock at stumbling upon this tiny deserted village, George had almost forgotten the trail of smoke he'd been tracking and now looked around to see if he could find the person or persons responsible for the fire.

At first he could see no sign of the smoke—he thought for a moment he had lost it completely and almost panicked—but after a few seconds he caught sight of a wisp drifting lazily up and out of a red-brick chimney that sprouted from the roof of a small log cabin to George's right.

The home was tucked into the very edge of the abandoned village and was clearly not part of the original town; it looked almost brand new. The construction appeared square and shipshape, with windows and a door and a farmer's porch running the length of the house.

George's heart leaped with the thought that he was about to get out of this mess, then the obvious question struck him like a hammer to the side of the skull: *who in the hell builds a home way out here in the middle of nowhere, at the edge of an old housing graveyard?*

Even Ted Kaszinski, the old Unabomber himself, the guy with the grudge against modern technology who had terrorized the country for a time in the 1990's with bombs delivered through the United States Postal Service, had lived in an area that was at least accessible to some conveniences.

What had George stumbled upon? Some antisocial lunatic who might chop him up into little pieces and then feed them to his equally antisocial dog?

George laughed uneasily to himself at such a ridiculous notion. He just needed a little help, that was all, and undoubtedly whoever lived here would be happy to provide it.

Of course they would.

Jesus Christ, get a grip, pussy.

But his nervous body refused to cooperate with his calm, rational brain. His breath came rapid and shallow and sweat dripped down his back as he stared at the strange village laid out in front of him. It was not a pleasant sensation considering he had been wet and freezing cold to begin with.

George couldn't imagine why he was so nervous and jumpy. He

wasn't a guy who spooked easily, and he should be jumping up and down screaming his damn fool head off in delight at the prospect of getting out of this mess, not standing motionless in the rain like some four-year-old kid afraid of his own shadow.

Grunting in disgust at himself but still unable to shake the feeling that something was terribly wrong, George forced himself to slow his breathing and made a concerted effort to calm his frayed nerves.

"Get ahold of yourself, dumbass," he muttered and began slowly walking toward the only recent construction, the log cabin. The smoke from the chimney had now almost completely disappeared, and George hoped the person or people who had been burning the fire inside the house wouldn't mind lighting it up again for him.

2

"That is totally disgusting."

Sharon Dupont shook her head, her pretty mouth drawing down into a frown as new Paskagankee Police Chief Mike McMahon attempted to navigate a large steak bomb in the passenger seat of their parked cruiser. He grinned at the petite officer's horrified expression as he chomped away.

He swallowed and licked his lips. "You're just jealous. You decided to pass up this traditional American feast and now you're sorry you didn't get something too, so you could join in the fun."

"Are you kidding me?" she countered. "After this…display, I might not ever eat *anything* again, never mind dead animal flesh."

McMahon reached across the seat and waved the partially eaten sandwich in front of her, eliciting another frown.

Then he nodded knowingly. "Jealousy. It's very unbecoming."

Mike McMahon had been in town for just over a week. He'd edged out a total of zero other applicants for the position of police chief in the isolated northern Maine town of Paskagankee, population four thousand. Give or take.

Outgoing Chief Wally Court—McMahon couldn't imagine a more fitting name for a law enforcement officer—had reviewed Mike's application and conducted a thirty-minute telephone interview followed by a two-hour personal meeting before hiring him, all within a matter of days.

In neither of the interviews had Court asked Mike the obvious question of why he wanted to move from Revere, Massachusetts—a hardscrabble community just north of Boston—to a sleepy hamlet like Paskagankee while still in the prime of his career.

For that Mike was grateful, if a bit surprised.

Maybe the chief had heard about the shooting last year and understood Mike's need to get away from Revere, or maybe he didn't give a damn why anyone would want the Paskagankee job and was just thankful someone did.

Either way, Mike had escaped his old life, which was exactly what he needed.

He had been surprised by the apparent contradiction that was Chief Wally Court. Court's office, where the in-person job interview had taken place, was neat to the point of obsession, the walls covered with the obligatory citations and photos of the chief glad-handing dignitaries, and with a shipshape desk devoid of any hint of clutter.

The outgoing chief's personal appearance, however, had been a different story. His graying hair badly needed a trim, as did his beard. He sported at least a three-day growth of salt and pepper on a face clearly unfamiliar with the intrusion. His uniform was heavily wrinkled and appeared slept-in, and Court sweated profusely throughout the interview, looking extremely uncomfortable, as if there was somewhere else he very badly needed to be.

Mike thought it all added up to something strange. There was clearly more to the story of retiring Paskagankee Police Chief Wally Court than met the eye. Perhaps the man was ill.

Whatever his situation, Mike had been notified three days after the unusual interview that the job was his if he wanted it. Furthermore, the town needed him to start as soon as possible due to the imminent retirement of Chief Court, a circumstance that fit Mike's desires perfectly.

The first thing the new police chief had done upon arrival was to introduce himself to his small roster of officers and announce he would not be changing any procedures or assignments right away, but rather that he would take the next month or two and accompany an officer on routine patrols in order to familiarize himself with the town and its people.

He had chosen rookie Sharon Dupont to train with for no particular reason other than she was a relative newcomer, so he assumed she would be less likely to raise a fuss about having to babysit the new boss than a more established veteran would be.

Now the two were trading barbs like partners and friends, despite the fact Dupont had been on the job just six months and McMahon brought fifteen years of law enforcement experience to Paskagankee, all of it on a busy metropolitan police force.

A light-falling mist drizzled around the cruiser as the two sat in the otherwise empty parking lot of the town's only funeral home. They were ostensibly clocking the speed of passing motorists with a hand-held radar gun, but the effort was mostly for show, an attempt to discourage townspeople from speeding rather than actually to ticket drivers.

Mike prepared to wave what was left of his sandwich in Officer Dupont's face again, just to enjoy her reaction, but before he could lift it a muddy, faded maroon Ford pickup flashed by. The truck was at least fifteen years old, losing the battle to rust and traveling a good twenty-five miles per hour over the posted speed limit of forty-five. It roared through a puddle, kicking up a rooster tail of spray and fishtailing momentarily before regaining traction on the wet pavement.

Dupont looked a question at Mike, her short black hair framing her face appealingly. She really was very cute.

"Go get him," he said, nodding, and she hit the gas, pulling smoothly out of the lot and overtaking the pickup within a quarter-mile, an impressive feat considering the truck's speed.

She hit her blues and the driver of the pickup traveled another several hundred feet before apparently noticing the cruiser and pulling to the side of the road without benefit of a turn signal.

Sharon eased up behind the truck and prepared to step into the falling drizzle.

Mike asked, "You want some help?"

"Nah. No sense in us both getting soaked."

"Good answer. You've really got a future in my department."

He grinned as she whacked him on the arm with her hat and climbed out of the cruiser. He admired her slim form as she walked away. She looked good even in the unflattering blue uniform blouse and dark grey slacks of the Paskagankee Police Department.

Mike was unsurprised to see the occupant of the battered

pickup hand his license and registration through the driver's side window without being asked. It was obvious he had fished the required documents out of his wallet and glove compartment during Mike and Sharon's brief conversation inside the cruiser.

"Had a little experience at this, have you?" Mike muttered to himself.

He sat up straight in his seat as the truck's door opened and a man stepped unsteadily to the pavement. His first instinct was to rush to the rookie's defense, but he forced himself to wait and watch, to stay in the cruiser and see how she would react to this unexpected development. Had he not been riding shotgun to learn the ins and outs of this small town, she would have been patrolling this remote stretch of road alone. It was best to let her handle the incident by herself.

Standard department procedure dictated that the officer instruct the driver to wait in his vehicle while she returned to her cruiser to check for outstanding warrants. Mike was certain she had done just that through the open window, so the man's exiting the truck in spite of that warning constituted an aggressive action and cause for concern.

Mike's concern turned to amusement, though, as the obviously drunk driver proved no match for Officer Dupont, despite his being at least eight inches taller and probably close to one hundred pounds heavier than she was. No sooner had his feet splashed down on the wet pavement than she grabbed him by the wrist, forcing his hand backward and using the resulting leverage to spin him around and slam him face first into the side of his truck. She kicked his feet apart and quickly patted him down for weapons, then slapped cuffs on his wrists and marched him to the rear of the cruiser, dumping him unceremoniously into the back seat while he sputtered indignantly about police brutality.

Eventually the man glanced through the cage separating the back seat from the front and saw Mike. He stopped complaining and slurred, "Who're you?"

"New police chief," Mike answered. "My name is Mike McMahon and I understand you have a problem with my officer?"

"You're damn right I do! You saw her beat on me for no good goddamned reason, and I want to file a complaint."

"That's certainly your right," Mike told him. "But you do understand I sat in this cruiser and watched the entire episode, and aside from the ease with which she subdued you, I didn't see anything out of the ordinary. I'll be happy to testify to that in court if necessary."

"But—"

"But nothing," Mike interrupted. "Did Officer Dupont instruct you to remain inside your vehicle?"

"Well, yeah," he reluctantly admitted.

"And you stepped out of your vehicle anyway?"

"Well, yeah."

"Then all I can tell you is you're lucky it wasn't me out there because you'd be on your way to the hospital right now, rather than to a warm, comfortable holding cell."

The man slumped back in his seat and shook his head petulantly, turning toward the side window as Sharon Dupont steered the cruiser off the side of the road and accelerated back toward town.

Mike winked at her and she smiled.

In the back seat, the man apparently found his second wind. "Hey, girlie, how's your daddy?" he taunted.

Mike glanced at Sharon and held his tongue. Her face reddened, and she stared steadfastly through the windshield as she drove, ignoring their passenger.

"I said, how's your daddy?" he repeated in a louder voice as if perhaps she hadn't heard him.

"He's dead, Earl, you know that. Now do yourself a favor and shut your mouth," she said sharply.

"Your new girlfriend tell you her daddy used to be one of my best drinking buddies?" Mike decided the man in the back seat must be addressing him. "Or at least he was before the pretty little thing sitting next to you replaced him. 'Course, I s'pose it goes without sayin' that he don't come around too much no more. You know, what with his being dead and all. Ain't that right, baby doll?" His voice resumed its taunting tone as he again addressed Sharon Dupont.

Mike glanced sideways at his officer and saw a hard set to her jaw. She was grinding her teeth and a vein throbbed in her forehead, and she looked like she might explode at any moment.

Enough was enough. For whatever reason, this drunken idiot was getting to the young officer, and it was time to put a stop to it.

"Hey dumbass, open your mouth one more time," he said, turning in his seat and staring down the man in back, "and we'll add assaulting a peace officer to the drunk-driving charge. You mull that over in your tiny little brain, but remember, just one more word and you're going to be sorry you ever opened your toothless mouth. That's a promise."

The drunk's mouth dropped open comically but the remainder of the fifteen-minute ride to the police station passed in silence. The pair brought the man into the station and deposited him into holding.

Mike sipped a coffee while Officer Dupont processed the drunk-driving suspect. One thing common to police stations everywhere, he mused, was the consistently bad coffee. It was as if the worst coffeemakers in the world were reserved for the cops, to be filled with the stalest ground roast and brewed with the nastiest water.

As he considered the feasibility of buying a brand-new coffeemaker and some fresh coffee with his own money in a gesture of mercy to his new employees, Sharon Dupont's shapely form rounded the corner.

She smiled tightly. "He's a barrel of laughs, isn't he?"

"Aren't they all," Mike replied, choking down the last of the bitter brew and following his temporary partner out of the station and back to their cruiser.

3

The drizzle turned to freezing rain and began falling more steadily as George Hooper crossed the uneven muddy track and approached the log cabin. The temperature had grown noticeably colder during the time he spent studying the granite foundations scattered around the deserted village.

George realized he'd been standing motionless in the cold rain for a long time. How long he didn't know. For some irrational reason, he was having trouble forcing himself to walk the short distance to the cabin to ask for help. The sense of dread and foreboding, which had begun gnawing at him almost the moment he stumbled into this clearing, had grown rapidly until it threatened to freeze him—literally—where he stood.

"Just do it, you freakin' wimp," George muttered to himself. His voice sounded somehow foreign and his breath crystallized in the chilly air, swirling into the rain and disappearing. He reluctantly resumed trudging through the mud and weeds. The ground was treacherously uneven and it crunched under his boots and George realized for the first time he was shivering violently.

How the hell long have I been standing out here?

The entire area felt deserted but obviously it was not. Someone had started a fire inside that cabin, and George was positive no one had left while he was standing out here.

Oh really? Are you sure about that? You were zoned out, you idiot. You don't have the slightest clue how long you've been staring at those gigantic granite blocks, now, do you?

The feeling of dread mushroomed, worming its way through George's intestines and growing in inverse proportion to his distance from the cabin. Finally he reached the front porch, and as he mounted the steps the panic exploded. It threatened to overwhelm him. He looked frantically from window to window, certain someone (*something*) was staring out at him, waiting and biding his (*its*) time until George wandered close enough to attack.

No one was visible in any of the windows; George could see that quite clearly because the glass in all of them had been cleaned to a smudge-free shine, and the rooms inside were as empty and vacant as the eyes of a zombie, a shambling undead monster intent on cracking his skull open like a coconut and devouring his brain.

Where in the hell did THAT come from? When have you ever watched zombie movies?

George's hands were shaking violently, and he knew it was not just from the lousy weather conditions. There was something evil about this whole abandoned village, he could sense it.

Sense it? Hell, I can almost taste *it.*

There was no point in kidding himself. He wanted desperately to leave, to run somewhere, anywhere, to get out of this cursed goddamned place while he still could, but he had no choice but to continue. If he turned around now he would freeze to death, his soaking wet clothes stealing his body heat and inviting hypothermia.

The porch creaked and groaned as George worked his way hesitantly to the closed front door. He thought it odd that the otherwise immaculate and solidly constructed log cabin would have loose floorboards for him to trip over. Had it been built that way intentionally?

George thought the only way things could get any worse at this point would be if he were to fall through the porch on one of those loose planks and break an ankle. That would leave him at the mercy of the malevolent force stalking him.

Stalking and preparing to attack, watching with red-rimmed eyes and stinking dead breath redolent of rotting flesh, watching and waiting for the perfect moment to rip your throat out.

After what felt like an eternity George reached the front door. His movements were becoming slower, clumsier, a sure sign of the onset of hypothermia; it was imperative that he shed his wet clothing and begin to raise his body temperature.

The cabin door stood before him and still George could not shake his conviction that something evil was lurking on the other side. It was just inches away. It was listening intently, exactly as he was, separated from him by nothing more substantial than a slab of oak with hinges on one side and a shiny brass knob on the other.

George raised one gloved hand and banged on the heavy wooden door and was surprised to see it swing slowly open. It creaked loudly, as if only reluctantly complying with the laws of physics. The noise sounded eerily like a scream.

George was certain that when he had examined the house from a distance the front door had been tightly closed.

Or had it? His mind seemed to be working just as slowly and clumsily as his body. Maybe he only *thought* the door had been closed. Maybe he had never really even checked at all. It was so hard to remember, so hard to think.

He eased his head through the partially open door, moving slowly. Warily.

"Hello?" His voice sounded fearful and hesitant, even to him.

He cleared his throat and forced a little more conviction into it. "Hello, is anybody in here? I got lost hunting and I could use some directions…"

By the time he finished speaking, George's voice had diminished until it was barely more than a whisper.

There was no reply. No indication anyone had heard him. If the cabin's owner was here, he clearly did not wish to reveal himself.

George took a hesitant step into the house, and then another, and then a third. He found himself in a spacious open room, a combination kitchen/living area with a short hallway branching off to the left. The hallway featured three doors placed side by side, presumably opening onto a bathroom and maybe a couple of bedrooms.

The entire home appeared empty, but it hadn't been for long. To George's right, a massive fieldstone fireplace took up most of the side wall, and inside the fireplace red-hot ashes still glowed, the flames only recently having been extinguished.

But where was the person who had been warming himself in

front of the fire? As far as George could tell there was only one entrance to the cabin, and he had been standing in front of it for a long time. Had the home's occupant departed just prior to George discovering the abandoned village? Or was he even now hiding in one of the rooms behind the three closed doors lining the hallway?

And if he was hiding, why?

Could it be he was afraid of George? Certainly he couldn't be any more fearful than George was right now. A strained chuckle forced its way out of George's constricted throat. He wasn't sure whose voice rang in his ears, but it sure as hell didn't sound like his.

Scattered throughout the interior of the cabin was the spoor of various small animals that had apparently taken up residence, and George was forced to step around their droppings as he made his way cautiously toward the hallway. He couldn't see any animals, but it was clear the embers cooling in the fireplace had not been stoked by any wild animal.

George hesitated, unsure of how to proceed, unsure whether he even *wanted* to proceed, but unable to stop himself from doing so. He had to see who or what was in here with him. His intuition screamed he wasn't alone, and he was not about to strip off all his clothes and spread them out in front of the fireplace without first scouting out the interior of this creepy house.

The question was simple—a cliché, really—but perplexing: which door should he open first?

The crushing silence weighed on George with an almost physical presence. The only sound he could hear was the rushing of blood in his ears. He felt (*knew*) if he chose the wrong door he would be trapped inside a room with no escape and some God-awful, red-eyed, foul-smelling monster closing in to do who knew what to him.

Oh, you know what. Yes you do, don't kid yourself, Georgie boy. It's a cold-blooded killer, and it will rip your head right off your body, and the last thing you hear before eternal darkness falls will be your skin tearing and your bones breaking, and the thing will drink your blood and snap your limbs one by one, and you will never be found, not ever.

Every fiber in George's terrified body was telling him to run, to sprint out of the cabin NOW into the freezing early evening drizzle and take his chances with a slow death from hypothermia.

The only reason he didn't bolt was he felt (*knew*) that if he tried to run, he would be pursued by the creature and taken down from behind, that he would never see it coming.

The die is cast, George thought, *with the emphasis on die*. He had no choice but to confront the monster now.

George unconsciously shrugged the Mossberg 464 lever-action hunting rifle off his shoulder as he stood in front of the three closed doors. He clutched the gun in front of his body like a shield with two stiff arms, knuckles white, hands shaking.

Decision time.

He chose the middle door to open first for no particular reason other than it was the one directly in front of him. Grasped the knob in one sweating, shaking hand and turned it slowly. He listened intently for the slightest hint of a sound from the other side of the door, something that would give him an indication whether anyone (*anything*) was inside the room.

Silence.

Deathly silence, George thought to himself as a hysterical laugh bubbled up from his gut. The laugh sounded suspiciously like a sob by the time he choked it off.

Predictably, the door creaked as it opened. George thought it was the most terrifying sound he had ever heard. It swung wide to reveal a bedroom, devoid both of furniture and of people. In fact, beyond the straw, animal droppings and other detritus of wildlife habitation, he could see nothing inside the room at all.

Relieved, George stepped into the bedroom and poked his head warily around the door, and when he did he leapt back as a strangled scream escaped his throat.

He was face to face with…*something*.

His panicked eyes registered a massive form, a mountain of shaggy hair covering an absurdly small-looking head propped atop a gigantic body. Straw and leaves and dead grass stuck at odd angles out of the filthy, unkempt head of hair and small worms or maybe even maggots appeared to be wriggling inside it as well.

And the smell.

The smell was horrific.

A stench of death, of rot and decomposition, assailed George with an intensity beyond anything he had ever experienced. In the back of his racing mind he wondered why he had not noticed it when he first opened the door, and he realized he had been holding his breath in fear.

He had to escape, to get away, to run. George tripped over his own feet and fell to the floor, heels scrabbling as he scuttled backward, his rifle useless and now forgotten after dropping it in his mindless panic.

One of his fingernails ripped off as he grabbed at the pine floor, and he didn't notice.

A splinter embedded itself deep into his palm, and he didn't notice that either.

A whimpering sound filled George's ears and he realized it was coming from him. He couldn't stop it and didn't care. His only conscious thought was to get away from that horrible thing stepping out from behind the door.

He shoved himself desperately across the dirty floor as the monster shambled after him, and he kept going until he smashed into the far wall.

The thing followed, eyes red as George had known they would be, breath stinking and foul as George had known it would be, and George now knew he was going to die; he was going to die all alone somewhere deep in the northern Maine woods at the hands of something alien and terrifying.

The creature kicked the Mossberg across the room, whether on purpose or by accident George couldn't tell. It clattered against the wall. For one brief moment George thought the shotgun might go off when it struck the wall, blasting the creature to kingdom come and saving his sorry ass.

But of course it did nothing of the kind.

The thing turned and advanced on George, a blood-chilling growl of fury issuing from deep in its monstrous chest. It grabbed George, slapping one meaty paw onto each ear and shaking his head violently from side to side. George heard a terrifying SNAP and knew it was the sound of his own neck breaking. He felt one instant of the most incredible pain he had ever experienced, and then a numb tingling filled his extremities.

He began to drift, to lose consciousness, and was amazed to discover the fear was gone. He could see blood splattering the floor, lots of it, and although he knew it was his own blood, he found he didn't care.

George's last conscious thought was that the creature's putrid breath wasn't quite as disgusting as he had thought it would be.

Then he was gone.

4

Mike McMahon and Sharon Dupont buckled themselves into the cruiser and Sharon prepared to drive out of the Paskagankee Police station parking lot.

"So," Mike said. "What was that all about?"

"What was what all about?"

"That guy we just tossed into a holding cell, the one you called by his first name even though you never looked at his driver's license, he taunted you about your father. You two know each other." Mike phrased it as a statement, not a question.

Officer Dupont was silent for a moment as she made a show of checking both directions for oncoming traffic. She pulled out of the lot and turned north on Main Street. The rear tires spun on the slick pavement and then gained traction.

Finally she answered. "Yes, I know Earl Manning. He was a couple of years ahead of me in high school. After he graduated—a minor miracle in itself—he became a regular at the Ridge Runner where my dad used to spend most of his time."

"The Ridge Runner is a bar, I assume."

"That's right. Out on Ridge Road. Original, huh?" The young officer flipped her hair behind her ear in what Mike McMahon was already beginning to recognize as a subconscious reaction to stress.

"Is this something you'd rather not discuss?"

Another hesitation, shorter this time. "No, it's okay. It's just that I'm not used to talking about myself. Besides, this shithole's a pretty small town, in case it had escaped your notice. Eventually you would hear all about my dad anyway."

She took a deep breath. "And about me, too, I suppose."

Mike watched two cars slide partway through a four-way intersection a couple hundred yards ahead. The storm was worsening as temperatures continued to plummet. Driving conditions were iffy now and weren't going to improve any time soon. He hoped people would have enough sense to stay off the roads, this being a Saturday, but doubted that would be the case.

"So your dad is pretty well-known around here?"

Officer Dupont coughed out a laugh, short and bitter. "You could say that. He held down a bar stool pretty much twenty-four hours a day at the Ridge Runner for most of the last ten years, starting the day after we buried my mother."

Mike looked down at the cruiser's bench seat and then across at Sharon Dupont. She stared straight through the windshield, concentrating on navigating the slick streets. If she noticed him looking at her, she didn't give any indication of it.

"I'm sorry about your mother," he said. "I didn't know."

"No reason why you should."

"How old were you at the time?"

"Twelve."

"So you went through your teen years with no mother and a father too busy drinking Budweiser to raise his daughter properly?"

"Yeah, that pretty much covers it," she said. "My dad was always an enthusiastic drinker, but after mom died, alcohol took over his life. I think he single-handedly kept one shift working overtime at the Anheuser-Busch plant down the road in New Hampshire."

The cruiser slid to a stop in front of the Unitarian Church on the corner of Main and Elm Streets. Officer Dupont angled into the parking lot and turned the car around so they could monitor traffic on the cross streets and stay off the increasingly dangerous roads for a while. She cranked up the car's interior heat.

Mike turned in his seat to look at the young officer. "Sounds like the sort of situation you'd be anxious to escape."

"Oh, I couldn't wait to get out all right, and eventually I left Paskagankee to attend the FBI Academy, but of course you know all of that from my personnel file."

"True enough," Mike answered. "But your file doesn't explain why you suddenly came back to this tiny little place in the middle of nowhere. Nothing against Paskagankee, but it seems to me you wouldn't be too quick to return, especially since you were doing well at the academy. I saw your performance scores, and you were kicking ass down there. What happened?"

"My dad was diagnosed with liver cancer a couple of years ago, and for a while he did okay. About six months ago he started going downhill fast. I have no brothers or sisters, and with my mother gone…"

She lapsed into silence and stared out the windshield at the empty streets, now rapidly glazing over with a thin coating of ice. Something like defiant regret hardened her features.

"You came back to care for your father."

Sharon nodded. She fiddled with the turn signal and looked everywhere but at Mike. "I made a promise to my mom before she died that I would look after my dad. She knew he would have trouble coping after she was gone. I came back for my mom, not for him."

Mike said nothing and she continued. "Then my dad died a few weeks ago, not long after I got hired by Chief Court, your predecessor. I haven't gotten around to leaving town for good yet. I don't know why. Inertia, I suppose."

She chuckled softly. "So now you know the sorry little life story of Sharon Dupont. Some of it, anyway. Would I be out of line asking my boss what *you're* doing here? Why you gave up a real career in a thriving city where you could actually make a difference to come here and take over a little Hicksville police force?"

Mike laughed. "Subtlety doesn't work for you, does it, Officer Dupont?"

"My friends call me Shari."

"Okay, Shari then. Yeah, it probably would be out of line, but I guess it would only be fair to dish a little dirt on myself since I have the scoop now on you."

The cruiser's radio crackled with an incoming call. Mike shook his head in mock remorse. "Looks like my little sob story will have to wait. It seems we have work to do."

5

Ida Mae Harper had lived in Paskagankee her entire life. Eighty-six years and counting, all spent in the little town a few miles south of the Canadian border. She had gotten married at age 16 to a young man by the name of Wallace Harper, eight years her senior, a laborer at the leather mill located hard by the Penobscot River. The couple spent nearly fifty years together before Wallace's sudden death more than two decades ago turned Ida Mae into a widow.

A stroke, they told her after Wallace buckled and fell to the floor one Sunday afternoon over boiled dinner. Ida Mae thought to herself that they could call it a stroke if they wanted to, but she knew what had really killed Wallace—too darned many decades of sixty-hour work weeks at the mill. Regularly scheduled double shifts, the occasional triple shift, week after week of working without a day off, you name it, and Wallace did it because he wanted to provide the best life he could for his Ida Mae.

The couple had never been able to have children, so Wallace's death meant Ida Mae was alone for the first time in her life. She had moved from her parents' home straight to Wallace's tiny but comfortable house when they married, and in that little house she still lived. Their inability to conceive had been a blow to Ida Mae and Wallace, but they had come to terms with the heartbreak after years of trying and had been happy for the most part ever since.

Following Wallace's death, Ida Mae bought a golden retriever puppy for company. His name was Butch, and upon his furry form she lavished all her love and attention. When the first retriever passed away, Ida Mae bought another, naming him Butch II.

Now, Ida Mae was on the phone to the Paskagankee Police Department, sobbing and requesting assistance immediately.

"What's the nature of the difficulty, ma'am?" the dispatcher asked.

"It's Butch, something's happened to my poor Butch," she wailed into the telephone receiver.

"Who is Butch, ma'am, and what has happened to him?"

"Just send an officer, please, and tell him to hurry," she said, tears running down her face. She provided her address to the bewildered dispatcher and hung up.

*   *   *

After what felt like forever, the cruiser finally arrived. It moved slowly up the long dirt driveway, sliding and lurching from one pothole to another, nearly bottoming out in spots but making steady progress. Eventually it eased to a stop in front of the house.

Ida Mae opened the front door and shivered violently as a gust of cold air blew freezing rain into her home, soaking her housecoat and plastering her hair to her head.

Two police officers exited the cruiser, simultaneously pulling the collars of their jackets up against the wind and rain and scrambling clumsily on the icy ground for the shelter of Ida Mae's living room. She opened the door further to allow them to enter, then she slammed it shut. She moved immediately to the thermostat and cranked up the heat, despite the fact the temperature inside the house already hovered around seventy-five degrees.

She turned to see the two officers, a man and a woman, holding their wet hats in their hands and dripping water on to the hardwood floor.

"Oh," she exclaimed. "Where are my manners? Please, come in. Have a seat on the couch, officers."

"We're fine, ma'am," the male policeman said. "What seems to be the problem? The only information we were given is that something has happened to someone named Butch. Is that your husband?"

"Oh, goodness, no," she said. "My husband was named Wallace, and he's been gone since probably before this little thing was born," she said, nodding at the petite female officer, who smiled back at her. "No, Butch is my dog. It's actually Butch II, but I just call him Butch. It's easier for me, you know, and he doesn't know the difference."

"I understand," said the man, who seemed to be in charge. "So, can you tell me what has happened to Butch?" he asked.

"Oh, dear," sniffled Ida Mae. "I put Butch out to get some air and, you know, to do his doggie business, earlier this afternoon. When he hadn't returned within a couple of hours, I went to the back door to call him and, well…"

She burst into tears, she just couldn't help it. She dabbed at her eyes with a Kleenex and led the two officers through the kitchen to the back door. Opened it and gestured bleakly toward the yard.

The two police officers crowded into the doorway, hips and elbows touching. They cringed simultaneously at the sight that greeted them.

In back yard, just visible in the waning grey late-afternoon light, were the gruesome remains of a golden retriever dog. The animal had literally been ripped apart, its remains strewn around a circle roughly ten feet in diameter. A portion of a foreleg had come to rest midway up the wooden steps leading to the door.

Blood was everywhere.

The dog's head was nowhere to be seen.

The petite young female officer placed her hand on Ida Mae's elbow and guided her back into the small living room to the couch. She sat her down and held her hand, doing her best to console her.

The other officer, the man who seemed to be in charge, closed the door and stood uncomfortably as Ida Mae wrapped an afghan tightly around her shoulders.

The little house seemed to have gotten much, much colder.

6

The auditorium on the University of Maine campus was big, old, drafty and—at the moment—nearly empty. Professor Kenneth Dye looked out at the smattering of college students seated randomly throughout the room and wondered if even one person was paying the slightest bit of attention to his lecture

Judging by the bleary looks on most of their faces, he guessed not.

It was 8:30 on a stormy, icy morning, which meant it was roughly four hours too early for most of these kids to be awake. The few that did seem chipper, large Styrofoam cups of coffee fueling their engines, seemed much more interested in text-messaging, game-playing, and whatever the hell else kids could do on their cell phones these days than in paying much attention to Professor Kenneth A. Dye.

The professor paused in his lecture, looking up from his notes, not even really needing them. He had been giving the same stock presentation for more years than he cared to remember. The only reason he was still teaching at this institution of higher education located in the middle of nowhere was that he needed a reliable source of income so he could afford the purchase price on his next bottle of Tennessee Sippin' Whiskey.

In fact, now that he really thought about it, Professor Dye decided he probably looked more bleary-eyed than most of the kids slumped in their seats in the unnecessarily large auditorium.

Lecturing in the monotone he had perfected over the past two decades about material he had been teaching for nearly that long, Ken Dye reflected on the incident that had become the turning point in not just his career but his life.

At one time, he'd been an up-and-comer, an aggressive young researcher rocking the academic world with controversial theories based on extensive research in his chosen field of Native American studies. Dye didn't just peruse historical accounts of life in North America prior to the European invasion of the 1600's and 1700's, he traveled extensively in the field, interviewing Native American tribal elders all over the United States and even going so far as to live with a number of different tribes in various regions of the country for several illuminating years.

After completing his research and reaching some controversial conclusions regarding the mysticism inherent in virtually all Native American cultures, Kenneth Dye made a fateful decision, one that would change his life forever and not for the better. He wrote a book detailing his findings and almost overnight was reduced to a laughingstock, both in his beloved academic community as well as the real world outside the ivied walls of academia.

Dye came to consider publication of the textbook the biggest mistake of his life. *Publish or perish indeed,* he thought wryly. *More like publish,* then *perish.*

Following the book's release, other professors gradually stopped coming by his office to discuss campus politics. Invitations to academic affairs dried up. Colleagues even began crossing to the other side of the quad when he approached so they wouldn't have to be seen with him.

Ken Dye became a pariah, the guy no one wanted to get too close to, lest his disease of insignificance rub off on them as well.

He had never married—who had time for romance when there was so much research to be done?—and after the release of his book, the professor became such a celebrated kook that the only women interested in dating him were either a little unhinged themselves or curious to discover whether he was really as loony as he was portrayed in the media.

Eventually, Professor Dye retreated into his solitary prison of semi-academia, lecturing bored kids who needed an easy elective with which to pad their schedules without expending too much effort. Administrators at the University of Maine at Orono were only too happy to let him keep his job—in the beginning—because he brought a measure of welcome attention to the out-of-the-way school.

After becoming the subject of near-universal academic scorn, the administration felt it even more prudent to retain Ken, if only to keep an eye on him. Out on his own in the world he could potentially do real damage to the school's academic reputation. Better to keep him under wraps.

Outside, the storm pounded the centuries-old building. High winds pummeled the campus, and the falling rain froze solidly on every surface within minutes. Professor Dye tried to convince himself that the low turnout for today's lecture was due in large part to the treacherous weather—*college students will take advantage of any excuse to ditch a class*—but he knew from long experience that even if the conditions were seventy degrees and sunny, there wouldn't be many more bodies in the lecture hall than were here right now.

Dye shot a glance at the portable alarm clock he had placed on the podium. It was important to track how many more minutes he must suffer through before he could get home and dive back into his bottle of Jack.

Eight-fifty-five.

Ten more minutes and the day's first class would be in the books. Only three more tedious, boring, mind numbing lectures to go. He wished he had poured some whiskey into his water bottle before leaving for work this morning. A powerful thirst was starting to build, and it was barely past breakfast.

7

"So, what in God's name happened to that poor animal yesterday?" Officer Sharon Dupont trained her deep blue eyes on Mike, her forehead crinkled.

He wondered if she had any idea how alluring she was and decided she probably didn't. Mike's theory was that most women seemed to think they were more attractive than they actually were, but every once in a while he ran into a real stunner made even more desirable by the fact she was completely unaware of her effect on men. He was starting to believe Sharon Dupont fell into that category.

He sipped his coffee in the passenger seat of the white and blue Paskagankee Police Ford Explorer and considered her question. They had switched to the four-wheel drive SUV for patrolling the streets today based on the severity of the weather and the fact that it was not forecasted to improve for at least three days. Local schools had already canceled classes for tomorrow and citizens were being urged to stay off the roads, but Mike knew plenty of people would ignore that advice and venture out anyway.

Steam curled out of the Styrofoam cup and Mike breathed in the coffee's rich aroma. "Bert Jenkins from Animal Control visited the Harper house last night to examine the dog's remains. What few were left, anyway. He says the animal was literally torn apart by something inexplicably strong and unrelentingly brutal."

"What, you mean like a bear? If one of those guys gets hungry enough or is disturbed during hibernation, it could get mighty testy, and we're approaching the right time of year for something like that. Maybe the dog stumbled across a really big black bear and ended up getting mauled before it could escape."

Mike shook his head. "I don't think so. Bert said there was no evidence of animal bite marks on the remains. He said it looked more like someone or something had pulled the dog apart like you might pull a drumstick off a roast chicken."

Sharon grimaced. She looked like she had bitten into a lemon. Her pinched expression was so comical he almost laughed.

"That's a pleasant thought," she said. "At least now I don't have to worry about what to have for lunch. I won't be able to eat for days."

She was silent for a few seconds. "What about kids? I know it's a horrible thing to contemplate, but is it possible a group of sadistic teenagers may have tortured and killed the dog?"

Mike shifted in his seat. "You mean like some kind of sick cult initiation ritual?"

"Stranger things have happened, right?"

"I guess so," he answered. "But this strikes me as a pretty close-knit community. People really seem to look out for one another living in isolation as complete as this. Don't you think we would have heard rumblings if there was a cult thing going on in Paskagankee? You've lived in this town practically your whole life, have you heard about anything like that?"

Sharon thought for a moment and then shook her head. "No," she admitted, "but I was never really in the loop anyway, even when I was growing up here, so it's entirely possible the kids could be into things that I wouldn't even have heard about."

"I guess we can't rule anything out, then," Mike said, "but considering the weather conditions, it just doesn't make sense to me that a bunch of teenagers would pick yesterday afternoon to go on a rampage. I don't know. I can't say why, exactly, but I have a bad feeling in my gut that's telling me it's not anything that simple."

"A bad feeling in your gut? Maybe it's just indigestion from that steak bomb you devoured in about five bites yesterday. I told you that you'd regret having that thing."

Mike laughed and then the police radio squawked and crackled and the voice of dispatcher Gordie Rheaume filled the vehicle, ending the conversation. "Unit Three, come in."

Mike lifted the mic from the rack on the dashboard. "This is Unit Three, go ahead Gordie."

"Chief, we got a call from a lady on Mountain Home Road by the name of Sally Crosker. She says her husband was out early this morning chipping ice off their driveway and now he's disappeared."

"Jeez, Gordie, maybe he went out for a cup of coffee."

"If he did, he forgot to take all of his blood with him because his wife says there's about a gallon of it splashed all over their driveway."

The dispatcher gave them the street address, and Mike answered, "We're on our way."

Sharon flicked a switch to activate the flashing blue lights atop the police SUV and carefully eased the four-wheel drive cruiser into the empty road. All talk of Ida Mae Harper's dog were forgotten, at least for the time being.

*   *   *

Officer Dupont eased the vehicle to a stop, parking at an angle across the end of the driveway at 32 Mountain Home Road. Mike could see even before exiting the SUV that some kind of violent confrontation had indeed taken place. The two officers opened their doors and walked up one side of the long drive, taking their time, examining the scene.

Before they had gotten halfway to the house, the front door opened and a woman dressed in jeans and flannel hunting jacket rushed out to meet them.

Mike turned his attention to her as she approached. Her face was heavily lined, either from advancing age or hard living. Her long brown hair was graying and tied up in a pony tail. He tried to guess her age and decided she could be anywhere from early forties to mid-sixties, it was that hard to tell.

"Thank you so much for coming, I know how treacherous the conditions are out here," she said, holding her hand out to Mike. "I'm Sally Crosker. I wouldn't have bothered you if I didn't think something was really wrong." Her voice broke at the end of her greeting. Her grip was firm but her hand was shaking.

"No problem," Mike answered. "This is why we're here, Mrs. Crosker. I'm Chief Mike McMahon and this is Officer Sharon Dupont. What happened out here? It looks like two dogs were fighting."

"I know," she said, staring at the blood-splattered ground and then looking away with a shudder. "I'm afraid something awful has happened to my Harvey. He's not well, you know. He shouldn't have been out here in this weather at all, but he wouldn't allow me to try to clear the driveway. He said it was man's work and he was bound and determined to do it." Sally Crosker looked at Sharon Dupont with a trembling smile, as if assuming she would understand.

Mike watched as the woman, who he was beginning to think was closer in age to sixty than forty-five, shivered in the slanting rain. "Mrs. Crosker, would it be all right if we talked inside? You really aren't dressed for this weather and getting sick won't help your situation."

She smiled gratefully. "Yes, please do come inside. I'm sorry for not offering. I'm just so worried about Harvey. Follow me."

The icy rain continued to fall, and although it couldn't have been more than eighty feet from the bloody ground to the front door, it took nearly a full minute to navigate the low-grade slope of the hill and reach the shelter of the house. Mike thought it was a miracle the woman hadn't taken a header on her way out to greet them.

Inside, the home was warm and inviting, the furnishings old but clean and well maintained. Mike and Sharon stood just inside the door, dripping water onto someone's living room floor for the second time in less than twenty-four hours.

Sally Crosker shrugged off her too-light jacket and turned to the officers. "Please, come in and sit down," she insisted, motioning them into the room. "Don't worry about the water. I can clean that up later. What do we have to do to find Harvey?"

Mike and Sharon sat side by side on the small couch in the Crosker living room. He was conscious of their legs touching and wondered if she noticed it too. "How long was your husband gone before you called for assistance, Mrs. Crosker?"

"It's hard to say for sure, because when Harvey went out to clear the ice, I puttered around in here for a while doing the dishes, washing the floor, folding laundry. After a fashion it occurred to me that Harvey should have been back inside. He's been suffering from cancer for several years now and his stamina isn't what it used to be. When I realized he hadn't come in yet, I looked for him out the picture window," she indicated the large window behind them, "and couldn't see him, even though the entire driveway is visible from here. So I threw on my jacket and took a walk outside, half afraid I would find him unconscious on the ground. Instead he was just gone and all that blood was everywhere…"

She took a deep breath and tried to choke off a sob and almost succeeded.

"Did you see anything at all, either while you were looking for Mr. Crosker out the window or when you went outside?" Mike asked. "Cars driving by, people walking along the road, anything unusual?"

"No, nothing," the woman replied, looking bewildered. "Nothing but all that blood. Who would have taken Harvey and for what purpose? We don't have much money. Harvey's cancer treatments have taken just about everything we *do* have except for the house, so it's not like we can afford to pay a large ransom demand."

"At this point, Mrs. Crosker, we don't know that he *has* been taken. Maybe he fell and hit his head, became disoriented, and wandered away. Why don't you let Officer Dupont and me get out there and take a look around. Maybe we can come up with something a little more concrete. Please try not to be too concerned yet. We'll put out a description of Mr. Crosker to all our officers and be on the lookout for him. In the meantime, if you hear from him or think of anything you might have forgotten to tell us, please don't hesitate to call."

Mike asked for a recent photograph of the missing man and Sally Crosker rushed out of the room, returning moments later with a picture of a graying, handsome man smiling into the camera. He was dressed in hunting gear and his face had the weathered appearance of a long-time outdoorsman.

Mike accepted the photo, then he and Sharon rose from the

couch and moved toward the front door. "We'll be in touch," he assured the woman, shaking her hand, before they pulled on their heavy winter parkas and moved back out into the escalating storm.

"Do you really think he fell and hit his head?" Sharon asked as they walked back to the Explorer. Mike noticed the smaller officer struggling to match his long strides on the icy ground and slowed his pace. The wind whipped the ancient evergreens surrounding the Crosker home. Trees were beginning to bend precipitously from the steadily accumulation of ice on their branches, and it was only a matter of time before some of them began snapping off and falling to the ground, making an already dangerous situation even worse.

"No," he answered, "I don't. Realistically, there's way too much blood staining on the driveway for that scenario. If a man, particularly an already sick man, had hit his head and lost that much blood, he would still be lying there. I didn't want to say what I really thought in front of Mrs. Crosker, especially with no proof."

"And what is it you really think?"

"I'm not exactly sure," he sighed, rubbing the back of his neck as they arrived back at the end of the driveway, re-examining the blood now being rapidly covered by an icy, slushy mix.

He looked at Sharon. "You tell me. Does this scene remind you of anything?"

"Sure. The mess behind Ida Mae Harper's house," she answered instantly.

"That's exactly right. And if Harvey Crosker was attacked by whoever or whatever ripped that golden retriever apart, he's in trouble. Big trouble."

8

Professor Kenneth Dye took a long pull on his JD and savored the sharp, smoky bite of the whiskey burning and churning its way down his throat before crash-landing in his belly. He had long ago reached the conclusion that the first sip of the day was the best but didn't mind testing that theory with plenty of other sips and the occasional enthusiastic gulp too, just for good measure.

He slid his frozen dinner into the oven and reflected on the day just past. Not too bad, all things considered. After struggling through that first interminable class in the typically empty lecture hall, he had hit his stride and burned through the remainder of his daily schedule with ease, setting his internal autopilot and noting with pleasure he could remember next to nothing from any of the remaining lectures.

Maybe not exactly the classic definition of job satisfaction, but under the circumstances, Ken knew it was the best he could hope for. A dead-end job teaching students who didn't care, for an employer who thought he was completely off his rocker, didn't do much for one's motivation.

As he waited for his frozen fried chicken dinner to bake—*Now there's a mystery,* the professor thought. *How can it be fried chicken if I'm baking it?*—he flipped on the local television news for no particular reason other than he appreciated the background noise. He could have microwaved his meal and been eating it in just a few minutes but why bother? He had all the time in the world, so whether the food was ready in eight minutes or forty-eight was irrelevant to Ken Dye. The extra time it took to cook in the oven would be put to good use anyway, as he could enjoy his drink a few minutes longer before digging in.

On the tube, the perfectly coiffed anchor gravely informed his viewing audience a water main had burst under Portland Avenue. "The plummeting temperatures," he intoned, "will cause the water to freeze, worsening the already hazardous driving conditions. Authorities are advising motorists to seek alternate routes and to stay home unless travel is absolutely necessary."

"Now you tell me," the professor groused. His drive home from work, normally no more than fifteen minutes from campus to garage, had taken almost forty-five this afternoon. The streets formed a passable imitation of a gigantic skating rink, with ice building up too quickly for the Town of Orono sand trucks to keep pace. Cars were sliding off roads into utility poles and each other with alarming frequency and predictable results.

For the time being, though, Ken didn't care. He was home for the evening. He had no place to go and in any event no intention of driving after enjoying his nightly medicinal dose of Jack Daniel's. The police had very little sense of humor about drunk driving, particularly in a college town, and Ken Dye knew his reputation was already damaged enough without adding the ignominy of a drunk-driving arrest to it.

On the TV, a perky blonde field reporter was transmitting a live breaking news report from the isolated town of Paskagankee, located fifty miles up the road, deep in the Maine wilderness. The woman was dressed in a dark green parka adorned with the station's call letters and a fur-lined hood that the wind kept ripping off her head. Her face was chapped and cold, stung by sleet that seemed to be flying sideways in direct violation of the laws of physics.

She looked miserable.

Ken wondered whether it was her idea or the producer's to broadcast the report from outside in the elements.

"This quiet, out of the way community was rocked today with news of the disappearance of fifty-eight-year-old Harvey Crosker," the reporter gamely shouted into the wind, which howled around the microphone like an out of control freight train. "The missing man was last seen by his wife when he ventured out into the storm this morning to clear his driveway. That was nearly twelve hours ago. A large amount of blood was found at the scene, and it is feared Mr. Crosker, sick with cancer, may have been abducted.

"This comes on the heels of a savage attack on a local elderly woman's dog last night. The animal, a full-grown golden retriever, was discovered with its body torn apart in the back yard of its owner's home.

"Police will not speculate on whether the two events are connected or if they have any leads on Mr. Crosker's disappearance, but anyone with information regarding the man's whereabouts is urged to call the Paskagankee Police Department immediately."

The report concluded with a photo of the missing man flashed onto the screen, a telephone number superimposed along the bottom of the image.

It was all lost on Professor Kenneth Dye.

He was no longer paying attention.

"Oh, my God," he whispered to the empty house, staring at the far wall and seeing nothing. "It's finally starting."

In the kitchen, the oven's timer beeped insistently, informing Ken Dye that his chicken dinner was ready and demanding he do something about it.

But suddenly he wasn't the least bit hungry.

9

"Who is this guy again?" Mike asked, giving dispatcher Gordie Rheaume a quizzical look.

"He claims to be a professor of Native American studies down in Orono at the university."

"And he claims to have information about our missing shoveler?"

"That's what he said. He wanted to talk to someone in charge, and I told him you would be in this morning. But he said he had to speak to you in person, that this wasn't something he could do over the phone."

Mike put his hands on his hips. "Did this guy sound rational?"

Gordie shrugged. "He sounded normal to me, but how can you really tell? He just said it was imperative he talk to the officer in charge of the investigation into the missing homeowner and the tortured dog, that he had information, and that it was critical you get that information as soon as possible."

Mike McMahon sighed as he watched the storm raging outside the police station's front window. It had taken three times as long as it should have for him to get to work this morning, and now he was looking at a three-hour drive down to Orono in this mess. He certainly couldn't ask the professor to drive up here, not with the conditions still deteriorating.

He turned to Shari Dupont, who leaned against a desk, arms folded, watching the exchange between Mike and Gordie with a look of amusement on her face.

"I don't know what you think is so funny," he said. "Guess who's coming to Orono with me?"

* * *

Back inside the police SUV, coffee in hands, the two officers warily eyed the two-lane blacktop that would take them south to Orono and a meeting with the university professor supposedly in possession of urgent information. Without any evidence to speak of or a single usable lead, Mike McMahon felt he had no choice but to make the trip and probably waste a good chunk of the day on what would likely turn out to be a wild goose chase.

The deserted road was covered with what looked exactly like the topping on a glazed donut. The ice continued to thicken by the hour and still the freezing rain fell in torrents that forecasters predicted would continue for at least another two days. Schools remained closed, and fortunately most people had finally come to the conclusion that staying inside and out of the storm was the best option.

"What are you thinking about?" asked Shari Dupont.

"Glazed donuts, if you must know."

She laughed. "Jeez, a cop with a thing for donuts. You're a walking cliché, did you know that?"

"Hey," he protested. "A man's gotta eat, right?"

"I wouldn't call what you do 'eating right,' not even a little bit."

"I'm a guy, remember? Donuts, takeout and frozen pizzas are the only things we know how to make."

"Then I'll have to make you a home-cooked meal," Shari said and stopped suddenly, obviously concerned about stepping over the line with her new boss. Her face reddened.

"That'd be nice," he answered quietly. "I haven't had a real home-made dinner in quite a while."

An awkward silence fell over the vehicle and the next few minutes passed slowly.

Finally Shari spoke. "Weren't you going to tell me why you decided to move up here to the outer edges of the inhabited universe when you had a thriving career going in a real city?"

"Oh, that," he said. "It's really not a very exciting story."

"Well," she countered, "it's not like we don't have time on our hands, right?"

"That's certainly true," Mike agreed, eyeing a tractor-trailer inching along the northbound side of the two-lane, wondering if there would be anything left of him and Shari if that behemoth were to jackknife as it passed, crushing them like a couple of bugs.

"We were negotiating a hostage release, or trying to, anyway," he started without preamble, not wanting to relive that day again but unable to stop himself from doing so.

"A father had snapped. He was separated from his wife and he entered a crowded bank with a semi-automatic weapon, taking the wife and their seven-year-old daughter hostage, along with a full complement of bank employees and, of course, all the customers inside the place at the time. It was early on a Friday morning and the building was full. The situation had the potential to get very ugly very fast. We evacuated the area around the bank and called a hostage negotiator to the scene. He stabilized the situation and slowed everything down, and it looked like we might get lucky and avoid a major tragedy.

"Along about the twelfth hour of the standoff, a customer tried to be a hero inside the bank building and made a play for the dirtball's gun."

Mike could feel Shari looking at him as he stared out the window of the SUV, seeing not the wilderness of Paskagankee, Maine, during an early November storm, but a blue-collar suburb on the outskirts of Boston on a sweltering July evening.

"I'm assuming the customer was unsuccessful?" she said finally.

"That's one way to put it. The perp put a bullet in the hero's head and then for good measure did his wife too, just to keep everyone else in line. That's when everything changed. We went from a posture of containment to one of attack. The moment he demonstrated his willingness to kill, especially multiple people at once, we knew we were out of time and had to take action."

Mike paused and tried to collect himself. The whole scene came flooding back so fully and felt so real. He lived it day after day and night after night. He dreamed about it; it permeated his entire existence: the grit of the dirty pavement under his feet.

The jitteriness and exhaustion.

The feeling of sweat running freely down the inside of his uniform shirt.

The knowledge that innocent people had died and more were likely to unless something was done, and soon.

"Mike?"

He jumped, startled. He had been a couple of hundred miles away. He glanced across the SUV at Shari and saw the concern evident on her face. Her eyes were big and blue and beautiful.

"Are you okay? You're white as a ghost."

He chuckled shakily. His mouth was dry and the inside of the police vehicle felt stiflingly hot. "I'm fine. Where were we?"

"You don't have to do this, you know," she said softly. "I understand if you just want to leave it in the past."

"That's exactly the problem. I can't leave it in the past. It's with me every day, a living, breathing entity. It's become a part of who I am. Maybe telling the story will help, I don't know. I've never really talked about it with anyone, not even the shrink the department made me see afterward."

"Okay. So, the father murdered two people inside the bank in cold blood."

"That's right." Mike's hands shook as he gripped the steering wheel. His palms felt sweaty and slick and his stomach churned. "Anyway, Lieutenant Blackburn, who was in charge of the operation, told us to take the guy down if we were able to get a clear shot. This particular branch office had a big plate-glass window fronting the street, and the suspect had been sighted numerous times over the course of the afternoon and evening walking back and forth in front of it. He became extremely agitated after shooting the two victims and cut off all communication with the negotiator.

"The SWAT guys were preparing to storm the bank, but the lieutenant wanted to wait just a little longer before sending them in. He was afraid once they hit the door that more people would get slaughtered by the guy before SWAT could put him down, even if they used flash-bangs to disorient him. There were so many people inside that damned building that even if the guy fired randomly, he was a lock to hit other people. Blackburn rolled the dice, hoping the guy would take another stroll in front of the big window and one of us could take him out before he killed anyone else. It was a calculated risk."

Mike wiped his sweaty hands on his pants.

"You took the shot, didn't you?"

Mike took a deep, shaky breath and blew it out forcefully. "Oh, yeah."

"And?"

"Well, the guy had been using employees as human shields all day. Whenever he walked around inside the bank, he pushed an innocent person around in front of him. This time, he did the same thing, but as he turned to retrace his steps, I had a clean shot for a split-second. So I took it.

"The thick plate glass deflected the path of the bullet even though it was almost a straight shot. It struck one of his hands, if you can believe that, and knocked the weapon to the floor. Several hostages jumped him after he fell and subdued him."

Mike felt Officer Dupont eyeing him closely as he continued staring straight ahead through the windshield. "So you were a hero. You saved all those people and, in the process, didn't even have to kill the suspect. All-in-all it sounds like a pretty good day to me."

"Yeah," Mike agreed bleakly. "A pretty good day. There was only one problem. After the bullet struck the perp's hand, it ricocheted at an angle down and to the left, where he had handcuffed his daughter to a desk leg. It struck the little girl in the head and she died instantly."

The inside of the SUV grew silent. The tension was electric.

"But you have to know that wasn't your fault," Shari protested. "That was nothing more than the worst kind of terrible luck."

Mike wiped his forehead with his uniform sleeve. He knew it wasn't hot in the car, but it felt like a sauna to him. This was the visceral reaction he felt every time he thought about that awful day in Revere, Massachusetts.

"Yes, I know that," he finally said. "The department conducted a full hearing afterward, just as they do whenever an officer is involved in a shooting. I was completely exonerated.

"Of course, the little girl's family didn't see it that way—what was left of her family, that is—and who could blame them? From their perspective the people who were being paid to protect her from harm were the ones that killed her. The grandparents filed suit against the city for millions—a lawsuit that's still pending, by the way.

"After that, the mayor's office informed the chief it would probably be best if I just went away quietly, so I did."

Shari Dupont sat motionlessly, mouth agape, her face flushed with anger and her eyes flashing. Even from deep inside his personal hell, Mike thought her emotion made her even more beautiful than before, if that was possible.

"You should have stayed and fought for your job," she sputtered. "You did *nothing wrong!* They couldn't just fire you for doing your damned job!"

"You're not getting it," he said, smiling faintly as he took in Shari's reaction. "I wasn't fired. They made a suggestion, one with which I agreed wholeheartedly, and I took it. I had been considering getting away for quite a while, trying something new, but my wife loved Revere and didn't want to move. It was where she had grown up, where her family and friends were and still are."

"I didn't know you were married," Shari said in surprise.

"Five years," he answered. "But after the shooting things were never the same. There was so much negative publicity, so much pressure on both of us, none of which was her fault. She just couldn't handle it. She left me four months later. I don't blame her, really," he said reflectively. "I wasn't the same guy after that shooting.

"Anyway, like I said, I had been wanting to do something different for a long time, I just wasn't able to decide what that something might be. I figured there was nothing holding me in Revere anymore, so when I read about the opening for chief here in Paskagankee, I decided to give it a shot. Little did I know the last guy to hold the job would want out so badly, I would be hired almost immediately. Now, here I am."

Mike breathed deeply. The temperature in the SUV was returning to normal for him, and the nausea he felt every time he thought about that horrible day in July sixteen months ago was beginning to ease.

"That's quite a story," Shari said quietly. "I remember seeing something about it on the news, even way down at the FBI Academy in Virginia, but I had no idea how horrifying the tragedy really was."

"You want to hear something funny?" he asked, not taking his eyes off the slick road. He still clutched the steering wheel with both hands like a drowning man holding a life preserver.

"Sure."

"That night was the only time I ever fired my gun on the streets. I drew it plenty of times, shot thousands of rounds at the practice range, but that was the one and only time I ever actually fired on someone. And I killed a little girl."

10

Carolyn Scherer pounded down the narrow path that wound through the thick woods. The steadily worsening weather made the forest floor slippery and dangerous, but Caroline barely noticed and didn't care.

She had fallen in love with running years ago, when doctors advised her she was grossly overweight. They told her in no uncertain terms that if she didn't begin exercising and slimming down, she could expect an early and exceedingly unpleasant death.

That was how she traded an obsession with eating for an obsession with exercise. Carolyn had started out cautiously, walking short distances at first and then increasing the lengths of those walks, discovering in the process that she loved being outdoors.

After dropping enough weight to run safely, she began jogging, slowly and over short distances at first. Now she was hooked. Carolyn Scherer was officially a die-hard distance runner. And die-hard distance runners didn't let a little thing like unpleasant weather interfere with their daily routines.

Today's run would take her on her favorite route. It would take her from the back yard of her Mountain Road home, through the woods along a little-used hunting trail, and then back to her house along the side of the sparsely populated road. The entire route was over six miles long, and Carolyn ran it practically every day.

She'd been running for twenty minutes and was now deep inside the massive forest pressing in on Paskagankee from all sides. The sleet and freezing rain coated every surface in ice and was thickening rapidly. Tree branches drooped, some blocking the path. Several times already, Carolyn had been forced to jump over or detour around huge limbs.

The disturbing thought crossed Carolyn's mind that should she slip on the ice and fall she might not be found until spring. Cell phones were useless because coverage was virtually nonexistent out here.

She shivered, only partly from the bitter cold and freezing rain.

Rounding a corner and concentrating all her attention on navigating the path, Carolyn almost missed seeing the large mass of dark red, partially frozen slush—it was more brown than red, really—flashing past in her peripheral vision under the trees to her right.

Several yards beyond the odd-looking splatter, some instinct she couldn't identify made her circle back. Curiosity overrode a vaguely formed feeling of dread.

She reached the spot where she had glimpsed the reddish-brown slush in a matter of seconds and peered into a stand of trees. She had glimpsed the strange sight for just a half-second and then only out of the corner of her eye, but she could have sworn it looked exactly like a pool of blood.

But of course it couldn't be a pool of blood.

That would be ridiculous.

Because how in the world would a pool of blood end up way out here in this isolated area?

Carolyn stopped and looked and almost couldn't find what she was certain she had seen just moments before. The freezing rain was driving hard now, slanting sideways, dripping off the brim of her New England Patriots baseball cap and obscuring her vision.

There!

Under an oak tree denuded by the season, a large puddle of what did indeed appear to be partially frozen slushy blood covered the ground. The hard rain was diluting the mess more and more with each passing minute, but it sure did look like blood.

She examined her discovery with equal parts curiosity and revulsion, easing closer to the sloppy mess. Then she leaped back, nearly losing her footing on the slippery ground as a drop of the liquid fell from above onto the growing puddle. It narrowly missed her neck and she choked off a scream.

Horrified and confused, Carolyn forced herself to look up into the trees as her heart pounded out a beat she was certain could be heard all the way down in Paskagankee.

And then she screamed for real. Alone in the forest and suddenly terrified, Carolyn Scherer gasped and sobbed and then screamed again.

Impaled on a dead branch high above her was a human head.

A man's head.

In the tree.

Its eyes were open and a look of terror frozen on its face as blood dripped slowly onto the ground at Carolyn's feet. Strings of tendons or muscles or ligaments, Carolyn didn't know which and didn't care, hung several inches below the grotesquely severed neck, and the blood rolled sluggishly along them before gathering into bulbous balls at the ends and falling thickly to the ground.

And Carolyn screamed.

11

Professor Kenneth Dye's house was located in a modest Orono subdivision of small ranch homes. The neighborhood was within easy commuting distance of the University of Maine, and Sharon guessed the homes had all been slapped together at the same time, maybe a half-century ago, to provide affordable housing for university students and staff.

The street was quiet as the Paskagankee Police Department Ford Explorer worked its way up the professor's driveway, easing to a stop behind what Shari assumed must be the professor's car, a Toyota Prius of recent vintage.

She checked her watch and smiled. "Only two hours and forty-five minutes. Not bad considering we had to travel almost fifty miles in this God-awful weather."

She had kept the conversation intentionally light after Mike finished relating the story of the Revere tragedy sixteen months ago. Shari was no medical professional, but she had become concerned he might suffer a nervous breakdown while he was talking. He had been deeply affected by the shooting and even though his head knew the little girl's death was nothing more than a horrible accident, she could see plainly that in his heart he refused to stop blaming himself.

12

Ken Dye paced nervously, glancing out his living room window as the freezing rain continued to fall. Power had failed in various Orono neighborhoods, and Ken wondered how long it would be before his house was plunged into darkness. He rechecked the candles he had placed around the room, hoping they would be sufficient to ward off the darkness when the inevitable occurred.

Of course, even if candles illuminated the room, they would do little to counter the darkness in his soul.

The professor sipped his Jack nervously and wondered for probably the thousandth time whether he had done the right thing in calling the authorities. He was almost positive that his hunch about what was happening in Paskagankee was correct, but Ken Dye was a man who had seen a promising career scuttled and a life ruined by discussing things people didn't want to hear. He had no desire to become a laughingstock again, this time to an entirely new segment of the population.

On the other hand, if the situation was what he believed, then he really had no choice but to alert the police, to tell all he knew and everything he suspected. If he remained silent and it turned out he was right, the bloodshed—and there would be plenty of it—would be entirely on his hands, and he simply could not live with that.

Ken took another sip—*be honest with yourself, Kenneth old chap, gulp would probably be more accurate*—and wished the damned police would just get here already. This waiting was the worst, even more so than dealing with the inevitable skepticism and maybe even downright scorn he would encounter from them.

The weather was terrible, though, and he thought it entirely possible they wouldn't show at all, at least not until conditions improved. It was a measure of how little the authorities had to go on regarding the disappearance of that poor man that they were even willing to *consider* coming all the way down here to listen to him in the first place.

He took another pull from his rapidly emptying glass and peered out his front window, and this time was rewarded with the sight of a white and blue Ford Explorer turning carefully into his driveway. On the side of the vehicle was emblazoned the words "Paskagankee Police." The front tires slid and for a moment Ken was certain the SUV was going to end up in the middle of his front lawn, then the truck gained just enough traction to complete the turn and park safely on the driveway.

A moment later both front doors opened, and a man and woman exited the vehicle dressed in police uniforms. Ken guessed the man might be in his mid-thirties and the woman, who was tiny and didn't fit any stereotype of a police officer Ken had ever heard of, looked considerably younger.

He hurriedly topped off his glass and opened the door to welcome the two into his home.

13

"You told our dispatcher you had some important information for us," Chief Mike McMahon said after introductions had been completed.

"That's right."

"I have to tell you," he continued as Ken ushered them into his living room, "that I expect to be impressed, since you insisted we come all the way down here in the middle of the worst November storm in at least a decade."

The professor cleared his throat and sipped his drink. He had offered refreshments to the officers but was unsurprised when they turned him down.

"I'm sorry about that, Chief McMahon, but if I told you what I had to say over the phone, I'm afraid you would have hung up on me before I even half-completed my story."

"You're not doing much to establish credibility with me so far," the chief told him. It was obvious the two officers weren't in the mood for idle chatter, having just completed a hair-raising trek along extremely icy roads.

Chief McMahon had done all of the talking for the two officers to this point, and Professor Dye wondered what, if any, purpose the young female officer's presence served.

"Let me just launch into it then," he said.

"Good idea."

Dye took another nervous sip and noticed a look pass between his two visitors.

"I know what you're thinking," the professor said, "and yes, I do enjoy my sour mash. After you hear what I have to say, you might just reconsider and have a belt or two yourselves."

"Get on with it, Professor, please."

"Okay. Yes. Well, I came to this country four decades ago to research Native American folklore after graduating from Oxford University. I've made the study of that subject my life's work, and I am convinced it has a direct bearing on what has begun happening in your town right now, Chief McMahon."

The police chief frowned. "You're saying a Native American kidnapped Harvey Crosker and tore an old lady's dog apart? How? And for what possible reason?"

"No, Chief, that's not at all what I'm saying." Ken took another drink with a shaking hand, the whiskey sloshing down one side of the glass.

"This is even more difficult than I had imagined," he mumbled, more to himself than to the two police officers.

"Listen, Professor," McMahon interrupted, clearly out of patience. "We came a long way in lousy weather because you said you could help with a missing-persons investigation. Is that the case or is it not?"

Ken took a deep breath and said, "Yes, I can help you."

"Then I suggest you start right now."

"Are you familiar with the history of the Roanoke Island settlement in what eventually became the state of Virginia in 1587?"

"I only know what little I learned in school and that was a long time ago. Wasn't that where the English colonists disappeared without a trace?"

"That's right," Ken answered, nodding. "The leader of the settlement, a man named John White, had returned to England to procure supplies when they became scarce. When he arrived back in England, he was forced by the British to assist them in their war against the Spaniards. By the time White managed to return to Roanoke, three years had elapsed, and he found that the colony had simply vanished, seemingly into thin air. No trace of any of the inhabitants, either living or dead, could be found anywhere although all of their personal belongings were left untouched."

"That sounds more or less like what I learned in school," Mike said. "It's all very interesting, but what does any of this have to do with an ongoing police investigation in Paskagankee, Maine?"

"The geographical area in which your town is located is home to a legend somewhat similar to the Roanoke Island mystery."

"Is that so?"

"The legend is much more obscure, but yes, it is so."

"Go on."

"In the early 1800's, when the town of Paskagankee was established, it was nothing more than a tiny village. A speck on a map, really. But back then the town didn't exist in its current location. The original village of Paskagankee was constructed on a piece of land some distance east of where the town square currently sits."

The chief gazed at Ken quizzically. The professor was glad to see he had at least gotten the man's attention.

He continued talking, his drink forgotten on the end table next to him. "The settlement existed in its original location only for a matter of perhaps a year or two, then…things…started happening to the residents, of which there were only a few dozen."

The young female officer finally spoke up. It was the first time she had opened her mouth since being introduced. "Things? What sorts of things are you talking about?"

"Bizarre, inexplicable things," Ken answered. "Things like animals being massacred in horrific ways. In those days, animals were much more important than mere pets. They were a critical element of survival, accounting for much of the village's food supply, and so the deaths were taken quite seriously, as you might imagine.

"Eventually, the massacre spread to residents. Villagers began being murdered, their bodies rent in horrifying fashion. The surviving members of the town, and remember there were only a few, abandoned the settlement. They picked up stakes and reconstructed Paskagankee where your town exists today."

Chief McMahon shook his head. "That sounds utterly ridiculous. They moved a whole town because of a couple of ritualistic murders? I don't think I'm buying that one."

"No, it's true," the female officer interrupted. "I've lived in Paskagankee most of my life, and there have been stories whispered for as long as I can remember about things happening hundreds of years ago in the area—things very similar to what Professor Dye just spoke of."

"Okay," Mike said reluctantly. "But were the perpetrators ever caught? Was the town massacred by Native Americans? Is that what you're getting at? And I still don't see the relevance to our situation today."

Professor Dye hesitated. "Well," he said, "here's where it gets a little hard to believe."

"You mean up until now you've been telling us the *believable* part?"

"Now you understand why I drink," the professor said with a crooked grin.

Neither of the two officers returned his smile, so he shrugged and continued. "I told you I've studied Native American folklore my entire adult life. Well, my research—and it has been extremely thorough—suggests that a deadly confrontation took place in the exact location of the original settlement of Paskagankee. It occurred in the late 1600's between a group of traveling missionaries and a local tribe of Abenaqui natives.

"As the legend goes, there had been a tryst between one of the missionaries and a young Abenaqui girl, who subsequently got pregnant and eventually gave birth to a baby girl. The missionaries returned to the area a couple of years later, and the young man who had fathered the baby discovered he had a daughter.

"He made the determination that no child of his was going to be brought up as an Abenaqui and somehow attempted to kidnap the child. A vicious battle broke out between the missionaries and the Abenaqui villagers, a battle in which nearly everyone from both sides was killed.

"As the Abenaqui tell it, one of the missionaries shot the young mother. Whether it was accidental or intentional depends upon what version of the story is being told and will undoubtedly never be known for sure. In any event, the musket ball ripped through the baby and then struck the mother. The shot basically tore the infant's head right off her body."

Ken paused, drinking from his glass of Jack Daniel's. His hand had stopped shaking and his voice was strong.

The two officers had been hanging on his words, clearly spellbound. Ken considered that a minor victory.

Now Chief McMahon said, "That's quite a story, Professor. But I still don't see the connection between a Native American legend from three centuries ago and a disappearance yesterday in my town."

"Yes, well, I was just getting to that," Ken explained. "You see, I said *almost* everyone was killed and that is true, but there *were* a couple of survivors. The legend has it that one of the missionaries—the man who shot the mother and her baby—survived, albeit with horrific injuries. The missionary, incredibly, managed to walk out of the forest. He was suffering grievously from his wounds but did, in fact, live, and eventually returned to England, never to see America again."

"And?" said Chief McMahon.

"And there was one other survivor. According to the Abenaqui legend, the medicine man from the doomed village, an ancient warrior possessed of powerful magic, leveled a curse upon the location of the massacre."

"A curse."

"That's right, Chief McMahon. The curse states that if a living human spends more than a very small amount of time in the location of the massacre, he or she will act as a host, allowing the mother to occupy the living body The mother's spirit will thus have the ability to extract retribution for her child's tragic death.

McMahon looked skeptically at the professor. "Retribution?"

"Yes. People will be torn apart, literally limb from limb, exactly as her child was torn apart. Legend says the spirit will possess tremendous power, far beyond what is understandable either through physics or physiology.

"This legend dovetails perfectly with the events that occurred in the original village of Paskagankee, which had the extreme misfortune of being constructed on the exact location where the massacre had taken place almost two hundred years prior. The young Abenaqui mother's spirit managed to inhabit someone from that town, perhaps more than one person, and caused the horrific deaths of numerous settlers, eventually forcing the panicked abandonment of the town. The granite foundations of some of the buildings from that haunted settlement still exist today. I know they exist because I've seen them.

"I believe, in fact I am nearly certain, that you will find this is what's happening now in your town." Professor Dye looked up at the clock hanging on his living room wall. Nearly two hours had passed since the police officers had pulled into his driveway.

Chief McMahon studied the carpet at his feet. Ken could see he was trying to decide how to proceed. "You expect me to believe that a three-hundred-fifty-year-old Native American woman is haunting my town?"

"Not haunting. At least not in the classic definition of the term. Rather, her tortured spirit has taken possession of some unfortunate citizen's body. That person, whoever it is, is under the influence of the curse and is not responsible for his or her actions. But here's the thing, Chief McMahon. The killing is not going to stop until the curse is neutralized. Until that happens, things are only going to get worse in Paskagankee. Much worse, I fear."

The police chief shook his head. "I've never been much of a believer in ghost stories," he said. "In my experience, flesh and blood human beings are capable of doing plenty of damage all on their own."

Now it was the professor's turn to shake his head. "That's exactly the point," he protested. "It *is* flesh and blood that's doing the damage. The spirit is helpless until she finds a host she is able to possess. Once that possession occurs, though, she becomes increasingly powerful and dangerous."

"I don't know," Chief McMahon said skeptically. "I appreciate you making the effort to contact us, and that's one heckuva story, but I have to be honest here. I'm not convinced that the spirit of a brokenhearted Abenaqui mother is kidnapping people in my town."

"Oh, no, no," Ken said. He shook his head vigorously. "I guess I didn't make myself clear. She's not *kidnapping* anyone. I told you, she's killing them. She's tearing their bodies apart."

At that moment, the chief's portable radio squawked to life. All three people in the room jumped at the same time. "Chief McMahon, come in."

McMahon pressed the transmit button. "Yeah, Gordie, go ahead."

The voice of the dispatcher came through, strained and upset.

"You need to get back here now," he said. "We've found Harvey Crosker."

"That's great news," the chief answered. "Is he okay?"

"Not exactly. Just get back here ASAP."

14

The water had been falling from the sky virtually nonstop for nearly three full days. At times it came down as mostly sleet with the occasional fat snowflake mixed in, at other times it took the form of freezing rain, and on very rare occasions the atmosphere warmed just enough to turn the whole mess back into plain old rain. But at no time did it actually stop, and now several inches of ice and frozen slush covered the ground, with more being added to it continuously.

The return trip to Paskagankee from Orono took Mike and Shari nearly thirty minutes longer than the drive south had taken, not because there was more traffic on the road; in fact, there was even less. But conditions had worsened to the point where even with a four-wheel drive SUV, Mike could not coax a speed of better than twenty miles per hour out of the Explorer without fearing he would lose complete control of the vehicle.

Darkness fell long before Mike and Shari finally limped into Paskagankee. They bypassed the police station and drove straight to the location where a passing jogger—*A jogger? In this weather?* Mike wondered what the hell people were thinking sometimes—had reported the gruesome discovery of a disembodied human head lodged high in a tree.

The jogger had been forced to run almost all the way back to her home before reaching an area where cell coverage was sufficient to permit a call for help, and she had been panicked and near tears when she finally managed to contact Paskagankee Police dispatcher Gordie Rheaume.

The moment Mike and Shari had reached the SUV after making their hurried departure from Professor Dye's house, Mike called Gordie Rheaume on his cell phone and received a briefing on the few details currently available. What he heard made him glad he had stayed off the radio. Gordie advised him that Officer Jimmy Hadfield had investigated the call from the hysterical jogger and could verify that the severed head did, indeed, fit the description of the missing Harvey Crosker.

Mike told the dispatcher to ensure Hadfield secured the scene and then instructed him to call the county medical examiner, as well as the entire Paskagankee police force. Everyone, including those on their days off, was to be called into work, to meet at the location where the gruesome discovery had been made.

It was now six-thirty p.m., and Mike and Sharon were hungry, tired and wired from coffee and raw nerves when they pulled the Explorer to the side of Mountain Home Road. The only access to the crime scene was via more than a two-mile hike into the forest.

An excited Jimmy Hadfield was waiting to escort them as they clambered out of the vehicle. "Chief, you're not gonna freakin' believe your eyes when you see this! It's a goddamn head in a tree!"

Mike raised his hands for Hadfield to stop, shaking his head and telling the young officer, "Don't say anything else, Jimmy, I want to see it for myself when we get there, okay?"

Hadfield turned sullen, saying, "Fine, whatever. I've been getting rained on out here for two hours waiting for you, that's all."

Mike looked at Hadfield's rain gear, still relatively dry, and said, "Well, you've been in your cruiser, right? I mean, you haven't been standing outside this whole time, have you?"

"No, of course not, it's just…ah hell, never mind. I've just never seen anything like this in the five years I've been on the force, that's all. It's unbelievable."

Mike asked, "You left someone at the scene, I assume?"

"Hell yeah, everyone's there by now, including the ME. They're all standing around waiting for you. What took you so long, anyway?"

Mike raised his eyebrows and looked up at the dark sky, freezing rain falling into his face. "You may not have noticed Jimmy, but there are rumors of a pretty serious storm in the area. We ran into part of it."

"Oh. Yeah. Right."

They started into the woods. Mike hoped Jimmy hadn't inadvertently destroyed evidence tramping around up there before anyone else reached the scene. The kid seemed to be a decent cop and a hard worker, but Mike had already discovered Hadfield might not necessarily be the smartest guy in the room, even when he was in the room all by himself.

Officer Hadfield started out ahead, picking his way carefully along the narrow, rutted, ice-covered trail. Mike could not believe that less than four hours ago a woman had been running alone through this remote and treacherous area. Judging trail's condition, he decided she had been extremely fortunate not to have fallen and broken a leg in her desperate rush to get help.

It didn't take long for a damp chill to begin seeping into his bones. He wondered if Shari felt the same way and figured she must. They were dressed in heavy all-weather gear stored in the back of the vehicle, so there was a measure of protection from the elements, but the dank blackness seemed a perfect match for his mood. Mike had come to Paskagankee, Maine, to get away from kidnappings and murders and horrific inhumanity. Now here he was, less than two weeks into his new job and he was waist-deep in…who knew what?

The little group slogged along the narrow path, the freezing rain soaking them and slowing progress to a crawl. The trail was littered with good-sized branches as trees buckled from the weight of the ice. Gigantic firs sagged against their neighbors, uprooted but lacking enough room to fall to the ground. Several times the officers were forced to abandon the path and pick their way around blockages caused by the storm.

Mike McMahon wasn't a guy who put a lot of stock in myths and legends. He had seen plenty of evil in his fifteen-plus years of police work and knew that spirits and demons weren't necessary to produce it. Mankind was quite capable of gross inhumanity all by itself. But as he picked his way through this vast, desolate forest, Mike found himself reconsidering Professor Ken Dye's incredible tale.

Was it really possible these woods had been the scene of a bloody massacre more than three hundred years ago and that the restless spirit of a grieving Native American mother was wreaking havoc on his newly adopted town? The idea had seemed ludicrous sitting in Professor Dye's cozy living room, watching the man sip whiskey and calmly and rationally speak words that amounted to utter nonsense.

But now, Mike discovered he was not so sure of certain. What had struck him as ridiculous and even laughable a couple of short hours ago now seemed, if not likely, then at least not entirely outside the realm of possibilities.

Mike chuckled. He must be more tired than he realized.

Up ahead on the narrow path, Officer Jimmy Hadfield led the way. Sharon Dupont followed, with Mike bringing up the rear. Hadfield trudged along, head down, still sulking over not being allowed to spill all the gory details of the grisly discovery.

The new chief of police found himself staring at Sharon, mesmerized by her shapely figure as she struggled along the trail. He was developing a strong attraction to the younger woman, even though he knew it would be asking for trouble to start anything. She was his employee for one thing, and he knew he was damaged goods thanks to the Revere shooting for another.

Still, he hadn't been with a woman since his wife picked up stakes and moved back to her parents' house almost a year ago, and Sharon Dupont was cute and smart and, as far as Mike knew, available.

He found his mind wandering, curious as to whether she felt anything toward him. *Stop it*, he told himself. *This is pointless. The woman works for you, for God's sake. Don't be an idiot.*

Finally a weak, hazy glow shone through the trees ahead. Seeing clearly for more than a few feet was impossible, as night had by now fully fallen and the heavy freezing drizzle formed a nearly impenetrable curtain. Flashlights helped cut into the heavy mist but were no match for the conditions.

The group worked their way around one last fallen tree and then found themselves amidst a crowd of nearly a dozen people, all holding flashlights and coffee and trying to keep warm as a portable generator lit the scene.

It was one of the eeriest things Mike had ever witnessed.

A tall, gaunt man in a dark trench coat stood in the middle of the clearing, tapping his foot impatiently. His collar was pulled up against the cold and an old-fashioned fedora was perched atop his head.

The man turned and said, "Finally. Can we get this show on the road?"

Dr. Jan Affeldt was the county medical examiner. He had been called to the scene by dispatcher Gordie Rheaume per Mike's instructions, and it was obvious he didn't appreciate having to hike deep into the woods on this pitch-black November evening in the middle of the worst ice storm the area had seen in decades.

Mike couldn't blame him.

The chief stepped forward and offered his hand and the tall man reluctantly shook it after a moment's hesitation.

"Dr. Affeldt, I'm sorry it took so long to get here. Thanks for waiting. I know you want to get back to your family, as do we all, so I'll try to move things along. I simply wanted to get a look at the scene in person before releasing the remains to you."

"Fine. Let's just get on with it." The doctor shuffled his feet, and Mike could see they were wet and muddy. The sight was a reminder of how cold and miserable everyone milling around out here must be.

He turned and took in the ghastly scene, bathed in the uneven artificial light provided by the generator chugging away in the background. Two portable lamps had been erected on metal stands, one on each side of the clearing. Each lamp featured a pair of automobile headlights, and both had been angled upward so their beams converged partway up an ancient oak tree.

Mike's gaze followed the light until he found what he was looking for—a disembodied human head.

The head was lodged in the tree, resting awkwardly ten to twelve feet off the ground in a joint where a large branch extended from the trunk. Following Mike's instructions, the crowd of officers had left it undisturbed where the unfortunate jogger, Carolyn Scherer, first glimpsed it.

One of the Paskagankee Police officers who had been cooling his heels—literally and figuratively—awaiting the chief's arrival spoke up. "How long do you suppose that thing's been up there?"

Mike gazed into the unseeing eyes of the late Harvey Crosker.

The victim's head was angled in such a way that he appeared to be peering down at the group of officers below.

"Well, according to the young woman who was running out here, the blood was still dripping when she came by. It's frozen into a solid mass now, so I would have to say whoever or whatever put that head up there did it not too long before Ms. Scherer passed by. I think it's safe to say she is extremely lucky her head isn't mounted up there next to Harvey's."

Another officer, Pete Kendall, spoke up. "What exactly is the point in sticking a severed heard up in a tree, anyway, especially way out here in the middle of nowhere? Whoever did it couldn't have expected someone to come by and see it?"

"It looks to me," Mike answered, "like the victim's head was *tossed* into the tree, believe it or not. It looks like an irrational act committed by an unthinking perpetrator."

After examining the scene and ensuring that the officers had taken photos from all angles, Mike sighed and said, "All right, let's get him down from there. I assume you people canvassed the area for evidence, did you find anything?"

Kendall spoke up again. "We did our best considering it's pitch black out here, but honestly Chief, this ground is frozen solid with inches of ice on top of it. We didn't find anything and it doesn't seem likely that we will."

"Okay," Mike nodded, "let's get Mr. Crosker down and bagged—what little of him we have at least—and carry the remains out to the road where Dr. Affeldt can transport them to the morgue for the autopsy. I'll pay Mrs. Crosker a visit and break the bad news to her. Everyone else can go on home, except the two of you who are still on duty, and we'll plan on meeting here tomorrow morning at eight a.m. for a thorough search of the area in the daylight. Or what passes for daylight while this damned storm is raging. Any questions?"

Mike looked around at the tired, cold faces. The officers appeared numb from shock—eyes downcast, feet shuffling. Many of them had known Harvey Crosker, at least by sight; Paskagankee was a very small town. The unthinkable fate that had befallen the man seemed to have had a profound effect on everyone.

Mike was pretty sure he knew what they were thinking. It

was the same thing he was thinking: this sort of thing was not supposed to happen in a quiet, out of the way community like Paskagankee, Maine.

The officers got to work on the grisly task of recovering the victim's head. Mike looked closely at Sharon, who was still standing next to him. She had barely moved and hadn't said a word for nearly the past hour.

Her eyes were haunted, and she gave voice to his exact thought: "What the hell is going on here?"

15

Mike's stomach twisted and churned. Telling a missing person's family that their loved one has been found dead was never an easy thing to do. It was physically and emotionally wrenching, for the law enforcement professional as well as for the family members.

In this case, though, compounding the horror was the fact that they had recovered only a severed head. Given the gruesome circumstances surrounding the notification, the job was beyond distasteful.

It was now almost 9:30 p.m. Mike wished there was some way he could put off this gut wrenching visit until morning, but that was nothing more than wishful thinking. Mrs. Crosker deserved to learn her husband's fate as soon as possible, even if that meant surely guaranteeing a sleepless evening followed by years of nightmares.

After hiking back out to the road, the officers dispersed quickly. Mike signed the body bag—ludicrously empty with just a head inside—over to Dr. Affeldt and then glanced at Sharon. She looked exhausted, pale and drawn, and he remembered that neither of them had eaten since breakfast.

"Listen," he said. "I was going to drive you back to the station to pick up your car, but maybe I should just drop you off at your house on my way to notify Mrs. Crosker. I can pick you up in the morning, and that way you don't have to navigate this icy mess in your little Toyota."

Her answer surprised him. "No," she said. "It sucks that you have to tell that poor woman what happened to her husband. If it's all right with you, I'd like to be there when you deliver the news. Maybe I can help soften the blow for her just a little."

Mike smiled at her, grateful for the offer. He had done this sort of thing before, many times, and knew it would be difficult no matter what. But having Sharon there for support would make the duty a tiny bit more bearable, at least for them. There was no way to spare Mrs. Crosker from the brunt of the terrible news.

"Off we go then, and thanks," he said. "Afterward, though, I insist on driving you home. You look exactly the way I feel, which means there's no way you should be behind the wheel of a car."

"You really know how to sweet-talk a girl."

They eased the Explorer into the Crosker driveway just before ten o'clock, and Mike wondered if they would be getting the woman out of bed to tell her she was now a widow.

His unspoken question was answered immediately, though. Before Mike and Sharon had even exited the car, the front porch light flashed on. He could see Mrs. Crosker's robed figure at the living room window as they carefully crossed the ice-covered ground to the house.

The freezing rain had nearly stopped, at least for now, but the footing was as treacherous as ever and the two officers were forced to move very deliberately. *Of course,* Mike thought grimly, *the task we're here to accomplish might have something to do with our slow progress, too.*

The front door opened wide as they ascended the stairs and a warm, inviting light spilled out, chasing away the brooding darkness for a precious few seconds. Sally Crosker's shadow loomed out the door and stretched into the front yard.

"Please, come inside," she said, trying to smile and failing.

The woman was composed, but the strain was plainly evident on her face. She knew a visit in this weather at this time of night from the people searching for her missing husband could not possibly be anything but bad news.

"You've found him, haven't you?"

Mike and Sharon removed their soaking wet hats at the same time and held them in their hands. Mike looked down for a moment and then into Mrs. Crosker's desperately searching eyes.

They were already red-rimmed and tearing up, as though she couldn't wait any longer to hear the bad news but needed to start grieving immediately.

"Perhaps you'd like to sit down, ma'am," Mike said gently. He put an arm around her shoulder and steered her to her couch.

"Oh my God," she sobbed. "He's gone, isn't he?"

"I'm so sorry," Mike said as she collapsed into his arms.

16

It was nearly eleven-thirty by the time Mike and Sharon left the Crosker household and once again hit the icy roads. Sharon had been indispensable after Mike broke the awful news. She made three mugs of tea, handing one to the woman and then draping an afghan around her shoulders before sitting next to her, quietly holding her hand.

Mike avoided specifics as much as possible regarding the condition of the victim's body, continually steering the woman's questions in other directions. After a while they made awkward small talk while waiting for Sally's sister and brother-in-law to arrive from across town.

The new widow seemed to have a need to tell stories about her life with her husband: their honeymoon, the children they could never have, how they fought about Harvey always forgetting to put the toilet seat cover down.

Anything to avoid considering the awful future now staring her in the face.

When the two exhausted officers finally walked out the front door and into the night, they found the weather, incredibly, unbelievably, had worsened again. The rain slanted down at a severe angle, pelting the icy ground and almost immediately freezing solid. It took ten minutes to scrape the windshield of the Explorer clear enough to drive.

"That was horrible," Sharon said as they pulled out of the driveway. The SUV's heater struggled to force lukewarm air through the vents and into the passenger compartment. "You've had to do that before?"

"Plenty of times," Mike answered, rubbing his hands against the chill. "I have to say, you were great in there with Mrs. Crosker. Excellent people skills," he said. "That's rare in a cop. Hell, it's rare in a person in any profession."

Sharon smiled and her face lit up. Even tired, hungry and cold she was beautiful.

"Yeah, well," she said. "You can thank my Bureau training for most of that. They teach you how to be empathetic, if you can believe it, for use in situations where information can be extracted from suspects using a soft touch. What you saw with Mrs. Crosker back there was actually nothing more than your federal tax dollars hard at work."

Mike laughed. It felt somehow foreign after such a strange day. "I think there's a little more to it than that. You want to be accepted as a woman in the macho world of law enforcement, so most of the time you have to shut off your feelings and emotions. And it's doubly hard for you, being so petite and beautiful. It's too bad, really, because when you let the real you come through, like you did back there, it's pretty special."

Sharon was silent as the truck fought its way through the night on the deserted and treacherous roads. They reached the driveway of her home and the house sat dark and empty as Sharon pulled on her gloves and hat and prepared to step one last time into the miserable night.

She hesitated for a moment. "Care for a nightcap?"

Mike studied her face. It was radiant, with big, blue, searching eyes.

"I don't think that would be appropriate," he finally answered.

"It's just a drink. Just one. Please."

"Ah, what the hell," he said after another short hesitation. "It's been a long day. A drink sounds great."

He shut off the Explorer's engine, and the two police officers sat side by side in the dark, the only sound the freezing rain pelting the roof of the truck. Mike wondered how long it would take to scrape the windshield this time when he came out to drive home.

They opened their doors and hurried to the front entrance,

slipping and sliding on the flagstone walkway, which was coated, as Mrs. Crosker's had been, with a thick slab of ice. The house had been deserted all day and the ice had continued building up until it was now so heavy Mike thought it might be spring before it melted completely away.

Sharon struggled with her key in the lock as the wind whipped the freezing rain sideways, soaking them both. Finally the door sprang open and they rushed out of the elements. They stood just inside the foyer in the dark as Sharon slammed the door and fumbled for the light switch.

Mike was intensely aware of Sharon's presence next to him in the pitch-black hallway—her breathing, heavy and labored from the rush to get inside, the scent of her perfume, citrus-y and soft, still lingering on her after a sixteen hour day, the rustle of her clothing as she searched the wall next to the door for the light switch.

He reached into the darkness to pull her into his arms. He knew it was wrong, that he was making a mistake, that nothing good could come from an affair between a supervisor and his employee, but Mike didn't care. He suspected she felt the same way and he needed to find out.

He would just take her by the shoulders, pull her into his arms, and—

The wall switch clicked and the lights blazed on. Sharon looked up at Mike with her big blue eyes locking on to his, her face flushed from the rush against the weather—or was it something else?—and he stopped himself.

Another awkward silence descended on the pair until Sharon chuckled nervously and said, "Well. We were going to have a drink, weren't we?"

They trooped into the kitchen, trailing water down the hallway as they went. It felt to Mike like they had been doing that a lot lately.

"Have a seat," Sharon said with a smile. "What's your beverage of choice? I have beer, scotch, vodka, rum. It's a regular alcoholic's paradise in here. My father always insisted the liquor cabinet stay well-stocked." She laughed uneasily.

"A beer sounds great," Mike volunteered, and Sharon pulled

one out of the fridge, grabbing a frosted mug from the freezer and pouring the beer into it like a pro.

She handed the drink to Mike and then moved across the kitchen to her coffeemaker and dumped some ground beans directly from the can into the basket. Then she filled the water reservoir and punched the "start" button.

"You're not joining me?" he asked, surprised. It had been Sharon's idea to stop for a drink in the first place.

"I, uh, I can't."

"Well, as you've already mentioned, I've seen your personnel file so I know you're over twenty-one," Mike answered. "What gives?"

"Actually, that's what I wanted to talk to you about," she said. "It's one of the reasons I invited you in."

One of the reasons.

Mike sipped his drink, savoring the taste as it worked its way down his throat and wondering what the other reason might have been. "Okay."

"Remember yesterday, when we stopped Earl Manning for speeding and it turned out he had been drinking, so we took him in?"

"Was that just yesterday? It seems like about a month ago."

"Yeah I know," Sharon answered and stopped talking. She distractedly twirled a lock of her short hair behind one ear.

Mike waited patiently as she seemed to be searching for the right words to continue. Silence didn't bother him. He was used to it.

"You asked me why I didn't get in Earl's face when he was harassing me."

"I remember."

"Well," Sharon said, taking a deep breath. "There's more to the story."

"There always is," he said. The aroma of fresh coffee began wafting through the kitchen. It was homey and reassuring. The coffee smell evoked a feeling of normalcy, making it almost possible to forget for a moment that someone was apparently running around Paskagankee brutally killing people and animals, tearing their bodies apart.

The coffeemaker burbled and hissed and steam rose into the air.

"Why don't you grab a cup and join me," Mike suggested.

As Sharon set to work preparing her coffee, he asked, "Why didn't you tell me the rest of the story yesterday?"

"It's not an easy story to tell," she admitted, blowing on the steam rising out of her coffee mug. Mike suspected she did it so she could avoid looking at him.

"I don't want to pry, Shari. If it's not job related, you're under no obligation to tell me anything."

"I'm a recovering alcoholic," she blurted out forcefully. Her face was red with shame.

"And I'm a Presbyterian," he said immediately. "So?"

Sharon burst out laughing. Mike decided it made her look even more beautiful than before, and he hadn't thought that possible.

"I'm not sure what reaction I expected," she said, stifling another round of laughter, "but that definitely wasn't it."

"Well, really," he said. "You're an alcoholic. So what? Have you been drinking at work?"

"Of course not," she answered, her face flushing again, this time from anger.

"Then don't worry about it. Nobody's perfect, right? The last perfect person to walk the earth died two thousand years ago. Maybe you remember the story. And they hung him on a cross, so if you think about it, things didn't go so well for him, either."

Sharon scuffled her foot and looked down at the kitchen floor. She still seemed uncomfortable. "Thank you for saying that; you have no idea how nervous I was to tell you. I quit drinking when I left town to go to the FBI Academy. It was the right time to do it. New job, new life, new me. Perfect."

Mike nodded. It was obvious there was still more to the story. "But…"

"But then my dad got sick and had no one to care for him. He was able to live in his home for a while before being moved into a hospice facility in Orono, but only if there was someone here twenty-four hours a day to look after him. So I came back. I had to return to the place I thought I had left behind forever, to all the people I knew when I was drinking, all the pettiness and foolishness and bullshit I thought I had left behind for good."

Mike studied Shari's face, her exhaustion outlined in dark

circles under her pretty eyes. "But why bother coming back here at all? You said your father basically left you on your own after your mother died. Why not just leave him like he left you?"

She shook her head emphatically, her black hair flying. "I couldn't do that. I was an only child and he didn't have any brothers or sisters. I couldn't stand the thought of him dying, alone and forgotten. He did the best he could after my mom died, really. He just wasn't equipped to be responsible for a child, especially a teenage girl. Hell, he could barely take care of himself, and I didn't make things easy for him, either. I guess you could say I was a handful for a long time after my mom died, drinking and partying and staying out all night."

"I guess I can understand you feeling like you had to come back," Mike said. "You have a strong sense of responsibility and family obligation, and that's a good thing. But I still don't see what the relevance is to right now, to tonight, to why you feel you need to tell me all this."

"Because," Sharon answered, looking miserable. "This is where I grew up, where I did all my drinking before I quit. It's where I was a wild child, and people like Earl Manning remember me that way. Makes sense. It's the only way they've ever known me. There were plenty of nights I closed the Ridge Runner sitting right next to Earl, each of us holding the other up as we stumbled out to our cars. I'm sure that's why he felt so comfortable mouthing off to me."

"I thought you handled that jackass just fine," Mike told her, "especially when he climbed out of his truck. I got in his face because I could see he was getting to you, but I'm confident you could have put him in his place with no problem whatsoever."

Sharon smiled. It was obvious she was grateful for the compliment, as well as the fact Mike was trying to make this as easy as possible.

"Thanks. But the problem is, now that I'm back in town, and for who knows how long, I don't know if I can resist the temptations this place holds. It's just a little hick town to you, but to me, it's where I learned all the bad habits I've worked so hard to escape."

She paused, clearly trying to figure out how to continue.

Mike sat motionless, letting her work through her issues.

She took another deep shaky breath, then exhaled and continued. "I wanted a drink so bad tonight when we were standing in the forest looking at Mr. Crosker's head in a tree, I could hardly stand it. It's all I could think about."

She looked Mike in the eyes, shamefaced and nearly in tears. "That's really why I wanted to go to Mrs. Crosker's house with you. I didn't trust myself to be alone."

"Is that why I'm sitting here now?"

"Partly," she admitted. "I won't lie to you, I still want a drink. But after you opened up to me in the car about what happened to you with that little girl…"

"Sarah," he interrupted.

"I'm sorry?"

"Her name was Sarah. Sarah Melendez. I'll never forget it, or her."

"Sarah, then," she said, nodding. "After you told me about what happened to Sarah, I just felt I had to be honest with you and let you know what was going on. I've needed to open up, to confide in someone about how hard it is, but who the hell could I talk to around here?"

Mike stood without a word, walked to the sink, and dumped the remainder of his beer into the ceramic basin. It foamed and hissed as it circled the drain.

He stood at the sink until it gurgled out of sight, then reached into the cupboard, grabbed a big mug, and filled it with steaming coffee.

Returned to the table, sat and took a sip. "I'd like to propose a toast," he said.

Sharon smiled, intrigued and amused. "What?"

"A toast. You know, where we raise our glasses and I say something corny and stupid. I want to make a toast."

"I know what a toast is, silly, but what are we toasting?"

"We're toasting this: here's to keeping the past in the past where it belongs and to making fresh starts."

"Wouldn't that be two toasts?"

"By God, I guess you're right," he said, clinking his mug into hers twice. Their fingers grazed lightly on each pass, and after the second one, Mike left his cup next to hers, the contact between them electric.

Sharon raised her gaze to meet his, her blue eyes impossibly large, her moist lips parted and inviting.

Neither one said a word as Mike stood and pulled her into his arms and kissed her, hard and passionate and filled with need.

She tasted like cinnamon and they melted together.

17

The worst part about being a traveling representative for a struggling replacement computer parts firm was having to drive through the God-forsaken North Country, which in some ways seemed to Frank Cheslo like it couldn't possibly have changed at all over the last several thousand years.

Of course, that notion was ridiculous and Frank knew it. For one thing, there were no paved roads thousands of years ago in the God-forsaken North Country. Or anywhere else for that matter.

But if you used your imagination just a little, Frank thought it was easy to see exactly what this area looked like way back when. Traveling didn't bother Frank—he had been a salesman his entire adult life and at forty-four years of age that meant he had done a lot of traveling and a lot of selling over a lot of years. The thing he had a problem with at this point in his life was *where* he had to do that traveling.

As the newest sales rep for Computer Solutions of New England, Frank had been issued the least desirable sales territory. He understood how things worked in the corporate world and knew that before too long someone higher up in the food chain would die or retire or contract some terminal illness or move on to bigger and better things, and when that happened Frank would have the opportunity to inherit a more lucrative—and less remote—sales route.

In the meantime, though, Frank was stuck schlepping around the northeastern United States in his company-issued Ford Focus sedan. His sector of responsibility included the entire geographical area north of Boston all the way to the Canadian border, which, by Frank's calculations, wasn't too terribly far away at the moment.

For a guy who enjoyed the nightlife and the company of as many different women as he could sample since his divorce, the assignment was roughly comparable to having an eyeball sucked out of his face with a vacuum cleaner hose.

Now, to make things worse, this excruciatingly bad weather was causing Frank Cheslo to question his decision to drive all the way home to the outskirts of Boston, rather than waiting out the storm in a motel and continuing on after the weather cleared.

If it ever did.

He had started out in Presque Isle, Maine, after concluding his business at seven o'clock in the evening when the driving conditions were poor but not unmanageable. The intervening seven hours had seen the weather deteriorate drastically, until now it was all Frank could do to keep his car from sliding off the road in an uncontrolled spin. He prayed that wouldn't happen because if it did, way out here in the middle of nowhere, probably no one would find him until next May.

Any thoughts of driving all the way home had vanished in a solid wall of freezing drizzle. All Frank wanted now was to find a motel—any rotting piece of crap would do—on the side of the road and hole up. But of course there *were* no motels because he was driving through some of the most desolate goddamned land this side of frigging Death Valley. He was currently creeping along a lonely two-lane at two o'clock in the morning with no sign of human habitation anywhere.

Never mind motels. Hell, there didn't seem to be any *towns* around.

He tried to puzzle out exactly where in the vast wilderness of northern Maine he might be, but this territory was still new to him, and he couldn't pinpoint his location with any degree of accuracy.

Goddamned company ought to provide their sales staff with GPS units, Frank thought. But of course money was tight and GPS units for ordinary working stiffs just weren't in the budget. Undoubtedly the big shots at the top of the corporate ladder had all the fancy shit in their cars, and they didn't even drive all over New England like Frank did. Pricks.

"So here I am," Frank muttered to himself, as was his habit, in between trying to keep his car on the road and attempting to find a radio station that would come in as anything other than toneless white noise. "I'm lost, I'm tired, and I have no freaking clue how far I am from a decent sized town. Or any town. God, I hate this job."

Frank continued cautiously along Route 24 because, really, what choice did he have? Pull over to the side of the road and hope someone would stop and take pity on him? Not goddamned likely, especially way out here in the boonies. Another car might not come along for ten hours, especially in this weather, and if one did, it would undoubtedly just cruise on by, its owner intent on getting home and out of the storm as soon as possible.

Plus, and here was the cherry on top of the ice-storm cake, Frank's car was dangerously low on gas. He had badly underestimated how much extra fuel it would take to drive so slowly in these conditions, and now he was paying the price for that miscalculation, or soon would be, anyway.

Freaking job.

Tree limbs and even entire centuries-old trees were down everywhere. Frank could see shiny ice coating them and it appeared in places to be three or even four inches thick. Considering the difficulty he was having just keeping his car on the pavement, Frank believed it was entirely possible that was exactly how much ice was on the branches, on the road, on the power lines, on pretty much everything.

His headlights fought a losing battle against the looming darkness as gale force winds whipped rain over and around the vehicle. It rocked on its springs from the force of the heavier gusts.

Frank fought the steering wheel, cursing himself under his breath for his stupidity in trying to get home tonight. He resolved to stop at the very first opportunity and sleep in the car if he had to. He would wait wherever he could manage to get off the road until the sun came out.

He rounded a corner and gasped. A massive upended oak tree filled his field of vision. The huge tree lay on its side blocking most of the road, and Frank slammed on his brakes, praying the car would somehow find enough traction to come to a stop before he plowed into it.

The car slewed sideways as the back end tried to pass the front. All Frank could do was hang on for dear life and hope the damage from the impending collision would not be so extensive the tiny piece of shit car stopped running entirely.

He had a fleeting vision of himself slowly freezing to death in his disabled car, a passing motorist discovering his dead body days from now lying on the front seat, alone and stiff from rigor mortis, and then he slammed into the big tree with more force than he would have thought possible considering how slowly he had been driving.

Metal crunched and shrieked, the crash sounding incredibly loud even over the screaming wind, and Frank found himself pulled taut against his safety belt for what seemed like hours but was probably only a second or two. Then everything stopped and silence covered the accident scene like a wet blanket. Even the wind seemed to subside for a moment.

Frank sat absolutely still, taking unconscious inventory and discovering to his surprise that none of his body parts seemed to be broken. His chest hurt when he took an experimental deep breath and he figured the safety belt must have bruised his sternum. Under the circumstances, Frank decided, he had been damn lucky.

Of course, now that the accident was over and Frank was alive and more or less unhurt, the concept of luck seemed relative. He was okay physically—if you excluded his frantically thudding heart and the adrenaline now coursing through his body—but unless the damage to his car was a lot less serious than it appeared at first glance, he was going to be stuck here in the middle of nowhere in freezing temperatures at two o'clock in the morning.

Fucking wonderful.

Frank's hands shook as he grasped the key in the ignition. He wondered whether the shaking was from the adrenaline rush or from the possibility of being stranded here for who knows how long. He wasn't a religious man, but he said a quick prayer—more like a desperate non-denominational plea just in case someone up above might be paying attention, as unlikely as that seemed—and turned the key.

The Focus's engine had stalled when the car slammed into the fallen tree, but now it started up on the first try and purred like a kitten. There was no guarantee it would continue to run, of course, what with the fact that the front grill seemed to be crumpled backward into the engine compartment, but Frank took the fact that the damned thing started at all as a very encouraging sign.

He pictured critical fluids spewing out of the engine block as he sat doing nothing and decided he'd better find out if the car would actually move. There was a miniscule opening on the far side of the road between the downed tree and the edge of the thick forest that looked as though it might be large enough to accommodate the car. Branches had tumbled across it but they looked relatively small, and Frank thought if he got up a little bit of speed and tried to crash through that the car might actually make it.

He had no idea what hazards the road held beyond the tree, of course, but at the moment was focused only on getting out of his current predicament. Everything else could wait.

Frank shifted into reverse and eased his foot down on the accelerator. The transmission caught with an audible THUNK, and the Focus lurched backward away from the tree trunk. Something screeched under the car's frame and then stopped. Frank realized he was sweating, although the temperature inside the car's cabin had already begun dropping.

Now that the car was moving backward, Frank was hesitant to stop in order to shift into drive. He had an irrational fear that if he changed anything he was doing at this very moment, anything at all, the damaged car would give up the ghost. It would sputter to a halt and go belly up right there in the middle of the road, never to move again.

He said another quick sort-of prayer to the same unknown being who had answered his first one, and then stepped on the brake. The car shuddered and ground to a halt, the brake pedal vibrating violently. Frank took aim at the opening on the far side of the road—it looked a lot smaller all of a sudden—and stomped on the gas. He knew he needed to build up enough speed to blast through the branches if he wanted to avoid getting stuck in the tangled mess.

The Focus hit the opening doing close to thirty, a dangerous speed on these icy roads even if he *wasn't* navigating directly into a downed hardwood tree. Frank put the odds at roughly fifty-fifty that he would spin off the road into the woods and end up even worse off than he already was but figured worrying about that was irrelevant now because he was committed.

The car rocked and squealed as branches grabbed at its front and sides like the grasping dead hands of a band of marauding zombies. A particularly large branch smashed into the windshield and cracks spiderwebbed in front of his eyes as Frank instinctively ducked.

He kept going. The car was slowing rapidly as the tree clutched and grabbed, unwilling to give up its newfound prize.

Then he was through. The little Focus burst through the tiny opening just as Frank had hoped it would, and even though the car slewed dangerously on the ice, miracle of miracles, it was sliding into the middle of the road, not the woods. Finally, Frank had caught a break!

His stomach felt like he had eaten too much of his ex-wife's chili and sweat poured down his face. He realized he'd been holding his breath and he chuckled tensely, his voice sounding strangled and foreign.

The road ahead appeared relatively clear, at least for the short distance he could see, and Frank allowed himself a glimmer of hope that maybe things were going to work out okay after all.

He straightened the car out, pointed the crumpled nose down the middle of the deserted road, stepped on the accelerator, and—

And the car ran out of gas.

The engine sputtered and coughed, the sound a perfect reproduction of his mother's Craftsman lawn mower when he forgot to fill the tank before cutting her grass. It almost died, caught for a second, almost died again, caught again, the little car lurching comically, before finally giving up and shutting down altogether, rebuking Frank with one final angry BANG!

He guided the disabled vehicle to a stop as far onto the shoulder as possible, not sure exactly why he was doing so. It wasn't like a caravan of vehicles was likely to come charging down the road, smashing into his piece of shit little car. He tried to recall how long it had been since he had seen any other motorist and realized he couldn't. It had been hours, and the storm wasn't abating at all. If anything, its fury seemed to be intensifying.

He pounded his fists on the steering wheel in frustration. It was so unfair! He had worked his way out of a dangerous frigging situation and the moment he did he was beaten down by fate.

As usual.

Frank felt like it was a pretty fair representation of his whole trip. He had driven ten long hours up to Presque Isle and sold less than half of the hard drives and other computer components he needed to unload to break even, and then he had to fight the worsening storm the whole way back and now this.

Plus, Frank was getting cold. The temperature inside the car was beginning to drop noticeably, and it had only been a few minutes since he had struck the tree, setting this fiasco into motion. He kept a bag filled with supplies in his trunk for just this type of situation, and although he had never needed it before, he was thankful he'd had the foresight to prepare for a worst-case scenario.

Getting to his bag was going to be a bitch, though, in this brutal weather. He pulled on his light jacket and prepared to get drenched. His heavy winter parka, the one with the fur-lined hood that he could zip until it enclosed almost his entire face, was packed away in the trunk along with the rest of his supplies because he hated driving with such a bulky coat on.

Cursing fate one last time for emphasis, Frank opened the door. At least most of the major damage seemed to be limited to the right side of the car rather than the left. He wasn't sure the passenger door would even open, crunched up as it was, but the door on his side was untouched and opened smoothly.

Rain poured in, soaking his head and neck and running under his shirt, down his chest and back. It was unbelievably cold. It took his breath away.

He leapt from the car and staggered to the trunk, fighting the gusty winds every step of the way. The freezing rain appeared to be flying sideways, and Frank wondered how long it would be before another tree fell across the road, crushing him like a bug and finally putting him out of his misery.

Probably not before I've suffered long and hard.

He popped the trunk and pulled out the duffel bag containing his emergency gear. He yanked it clear and began trudging back toward the driver's side door. He'd foolishly left it open, and now the rain was soaking the interior of the car. Frank shook his head in disgust and out of the corner of his eye saw what he would have sworn was a flash of dull red off to the right, moving rapidly through the trees.

A split-second later, a sharp *crack!* echoed through the wind and freezing rain. It seemed to Frank like the noise originated in the general vicinity of that flash of red he wasn't even sure he had just seen. It was loud, almost like the sound of thunder. But of course it wasn't the sound of thunder. It couldn't be. This wasn't a thunderstorm.

He stopped in his tracks, a feeling of irrational dread filling his gut. Something was out there, just out of sight in the woods, and it seemed to Frank's feverish mind to be tracking him.

A bear, maybe? He had heard that black bears could be vicious and this was definitely black bear territory. Whatever it was, he was making himself too easy a target standing in the driving rain and wind like an goddamned idiot.

He turned toward the open driver's side door, and when he did he ran headlong into a gigantic figure. It appeared almost but not quite human and was monstrously large, clad in a tattered reddish-plaid wool hunting coat and soaking-wet, muddy jeans.

Frank let out a yelp of surprise and jumped back instinctively. He opened his mouth to say, "Thank God, I need some help here," and then realized the man—if it even *was* a man—was staring at him, staring *through* him really, with eyes black and dead and devoid of any spark of life.

They looked to Frank like the eyes of a shark sizing up its prey.

Panic took over and Frank turned to sprint in the opposite direction, away from the thing with the shark eyes that may or may not be a man. This would take him away from the shelter of the car, but Frank didn't care. He wasn't thinking about cars or shelter or anything else at the moment. Right now, all that mattered was getting away from that awful shambling thing behind him.

Three running steps later, the thing pulled him off the ground from behind. It grabbed his jacket with two hands and lifted him high into the air.

How that was even possible, Frank had no idea. He was a large man, tipping the scales at well over two hundred pounds. He couldn't believe how quickly the monstrosity moved, especially considering its massive bulk. The thing had to be close to seven feet tall if it was an inch.

Frank looked down at the thing and decided it definitely resembled a gigantic beast now more than an actual human being, although its features seemed semi-human. Its hair was greasy and stringy and unwashed and its beard was the same. Clumps of straw and dead grass protruded at odd angles out of that shaggy hair, nestled securely into the tangled mess despite the high winds and driving rain.

The dark red wool coat hung unbuttoned, flapping loosely off the giant's frame in the shrieking wind, and its jeans were torn and filthy. The thing hefted a terrified Frank Cheslo onto its shoulders, letting go of him momentarily but only to adjust its grip.

Then it lifted Frank high above its head and slammed him down onto the pavement.

Frank's head bounced off the hard surface with a sickening wet SMACK! Bright lights flashed and danced in his vision, and he had a vague notion of blood splattering and mixing with the icy wetness in the road. It was an impressive amount of blood, and Frank realized it was all *his* blood.

The pain was immense and the computer parts salesman kicked once, violently, and then his own internal hard drive failed and he was still.

18

Mike McMahon waved wildly at a mosquito flying around his ear. He missed and it continued circling, over and over, buzzing relentlessly. He swatted again and smacked himself in the head, waking himself enough to realize that the annoying mosquito was actually Sharon Dupont's alarm clock.

The offending clock sat on the nightstand next to his head, buzzing patiently, determined to torment him until switched off which, unfortunately, Mike had no idea how to do. He slapped at buttons and twisted knobs and succeeded only in turning on the radio, adding to the frustrating cacophony.

Finally, in a crushing admission of defeat, he nudged Sharon awake. She crawled over the top of him to turn the clock radio off before falling back to sleep with her head resting on his chest.

Mike tried to decide which sensation he preferred, the blessed silence from that damned alarm stopping or the feeling of Shari's warm body lying on his and decided it was a no-brainer.

"Hey, sleepyhead," he said, shaking her slim shoulders until she reluctantly reopened her eyes. "How do you ever make it to work on time when there's nobody here to wake you up? There *is* usually no one here to wake you up, right?"

She smiled, her tired eyes brightening. "No, there's not usually anyone here to wake me up. When I'm by myself I have to move the clock to the top of the dresser across the room. That forces me to get up to turn it off or else I'd never get to work before noon."

She slid out of bed, Mike enjoying the view as her silk

nightdress caught on the covers and pulled up to her hips before slipping back into place. Then she wandered across the room and into the master bathroom, stifling a yawn. Seconds later he heard the water running in the shower.

After the incredible electricity that had passed between them when they touched hands last night, they had left a trail of clothing from the kitchen to the bedroom. He understood that putting himself in the potentially damaging position of sleeping with a subordinate was not the way to start his career as police chief in Paskagankee, but both he and Shari had desperately needed to make a connection with another human being last night.

It had felt right then, and it still felt right this morning.

There was no awkwardness, no sense of regret on Shari's part, at least none that he could detect. There certainly wasn't any on his part. Mike hadn't been with a woman since Kate divorced him nearly a year ago, and the only emotion he felt right now was happiness—happiness that this beautiful young woman found him attractive, happiness that he had found someone he could talk to and happiness that he was finally able to enjoy intimacy again, even if it was only temporary.

Sharon had confided her deepest secrets and darkest fears to him last night but rather than driving him away as she had clearly feared they would, they served to make her all the more attractive to him.

And that only made sense. After all, he was damaged goods himself. He knew from bitter experience with Kate that it took a special woman to fight her way past the burden of guilt he carried around like a ball and chain.

The way Mike saw it Sharon's battle with alcoholism was a direct result of her unfortunate upbringing and thus not really her fault at all. He, on the other hand, had made a conscious decision to take the disastrous shot back in Revere. He wondered how she could even stand to be around him without judging him as harshly as he judged himself.

The sound of the shower stopped in the master bathroom and a few minutes later Sharon walked out, water dripping off the ends of her short black hair, bath towel wrapped around her otherwise naked body.

Mike wolf-whistled and Sharon curtsied.

"Take it all off!" he said, but she blew him a raspberry and disappeared back into the bathroom after pulling a clean uniform out of her closet.

Mike would have to dress in yesterday's uniform since there was not enough time to stop at his apartment before going to the scene of Harvey Crosker's grisly murder to start the eight a.m. search for evidence, but he didn't care. It seemed a small price to pay in exchange for the evening he had spent with this beautiful, alluring woman.

Sharon opened the bathroom door and stepped out, dressed in her blue and grey Paskagankee Police uniform. Mike admired the way the fit of the trousers and button-down blouse accentuated her figure and decided that if her picture were ever placed on a poster for recruiting, the ranks of law enforcement everywhere would skyrocket.

"You planning on lazing around in my bed all day?" she teased.

"That all depends," he shot back. "Will you join me if I do?"

"Some of us have work to do."

"Man, your boss must be a real bastard," he said.

Sharon laughed. "You have no idea."

He grunted in mock indignation and finally arose, padding to the bathroom. The air was heavy and moist from Sharon's shower and smelled vaguely of cinnamon. Mike was reminded of the taste of her kiss and smiled.

"Black, no sugar," he shouted through the door.

"You'll take it the way I give it to you," she shouted back.

"Now you're talking my language," Mike answered. He pictured Sharon simultaneously grinning and blushing.

He shaved quickly using Sharon's razor and hoped it hadn't been too long since she'd replaced the blade. He pictured himself trying to explain to the rest of the department why his face was cut to ribbons but was relieved to find the blade sharp.

After his shower, Mike walked into Sharon's bedroom wrapped in a towel and found his uniform, his underwear and even his socks lying on her bed freshly laundered and wrinkle-free.

He smiled in appreciation and pulled on his clothes as Sharon wandered into the room carrying two large mugs of coffee. She handed him one and he asked, "When the hell did you get around to washing my stuff?"

"I got up last night and threw it all in the machine while you were sleeping and then again an hour later to transfer it to the dryer." She shrugged. "It's no big deal."

"I can't believe I didn't wake up while you were running around working so hard."

"I can," she said, laughing. "Did your ex-wife ever tell you that you snore like a freight train?"

"She never mentioned it. And how does a freight train snore, exactly?"

"You know what I mean. It sounds like a logging train is passing by every time you breathe. I could bring a heavy metal band in here and you wouldn't wake up."

"Hmph," he grumbled. "As long as you're only bringing them in to play music."

They moved to Sharon's kitchen and bantered back and forth easily as they drank their coffee and prepared to start the day. Mike felt more normal than he had in a very long time, and if Sharon felt any guilt or regrets about last night, she didn't show it.

They stepped outside under clouds roiling black and low and menacing. The wind-whipped freezing rain threatened to resume at any moment, but for now nothing fell from the sky, a welcome change from nasty weather of the past few days. Ice glittered on every outdoor surface. It was on tree branches, on the ground, and on power lines sagging dangerously from the poles out by the road. Mike was amazed Sharon hadn't lost power yet, and as far as he knew nobody in Paskagankee had, which seemed a minor miracle.

The road conditions had improved little over the past eight hours even though the freezing rain stopped falling sometime overnight. The four-wheel drive Explorer slipped and slid along Route 24, eventually arriving at the turnoff where the officers were gathering to hike to the crime scene.

Mike was thankful for the slight improvement in the weather but concerned the people of Paskagankee would interpret it as a sign they could safely take to the roads again. They were still icy, and auto accidents would follow, inevitably accompanied by injuries and property damage.

If that happened he would be forced to sacrifice valuable man-power from the search for evidence in the Crosker murder.

The last officers were just arriving as the Explorer rolled to a stop. Mike and Sharon stepped out and he saw looks pass between several of his officers, even a smirk crossing the face of one or two.

For now he decided to say nothing. There were more important matters to consider at the moment than who was sleeping with whom.

Mike gathered the group of officers in a semicircle around him at the forest's edge. "Okay, here's what we're going to do," he said. "We'll start at the site where Mr. Crosker's remains were found and fan out in each direction, moving north initially and repeating the procedure as many times as necessary to cover three hundred sixty degrees. Everyone will stay in sight of at least one other officer at all times.

"We're looking for footprints or possibly a piece of clothing that might have caught on a branch and torn. Anything, really, but especially be on the lookout for blood evidence. This man's head was torn completely off his body. It strains the limits of credulity to think there is nothing for us to find. I don't care how much rain fell or how windy it was or how much ice is on the ground, there has to be evidence out there and we're going to find it.

"But remember, and I can't stress this enough, until we know who or what the hell we're dealing with here, I want every single officer to remain in sight of at least one other member of this force at all times. Is everyone clear on that?"

Heads nodded and feet shuffled; the smell of coffee filled the air as practically everyone clutched a Styrofoam cup.

"Okay," Mike said after a moment. "Any questions?"

Someone to his right said something under his breath and a few men snickered.

Mike was instantly furious. He knew the anger showed on his face because the laughter died out quickly. "A man was decapitated in these woods yesterday less than two miles from here. Anyone who finds that humorous can step to the front of the line and hand me your badge and gun right now. Who wants to be first?"

More feet shuffled and this time eyes drilled holes in the ground as everyone found cause to examine their footwear.

"I didn't think so," he said. "Now let's get moving and find something that will help us determine what the hell happened out there yesterday."

The group trudged single file into the forest along the narrow trail. The department owned several ATV's for use in this type of situation, but Mike had decided the terrain in this part of Paskagankee was so treacherous, so littered with downed trees and branches, so slippery with ice, that it was simply impossible to reach the area where Harvey Crosker's remains had been discovered by any means other than on foot.

The skies, though dark and threatening, had yet to resume pelting the area with freezing rain, so the trip to the crime scene went much faster than it had yesterday. They reached the clearing relatively quickly and immediately formed a line, each officer approximately eight feet from the next.

The officers moved slowly and deliberately into the forest, sweeping the terrain with their eyes. It was exhausting work, with scrub brush, dead trees and branches, stumps and other forest debris to climb over, through and around.

They worked slowly and for the most part silently, concentrating on the job at hand. Occasionally someone would mumble something to a neighbor, but the search was largely a solitary undertaking despite the fact that a dozen people were taking part.

They moved farther and farther away from the scene of the gruesome discovery, finally suspending the search after two hours without a single positive result. They returned to the oak tree at the center of the investigation and took a short break, preparing to resume the search in a different direction.

"How are you doing?" Mike asked Sharon as they leaned against a tree to catch their breath.

"I'd be doing a lot better if we actually made some progress," she answered, smiling wanly up at him.

"Well, we're looking for the proverbial needle in the haystack," he replied. "Although this forest is so vast, it's more like searching for a needle in a hay *field*. We'll find something eventually, though, I'm sure of it. There's got to be blood evidence if nothing else. If we're lucky, whoever did this trailed some of that blood behind when they took off after tossing that poor guy's head into a tree. If we can determine which way he went, it'll at least give us something to work with."

Sharon scuffed her hiking boot on the glazed ground.

"I'm sorry about this morning," she said, looking off into the trees.

"Really," Mike answered. "Which part are you sorry for, the part with the mind-blowingly great sex or the part where we totally enjoyed each other's company? Or was I imagining things, and that enjoyment was only on my side of the equation?"

"No, no, it was on my side too. I'm pretty sure you could tell. I'm talking about after we got here, when those idiots played their stupid little junior high games. You know they were talking about us, don't you?"

"Yeah, I know," Mike said with a shrug. "So what? I don't live my life to please everyone else, do you?"

"Of course not," answered Sharon with a flip of her head. "But some of these yokels could cause a lot of grief for you if they decide to. Dating a subordinate is a no-no, remember?"

Mike grinned. "So we're officially dating, then? Awesome."

Sharon shook her head in frustration but couldn't help smiling too. "You're hopeless. They haven't decided what they think of you yet so they're giving you the benefit of the doubt, but that could change at any moment. Trust me, I know what I'm talking about. I've known most of these dopes my whole life. Some of them aren't a whole lot brighter than the people we have to arrest, you know."

"Well then," Mike told her. "I'll just have to do a damned fine job of running this department so I don't give anybody any ammunition." He paused a beat. "No pun intended."

"I'm just saying you need to be careful, that's all."

"Thank you, I appreciate the thought," Mike said, winking at her. "I'm pretty sure I can handle these guys. Now, I think break time is over. Let's go catch a killer."

19

Four long hours later, the search had turned up nothing but a badly rusted beer can. Everyone was frustrated and tired, and the small group of officers was in the middle of a late lunch break when dispatcher Gordie Rheaume's voice crackled out on Mike's radio.

Mike had stayed in touch with the station all day and was relieved to hear that most of Paskagankee's citizenry still had not taken to the roads, probably due to the dark clouds hanging low and ominous in the sky. The freezing rain had not resumed, but the temperature hovered just under thirty-two degrees, and it looked as though the skies might open up again at any moment.

Mike keyed the transmit button. "Go ahead, Gordie."

The dispatcher responded immediately, his voice tight with tension. "Harley is on the outskirts of town on Route 17, not far from the Ridge Runner. He says you need to get out there right now."

"Dammit, Gordie, now what's going on?" Mike asked. "He knows we're kind of busy here, right?"

Harley Tanguay was the only member of the force that Mike had left in town on routine patrol, and Mike had already reached the conclusion Harley was not a particularly sharp specimen. Mike suspected Harley might be one of the people Sharon had told him to watch out for a few hours ago.

"Yes, he knows," the dispatcher said, his voice on the radio's little speaker distorted by static. "But he says there's been another murder."

20

Mike left Officer Pete Kendall in charge at the crime scene and took only Sharon with him when he hiked back out to Route 24. Until he knew exactly the situation out on Route 17, there was no reason to pull everyone out of the forest when there were still a few hours of daylight left in which to continue the search.

This time, when he selected Sharon Dupont to return to Paskagankee, there was none of the snickering or the barely-disguised looks of amusement the officers had displayed this morning.

This time there was actual grumbling, and it was louder and more direct. No one quite went as far as to say anything to Mike's face—or to Sharon's either, for that matter—but it was clear the officers were unhappy with the rookie's favored status, and it would not be long before a confrontation boiled over.

Mike made a mental note to deal with the situation head-on when he had a chance, which, if Harley Tanguay was to be believed when he said there had been another murder, would not be any time soon. He didn't care what the other officers thought—although he understood their anger, having been a patrolman himself for many years in Revere—but right now he needed someone by his side that he felt he could trust, and Officer Sharon Dupont was that person. It didn't matter that she was the lowest ranking member of the Paskagankee Police Department in terms of seniority, she was sharp and intuitive and he needed her help.

Plus, he wasn't sleeping with anyone else on the force.

"What exactly did Harley say?" Sharon asked. She had been

off in the woods peeing—"Sometimes it's a drag to be a girl," she said upon her return—when the call came in on Mike's radio and hadn't heard any of the conversation.

"It was all pretty vague," Mike answered. "He told Gordie there had been another murder out on Route 17 near the Ridge Runner at the scene of a car accident. I didn't ask for any more specifics because anyone can listen in on the police band, and I don't want to incite a panic, especially since I don't necessarily trust Harley's version of things. I'd like to see for myself what's going on before I reach any conclusions."

Flashing blue strobes lit the mist around a corner in the distance, and Mike knew they were almost there. He called dispatch and advised Gordie to have the public works department close off this portion of Route 17 so they could examine the scene without being forced to dodge passing cars, although from the looks of things, traffic was mostly a non-issue. They had only passed two other vehicles on the drive over, both sanding trucks frantically working overtime while the weather held.

Mike rolled the Explorer to a stop behind a Paskagankee Police cruiser slewed across the middle of the road. It was parked at an angle in front of a dark blue Ford Focus with a crumpled front end. The Focus had been pulled nearly, but not entirely, onto the right shoulder.

Mike looked for Harley Tanguay as he stepped out of the SUV onto the slick pavement but didn't see him anywhere.

Walking around the damaged car, Mike thought he could imagine what had happened. He looked at a sharp curve beyond the far side of the tree and envisioned the Focus coming around the corner at a rate of speed too fast for the conditions and being unable to stop in time when confronted with the mammoth downed tree, smashing right into it.

The driver had then apparently managed to squeeze his damaged car past the tree, but for some reason had stopped on the other side. Had he been too injured to continue, or was the damage to the car too severe? Or had he stopped for some other, unrelated reason?

The driver's side door stood open, and partially frozen water soaked the front seat and dashboard of the vehicle. It was pooled on the floor under the accelerator and brake pedal, a testament to just how heavily the freezing rain had been falling when the driver stopped and exited his car.

But that was the question. *Why* had the driver of the Focus extricated his vehicle from the mess on the far side of the tree, driven around the branches to the other side successfully, then stopped his car and gotten out?

And where was this supposed murder victim? For that matter, where was Officer Harley Tanguay? Mike had left specific instructions for Tanguay to remain at the scene until he arrived, and the officer was now nowhere to be seen. He turned to Sharon to ask for her insight into Tanguay's reliability and saw her staring intently into the woods on the far side of the road.

"What is it?" he said.

She responded simply by pointing to the area just beyond the shoulder on the far side of the two-lane county road. Officer Harley Tanguay crouched on his hands and knees, retching into the scrub brush.

Mike trotted over to the policeman as Harley wiped a string of gooey yellow saliva off the corner of his mouth with the sleeve of his jacket, which he had taken off and was holding in his hands. He was sweating profusely and all the color had drained out of his face.

Mike suddenly understood the expression, "White as a ghost."

"Harley, what's the matter? Are you sick?" Mike asked as he put a hand on the officer's shoulder.

Tanguay shook his head mutely and spit another gob of yellowish-green gunk onto the ground. He swayed, bent at the waist with his hands on his knees, then rose slowly and shakily to his full height and turned to face them. His face looked pinched, like he had just eaten some bad fish.

Harley pointed to the forest floor about ten feet from where the three of them stood. "Go take a look," he croaked and stumbled over to his cruiser, collapsing into the driver's seat and resting his head on the steering wheel.

Mike almost reminded him not to leave the scene, then decided there was no way Harley Tanguay would be going anywhere for a while. He looked too ill to drive.

Mike and Shari glanced at each other apprehensively. By now Mike had a pretty good idea what they would find when they stepped into the scrub brush, and it was obvious, by the look on Sharon's face, that she did too. They were about to find the driver of the wrecked car, and when they did it wouldn't be pretty.

"Why don't you stay here," he said, taking a step in the direction Harley had indicated.

Sharon said nothing, shaking her head with grim determination and following Mike. Her lips were set in a thin line, and Mike decided there was a lot more to this young lady than he had first realized.

They ventured a few steps farther into the woods and then stopped in their tracks, stunned. Scattered on the frozen ground over a diameter of twelve to fifteen feet, torn limb from limb, was the body of a middle-aged male, presumably the unknown motorist who had abandoned his car on the side of Route 17.

Blood was everywhere. It was scattered and splattered over trees, brush and the icy ground. It pooled under the thick part of an upper arm that had been ripped off the man's torso and tossed like a stick. It lay frozen on leaves and twigs littering the ground. It appeared to be far too much to have come out of just one man, although Mike knew blood evidence could be deceiving. The devastation was astonishing; it looked as though a bomb had blown up the victim from the inside.

Sharon turned and puked onto the ground, and Mike felt the contents of his own stomach rising into his gullet. He forced himself to choke it down and get a grip. He had seen a lot in his fifteen years of police work, but this was worse than any of it. The brutality, the sheer viciousness of the attack was stunning and unsettling.

The scene looked how Mike imagined a bear mauling would look—the worst bear mauling imaginable—but of course it wasn't a bear mauling. Even the most cursory examination of the scene and the horribly rent body showed no bite or claw marks, of which there would have been plenty had a bear ripped this man apart.

This would be another case for Dr. Affeldt, who probably had not seen two days like these in his entire career as medical examiner.

Sharon apologized. "I didn't expect anything like this," she said. "I'm so sorry, that was unprofessional as hell. I just couldn't help it, I threw up almost before I even realized it was coming."

"Don't worry about it," Mike told her, his voice strained and soft. "I was about two seconds from joining you in a little puke party. Besides," he said in an attempt to lighten the mood, "Harley's got you beat for sure. He looked like he was barfing the whole time we were on our way over here."

The officers retraced their steps to Route 17 and stood on the edge of the road, breathing deeply.

Harley walked over from his cruiser and joined them. He appeared to have rallied a bit, although his face was still chalk-white and his features drawn. "Pleasant little scene in there, isn't it?"

Mike nodded. "How did you find him?"

"I took a call from Gordie about an abandoned car that looked as though it had been involved in an accident. We've had a few of them this morning, just like you said we probably would. Well, when I arrived on the scene the car was sitting with its door open and all that water inside. It was obvious to me this wasn't any typical fender-bender. That car door must have been open for hours to let that much water in."

Mike nodded. "Nice job."

"Thanks," Harley replied. "Anyway, I decided to take a walk around the area to see if maybe the guy had gotten injured and disoriented in the accident and somehow stumbled into the woods and collapsed. That's when I found him."

He looked like his stomach might be mulling over the pros and cons of another round of projectile vomiting, and Mike took what he hoped was an inconspicuous step backward.

Harley smiled weakly. "Don't worry, boss, I've got nothing left inside to come out at you."

"Listen," Mike told his officer. "I was close to losing it myself when I saw the mess back there, so don't feel bad."

"What do we do now?" Harley asked.

"It's almost dark so there's not much point in continuing the search at the Crosker scene. I'm going to pull everyone back and send them home until tomorrow. The whole crew has been working hard tramping all over the forest, and they are probably about ready to fall over from exhaustion. In the meantime I'm going to call Dr. Affeldt and get him out here."

Mike ran a hand through his hair and sighed. Then he turned to Harley and said, "If you don't mind, you can go to the station and bring back some of the portable spotlight units so I can examine this car, inside and out. I need to figure out what happened here."

21

Artificial light, bright and reassuring, blazed from automobile headlamps mounted on metal stands. The spotlights were identical to the ones used last night at the Crosker scene—adjustable both by height and by direction as well as by angle of attack. Right now the light was being directed at the damaged blue Ford Focus.

The wind had begun increasing again and the temperature was steadily dropping as darkness descended. Mike turned up the collar of his parka although doing so seemed pointless. He was chilled to the bone from something much more than the temperature.

The last two days were beginning to seem endless and more than a little unreal. Mike almost felt sorry for himself—he left Revere for this?—and then a wave of disgust washed over him. Two people were dead, killed in the most gruesome manner he had ever seen, and he was worrying about how it affected him?

"What the hell's wrong with you?" he muttered to himself. He had sent Sharon out in the Explorer for two large coffees and sent Harley Tanguay home, so for the moment, Mike was alone with his thoughts.

After Sharon's departure, Mike trudged reluctantly back into the forest to the mangled body, snapped on a pair of latex gloves, and carefully removed the victim's wallet from the back pocket of his ripped and soiled dress slacks.

The driver of the car was a man named Frank Cheslo. He was forty-one years old and, according to the business card in his wallet, had been employed as a salesman for a company called Computer

Solutions of New England. Mike could find nothing in the man's wallet or in any of his other pockets indicating a next of kin or even a close friend the Paskagankee Police could call to inform of his tragic death.

That meant Mike would have to call Computer Solutions of New England, but considering the time of night and his more pressing priorities, he decided that telephone call could wait until tomorrow morning.

Mike examined the scene as closely as he could with just his flashlight. Although the devastation was worse here than at the Harvey Crosker scene—more blood, more body parts—the two crime scenes were similar in that the attacker had left behind no obvious evidence indicating why the attack had taken place or who (what?) might have committed it.

He dropped Frank Cheslo's business card into his jacket pocket and wandered back to the man's disabled car. Then he stood beside the trunk, chin cupped in his left hand, thinking about how unlucky the man had been. It appeared he had survived the initial impact with the tree and managed to work his way through the branches to the other side, only to run out of gas.

Mike theorized the man had then jumped out the driver's side door in the pouring rain and sprinted to his trunk, where he retrieved a duffle bag filled with emergency supplies, leaving his door open so he could make a quick dash back into the car. The duffel bag and its contents had been scattered all over Route 17 and included a heavy winter coat, hat, warm leather gloves and a liberal supply of food and water.

Cheslo had taken the time to close the trunk, so whatever horror had befallen the man must have occurred during the few seconds between retrieving his supplies and returning to the front seat.

Unless the killer had been traveling with Cheslo, a possibility that seemed absurdly unlikely given that there had now been two murders committed in the same grisly fashion in the past two days in Paskagankee, Mike now knew without a doubt a terrifyingly sadistic killer was operating in and around town.

That thought made him aware of just how alone and isolated he was right now. Mike gazed into the inky blackness of the northern Maine night and felt a sense of security from the heft of the service pistol sitting on his hip. He had consistently ranked in the top ten percent on the practice range in Revere and was glad he had worked hard over the course of his career at maintaining his proficiency with his weapon.

A set of headlights approached slowly and deliberately from the direction of town. Mike hoped it was Sharon returning with the coffee. He needed a shot of caffeine, not to mention the lift he got from looking at the pretty young officer he was now, he supposed, dating. The thought made him smile.

A light green minivan roughly the color of the stuff Sharon had puked up a couple of hours earlier pulled to a stop a few feet from the Focus. The van's driver doused the headlights and killed the engine, and then the gaunt figure of County Medical Examiner Jan Affeldt stepped out of the vehicle.

Mike offered his hand when Affeldt approached and the obviously annoyed doctor looked at it with distaste before reluctantly shaking it. "Would you mind explaining to me why I have to keep coming out to the middle of nowhere to hold your hand when my work can best be done in the morgue?"

Mike glared at Affeldt as his smoldering temper flared.

"Listen to me, Doc," he said. "I'm exhausted, I'm cold, I'm hungry, and I'm tired of finding people in this town ripped apart like so many paper dolls. I'm sorry for making you leave the warmth and comfort of your office and taking you away from your tea and crumpets, but I need to talk to you, and I don't have time to drive all the way over to the morgue and sit around waiting for you to find the time to see me. So here's how we're going to do this—you're going to answer my questions and if I need to see you again, you'll come to me again. Do we understand each other, doctor?"

The man stood silently for a moment as his eyes bulged and his face flamed red and then he said, tightlipped, "What do you want to know?"

"I assume you've completed your preliminary examination of Harvey Crosker's remains?"

"You mean his head? The tiny portion of him you gave me to work with? I have."

"Well, what can you tell me? Was he killed by an animal?"

"I can't say for certain because I have not yet nailed down a specific cause of death for the victim. He may well have been dead before his head was torn off. Let's hope so, at least. But I can tell you this much, his head was not removed by an animal, and he doesn't appear to have been decapitated in an accident, either."

"So another human being pulled the man's head off his body?"

The medical examiner grimaced. "That's not exactly how I would phrase it, but it would appear so, yes."

"How did you reach that conclusion, doctor?"

"Well, there was deep bruising in the area immediately surrounding the jawline."

Dr. Affeldt paused and Mike asked, "What does that signify?"

The ME said, "The bruising is specific and clearly in the outline of human fingers. Not claws, not teeth, but fingers. Someone tore the man's head off with his bare hands, Chief."

"How is that possible, doctor? Is there any technique of which you are aware that would allow a human being to remove another person's head from his shoulders by hand?"

"Of course not."

"Then what are you telling me?" Mike shook his head in frustration. "I'm not following you."

"I'm telling you the medical facts as I see them," Affeldt answered curtly. "That's what you asked me to do. It's not my job to interpret them. Now, is there anything else you need from me? It's cold out here and I have work to do."

Mike paused. He was dumbfounded and literally had no idea how to proceed. The information he had just received from Jan Affeldt was specific and straightforward; the ME had not hedged at all. You couldn't ask for more than that in a homicide investigation.

The only problem was that his conclusion was impossible.

"No, that's all I have right now," Mike finally answered, shaking his head tiredly. "The remains of this victim will be transported to the morgue soon. It looks like we have a complete body this time, although it's in a number of different pieces. I'd appreciate it if you could make this autopsy a top priority and get your conclusions to me as soon as possible."

"Of course," the doctor replied. He turned without another word, striding briskly back to his minivan. He started it up, executed a neat K-turn, and accelerated away toward Paskagankee.

As the taillights disappeared into the distance, Sharon passed him in the Paskagankee Police SUV, returning from town with the hot coffee. She parked on the side of the road and emerged from the vehicle carrying two oversized Styrofoam cups. She handed him one and looked at him with concern.

"Are you all right?" she asked. "You look terrible."

Mike smiled, gamely attempting a comeback. "Hey, thanks for the vote of confidence. I just need a caffeine pick-me-up, that's all. My conversation with Dr. Affeldt, Penobscot County's Mister Happy himself, didn't clear much up. In fact, I have more unanswered questions now than I had before he blessed me with his presence."

"What did he say?" she asked, blowing away the steam rising off the top of her coffee cup and looking up at him over the plastic cover.

Mike frowned and shook his head slowly. "It's time to call in reinforcements."

22

"Are you sure you want to get the Staties involved?" Sharon asked. "You know how it's going to go if you do: they'll take over your investigation and more than likely shut you out."

She was dressed in a short silk negligee, brushing her hair in front of the vanity mirror in her bedroom while Mike lay on top of the bedcovers. He was propped against her maple headboard on two pillows, watching her and having trouble concentrating on the conversation.

"No," he said, "I'm quite sure I *don't* want to get them involved. That's the last thing I want to do, precisely for the reason you just stated, but I also know I have no choice in the matter. A single murder is something I can investigate, but now that there's concrete evidence we have some kind of serial killer psycho stalking Paskagankee, I've got to get help in here. We're just not equipped to deal with something like this, and I'm afraid more people will die before we catch this guy."

The pair had remained at the most recent murder site until the victim was bagged and transported to the morgue just outside Orono. Once again they strung yellow POLICE CRIME SCENE - DO NOT DISTURB tape around the area where the body parts had been discovered.

The wrecker Mike had called after he finished examining the disabled Ford Focus arrived thirty minutes after Dr. Affeldt drove away and in short order had winched the car onto the back of the flatbed and begun transporting it to the State Crime Lab in Portland.

By then it was nearly midnight and Mike and Sharon had been on the go nonstop for over sixteen hours. They fell into the Explorer and drove toward Sharon's house.

The road conditions had improved slightly due to the fact that no freezing rain had fallen for nearly twenty-four hours and the salt and sand trucks were able to cover all of the town's roads at least once. A silence born of exhaustion and a touch of awkwardness permeated the vehicle, with each of its occupants lost in their own thoughts.

"So," Sharon started.

"Yeah. So."

"What are your plans?"

Mike pulled his hat off and ran his hands through his thick brown hair. "I'm going to call the State Police in the morning and get an investigative unit up here as soon as possible."

Sharon laughed, the sound filtering through Mike's exhaustion and lifting his spirits.

"Thanks for confiding your official police business to me, boss," she said, mock-seriously, "but that's not what I mean. I'm talking about your more immediate plans. Are you coming back to my house tonight?"

Mike chuckled. "And I'm supposed to be a trained investigator. I must be more tired than I realized. Well," he said, "do you want me to?"

"Are you crazy? Of course I want you to. Assuming you want to."

"Then that's where we're headed," Mike told her. "Let's just swing by my apartment first so I can grab some stuff. That way I don't have to try to scrape my face with the razor you use on your legs, and you won't have to sneak away in the middle of the night to wash my laundry."

"I've got news for you," she laughed. "I didn't have to sneak anywhere. You sleep so soundly a bomb could go off next to you and you'd never even know it."

They drove across town to Mike's apartment building and within a few minutes he had packed a duffel bag not unlike the one found on the ground outside Frank Cheslo's disabled Focus. Then they drove to the police station so Sharon could pick up her car.

Now, back in Sharon's warm house, Mike gazed at the young woman as she prepared for bed. He considered the unreality of the situation—investigating some kind of superhuman demon stalking this tiny town, murdering people in the most gruesome manner imaginable, while at the same time starting a relationship with this beautiful woman.

But that's not the whole story, is it? She's not just a beautiful woman, she's a beautiful member of your police force.

A subordinate.

Mike forced that thought to the back of his mind. He knew the time would come when he would have to confront the issue of dating a member of his own police force, but right now he just didn't have the energy to think about it. The two were providing each other something they both needed—for Mike, Sharon offered a valuable sense of normalcy that his life had been missing since the tragic shooting on that sweltering July night in Revere a year and a half ago, and for Sharon, he was an anchor, a way to resist the siren song of addiction that returning to the town of her youth had reawakened.

"How long do you plan on brushing that hair?" Mike asked. "It looks pretty damned good to me right now and so does everything else, for that matter."

Sharon smiled and placed the hairbrush on the vanity table. She turned out the light, padded softly to bed and slid under the covers next to Mike.

23

The lights inside the Paskagankee Police station seemed unnaturally bright to Mike after spending virtually all of the last forty-eight hours in the field, much of it in the dark of night or muted grey daylight under overcast skies. Few of the day shift officers had arrived yet, but Mike had come in early because he wanted a little time to organize his notes on the two murders.

The State Police investigative team was due in Paskagankee by nine a.m. and would require a comprehensive briefing. The responsibility for conducting that briefing fell to Mike as chief of police, even though it was the last thing he wanted to do. Conducting a meeting when there was nuts-and-bolts investigating to be done seemed to Mike to be a waste of valuable time, but there was no way to avoid it.

The sooner the briefing was completed, the sooner he would be able to return to real police work.

He kissed Sharon on the forehead before leaving her house for the drive to the station. Her shift was not due to begin until eight o'clock, and Mike knew she was exhausted, so he decided an extra hour's worth of sleep would be something she might appreciate.

Plus, if he was being completely honest with himself, he knew it would look better and result in fewer hassles—less questions and juvenile comments and knowing looks—if they came to work separately than if they arrived in the same vehicle for the second day in a row.

Mike's reluctance to call in an outside investigative team turned out to be irrelevant. He had received a call in the middle of the night on his department cell phone from the Maine attorney general advising him that a two-man serial murder task force would be arriving in the morning per specific orders from the governor, and that was that.

Whether he wanted help or not, he was getting it.

At ten minutes to eight, as the day shift filed in, most of the officers subdued and quiet, Sharon entered and flashed a dazzling smile on her way past his office.

He winked at her and looked forward to seeing her after conducting the task force briefing. Mike still had a lot to do before it, however, and dived into the material, forcing himself to push aside the pleasant memories of last night.

He had no sooner resumed working than a tall, willowy, red-haired woman barged into his office. Somehow she had managed to bypass the front desk. She offered a single perfunctory knock on his closed door before charging in like she owned the place.

She looked vaguely familiar, but Mike couldn't put his finger on where he had seen her. She stood before his desk expectantly, saying nothing.

He said, "May I help you, Ms…"

"Melissa Manheim, *Portland Journal*."

Mike reluctantly stacked his notes into a neat pile and slid them to the far corner of his desk, then rose and shook the reporter's hand. The uninterrupted prep time he was counting on before the arrival of the State Police investigative team had suddenly been shortened considerably, maybe even eliminated, depending upon how persistent this young woman turned out to be.

Mike pegged her as maybe thirty years old. She waited in anticipation.

Of what, he wasn't sure.

Finally he broke the silence. "I'm Mike McMahon. I'm the new—"

"Yes, I know who you are," she interrupted. "You're the new Chief of the Paskagankee Police Department, taking over for the recently retired Chief Court. I must say," she purred, her voice low and seductive, "this is definitely an upgrade. Chief Court was a fine man and a good administrator, but you're much easier on the eyes."

Mike blinked in amazement. Had he just heard what he thought he heard?

He glanced involuntarily out the glass walls of his office to the bullpen, where the day shift officers were gathering, and saw Sharon watching, her eyebrows drawn together with a look on her face that Mike could not decipher.

"Listen, Ms. Manheim, it's nice to meet you and all, but—"

Again she interrupted him. The trait seemed habitual. Mike decided it would become tiring very quickly if he were to be around this woman for any length of time.

"But you're very busy investigating these horrible murders in your town and you don't have time for freedom of the press, is that it?" she asked with the smug look of a woman used to bulldozing people into giving her what she wanted. "You've heard of the First Amendment, I presume, Chief?"

Mike wondered through his growing impatience where the leak to the press had originated. Did it come from his department, or perhaps Dr. Affeldt's office? Right now, of course, the source was irrelevant, but Mike knew he would have to find it and seal it at some point.

"Ms. Manheim," he responded. "When we have anything to report we will be more than happy to announce it at a press conference, which you or a representative of your newspaper will of course be welcome to attend. Until that time, I have to tell you I don't appreciate my workspace being invaded, and I don't appreciate your sneaking past my front desk clerk."

"Well," she said indignantly, "Chief Court and I had an understanding, and I expect—"

Now it was Mike's turn to interrupt the reporter. He had to admit it felt good.

He raised one hand to stop her tirade and said, "I understand the First Amendment and freedom of the press much better than you probably realize, but you need to understand something, too. Whatever agreement you had with Chief Court regarding information to be funneled to your newspaper, or giving you unfettered access to this office, or about anything else for that matter, is hereby officially and unequivocally revoked. If you want to talk to me about the situation in Paskagankee or about anything at all,

I expect you to make an appointment beforehand. The next time you barge into my office unannounced, you will be arrested and escorted immediately to a holding cell where you will be charged with disturbing the peace and obstruction of justice. Am I making myself clear, Ms. Manheim?"

"Crystal," she said. A frosty look transformed her appearance from one of almost carnal anticipation to icy, barely controlled rage.

"I've been doing this a long time," she continued, "and I have developed quite a robust following among the population of this region. It would be a mistake to make an enemy of me."

Mike picked up his stack of notes and began riffling through them. "Thank you for the warning. If you've finished threatening me, I have quite a lot of work to do."

He looked from Melissa Manheim to his office door and let his gaze linger on it until—eventually—she took the not-so-subtle hint and marched through it, pulling it closed behind her author-itatively in what was almost but not quite a slam. She wound her way through the bullpen staring resolutely forward, looking at no one, until exiting the building and disappearing.

Mike sighed.

"Great," he mumbled to his empty office. "Just what this inves-tigation needs, a crusading journalist."

He spread his notes out on the desk and got back to work.

24

At nine o'clock precisely, the front door opened and the two-person Maine State Police investigative team entered the station. Like Melissa Manheim before them, the pair moved directly through the building to Mike's office.

A tall, silver-haired man dressed in a sharp blue suit knocked once on the door, sharply, then the pair entered without awaiting an invitation. Mike rose, noting immediately the smug attitude radiating off the silver-haired man.

After completing introductions—the men's names were Detective O'Bannon and Detective Shaw, or perhaps Shore, it wasn't easy to tell thanks to the man's thick down-east accent—Mike passed a copy of his notes to each investigator and began filling the pair in on the events of the past two days.

"So, let me summarize," Detective O'Bannon said. He was apparently the lead investigator. "You've got no suspects, no concrete leads and no idea where this person, if it even is a person, is hiding?"

"That's about the size of it. Our ME assures me that the pattern of bruising on the first victim's neck was most likely made by human hands. The results of the autopsy on Victim Number Two, Frank Cheslo, should be available soon. Hopefully we can get the doctor to provide us with preliminary results as early as this afternoon. I asked him to put everything else on the back burner until he completes this examination."

"Well, that's wonderful," O'Bannon replied snidely. "Have you ever heard of a single case where a human being, using only his hands, has ripped another man's head clean off his body, Chief?"

Mike gazed at the man for a long moment, trying to decide on a response. For the time being he elected to take the high road in hopes of remaining part of the investigation once the Staties started calling the shots. He knew he was facing long odds, but he had come to think of Paskagankee as his town already, and Mike didn't want to be an observer when the killer was finally brought down, although he had every expectation that would be the case. Jurisdiction wasn't something easily shared, and the Maine State Police possessed a lot more clout than he did.

"I'm relating the facts as they've been presented to me by the medical examiner," he said. "You can interpret them as you choose, but I thought you should know where this investigation stands.

"And by the way," he added, "there was nothing 'clean' about how Harvey Crosker's head was ripped off his body or how either of those men died."

"Right. Sure. Investigation?" O'Bannon huffed. "Is that what this is? Because all I see is a couple of stiffs and nothing much being done in terms of investigating at all."

Mike glared at the man, doing his best to keep his temper under control. "I know you look at this town and see a little Hickville police department and think you can come in here and intimidate me, but let me tell you something, we know what we're doing. I understand we don't have the resources to handle this type of investigation, and I understand the governor himself sent you boys up here, but from here on out you'll keep your opinions of me and my department to yourself or you'll find yourselves returning to Portland so fast you'll be back in the city before you've finished admiring your reflection in your hotel room mirror. Am I making myself clear, detective?"

O'Bannon looked at his partner, a smirk passing over his face and then disappearing. Mike was getting tired of seeing that look on people's faces.

"Sure, Chief, whatever you say," he answered. "Is there somewhere in this tiny shoebox of a building Detective Shaw and I can set up shop?"

Mike showed the two men to a corner at the far end of the

station where a couple of desks had been thrown together and stocked with computers and file cabinets. He still wasn't sure whether the second guy's name was Shaw or Shore and decided it really didn't make much difference. These two were trouble, but he was just going to have to put up with them for the time being until they caught the murderer, which, hopefully for his rapidly evaporating patience, would be soon.

As the two men began organizing their workspaces, Mike turned back toward his office.

Detective Shaw/Shore spoke up. It was the first time he had said a word since introducing himself. "I assume we can count on the full cooperation of you and your department, Chief?" The inflection he imparted to the words let Mike know it was meant as a statement and not a question.

Mike stopped and debated telling him that *he* expected cooperation from the Maine State Police rather than vice-versa, but then he bit his tongue and said only, "Of course," without turning around.

He stalked into his office and closed the door. It was starting out to be another long day.

25

Back inside the relative peace and quiet of his office, Mike decided he might just as well tackle another piece of unpleasant business. *No reason to let the bitter taste in my mouth go to waste.*

He picked up his phone and dialed the number listed on Frank Cheslo's business card for the home office of Computer Solutions of New England.

A relentlessly perky female voice answered on the second ring with a scripted, "Thank you for calling Computer Solutions of New England. What solution can we provide for you?"

Thankful he had gotten a real person and not a recording, Mike identified himself as Chief of the Paskagankee, Maine, Police Department and asked to speak with the man or woman in charge.

The voice came back, "May I ask what this is in regards to?"

"It's a confidential matter regarding one of your employees, Mr. Frank Cheslo," Mike answered.

"Mr. Cheslo is out of the office right now and is not expected in until at least tomorrow, perhaps the next day," the perky voice told him.

"I understand that," Mike said evenly. "Now, please connect me to the person in charge immediately. This is an urgent police matter."

Coolly, the voice replied, "Hold please."

Mike listened to two or three minutes of elevator music that quickly convinced him it would be more pleasant to continue his conversation with the two Statie jokers outside his office than have to suffer through this musical torture. He wondered idly how many customers Computer Solutions of New England lost every day just because the callers couldn't stand having their ears assaulted on the telephone by bland Muzak versions of ABBA and KC and the Sunshine Band while waiting on hold.

At last an authoritative male voice came on the line and without introduction asked brusquely, "What's Frank done? If it's something stupid like drunk driving again, this company won't be held responsible."

Mike introduced himself and asked, "Who am I speaking with, please?"

"This is Earle Stanley. I'm the owner and CEO of CompuSol New England. This is a small business and I'm very busy, Chief… I'm sorry, what did you say your name was again?"

"McMahon," Mike replied. "Mike McMahon." He wondered how Stanley's company remained in business given the lack of telephone etiquette that seemed to be in evidence from the top man on down.

"So, Mr. Stanley, Frank Cheslo is an employee of yours, is that correct?"

"Yes, that's right." Mike could imagine the man holding his telephone handset away from his ear and fuming at his inability to rush things along.

"We're not calling you about a drunk-driving situation."

"Then what is it? What has Frank gone and done now?"

"He's gone and gotten himself murdered, Mr. Stanley."

There was a short silence on the other end of the line while Earle Stanley digested the information. "What? Murdered? What are you taking about? Where are you calling from again?"

"The name of the town is Paskagankee, Maine, Mr. Stanley, and you've probably never heard of it. We're on Route 24, roughly halfway between Presque Isle and Orono."

"I don't understand," Stanley said. "What was he doing in a hick town in the middle of nowhere anyway? What happened to him?"

Mike swallowed the sarcastic retort that tried to leap out of his mouth and said, "Mr. Cheslo was involved in a car accident on a remote section of road during the terrible ice storm that has been ravaging the area for the last few days. We believe he stepped out of his vehicle to retrieve some survival gear from the trunk and was ambushed."

Mike decided the man didn't need to know the condition of Cheslo's body when they found him. He almost wished *he* didn't know.

He concluded, "That's all the information we can really divulge at the moment, but the investigation is ongoing. The reason I'm calling, sir, is that we could find no contact information of a personal nature in Mr. Cheslo's possession. Does he have a wife, girlfriend, or some other relative we could notify?"

"Well, Chief McMahon, Frank just started working here a few months ago, and as far as I'm aware, no one has gotten too close to him. Our sales force works long hours and each member has quite a large territory to cover, so contact between our employees is spotty and rather random at best. I don't know offhand if Frank ever mentioned a wife or girlfriend, but I will certainly check our records and notify the appropriate next of kin. That would be the person Frank listed as his emergency contact in our employment package."

"I would appreciate that, Mr. Stanley. If you think of anything you believe might be of help in our investigation," Mike said optimistically, still hoping the State Police team wouldn't shut him out, "no matter how trivial it might seem, please call at any time of the night or day. Thank you for your time, and I'm sorry to have to deliver such terrible news."

He hung up the phone and sat back in his chair, relieved to have gotten the call out of the way but disappointed with its result. A man had been brutally murdered and there didn't seem to be anyone who would even notice, much less give a damn.

Kind of a depressing prospect, Mike thought sadly.

26

Mike hung up the telephone and almost immediately was interrupted by an abrupt knock on the door.

Again.

The two State Police investigators—Mike had already begun to think of them as Huey and Dewey—reentered the office, for the second time without waiting for an invitation.

Mike tried not to show his impatience. "Are you gentlemen all set up?"

O'Bannon answered curtly. "Yes. What we'd like to do now is interview the wife of the first victim, Mrs..." he consulted his copy of the notes Mike had given them, "...Crosker. She was alone with her husband when he disappeared, is that right?"

"Yes, but—"

"Then we'd like to see how she tells her story."

"Listen, guys," Mike said. "That woman had nothing to do with her husband's disappearance."

"If you say so," he responded. "We're going to talk to her anyway."

Mike wanted to tell the two investigators there was no way the dead man's petite wife could have inflicted the kind of extensive damage on her husband's body that he had suffered, that *no one* could have ripped Harvey Crosker's head off, much less a five-foot, two-inch middle-aged woman.

He knew already, though, that he would be wasting his breath. These two jokers were going to do whatever they wanted, regardless of his input, regardless of common sense, so he held his tongue. Huey and Dewey would understand soon enough. Once they got a good look at the condition of the two victims, it would become patently obvious.

"And about your men," O'Bannon continued.

"You mean my *officers?* I have a female on this department, too," Mike interrupted, just to tweak the pompous ass.

"Oh, well, excuse me. Your *officers.* I want them to split up into two teams and canvass the two crime scenes. They will start immediately and work until I decide they are finished. The moment they find any evidence, I don't care how insignificant it seems to them, I want to be notified right away, and I don't want the evidence disturbed until my partner and I have had a chance to examine it. They won't move it, touch it, breathe on it, or in any way contaminate it. Is that clear?"

Mike glanced between the two men with an amused look. "Anything else?" he asked.

The two investigators either didn't notice the sarcasm in his tone or chose to ignore it. "No, that will do for now. We'll advise you as soon as there's anything else, don't worry."

Mike couldn't help himself. "You know, my people *do* understand how to do their jobs."

"If you say so," O'Bannon replied, the second time he had used that retort on Mike. It was becoming clear creativity wasn't his strong suit. "Later this afternoon Detective Shaw and I will speak with the medical examiner regarding the result of his autopsy on the second victim."

"I was planning on paying a visit to Dr. Affeldt myself as soon as we were done here," Mike said, knowing what was coming next.

"Don't bother," O'Bannon replied. "It would only be a duplication of effort. Your time would be better spent elsewhere."

He didn't specify exactly where that would be. "Of course, we will keep you abreast of our progress to the extent possible."

To the extent possible, Mike thought glumly. *So much for being a part of the investigation. What the hell do I do now?*

27

Sharon poked her head through the door as Mike was plowing through some of the mountain of paperwork generated by two murders.

He rubbed his hands across his face—was it really only ten o'clock in the morning?—and smiled when he saw the ice-blue eyes regarding him from around the edge of the door.

"Doing anything important, boss?" she asked, "because I don't want to interrupt."

"Important? Those two State Police clowns are going to make sure I don't have *anything* important to do from now until they leave town. And before you say it, I'm already well aware that you told me so."

Sharon smiled. "I wasn't going to say 'I told you so.'"

"Really?" Mike asked, surprised.

"Nah. That would be too easy. I like a challenge."

"Thanks a lot. Even my only ally is giving me the business."

Mike straightened the stack of official forms that were destined to end up gathering dust in filing cabinets and cardboard cartons and messy closets all over the State of Maine and moved them to the corner of his desk.

"I need an 'out' basket," he said, "so I can feel like I'm accomplishing something as I sit at my desk with my thumb up my ass for eight hours a day."

He sighed. "I'm not sure I'm cut out for administrative work."

"Feeling sorry for yourself, are you?"

"Damn right," he answered. "I've got to get out from behind this desk. Want to help me?"

"I know you're getting old," she said with a sardonic grin, "but I'm pretty sure you can at least get out of your chair without my help."

Mike laughed. "Okay, okay, you win. I'll agree to stop feeling sorry for myself if you'll agree to stop making me feel like an idiot."

"Fair enough. So what is it you really want my help with?"

"I'm going to take a ride out to the morgue to speak with Mr. Happy himself, Dr. Affeldt, even though Dumb and Dumber from Portland told me not to bother, that it would just be a 'duplication of effort.' Idiots."

"You really don't like those guys much, do you?"

"Is it that obvious? They've been here half a day and they don't want any input at all. They're running around covering bases we've already covered and meanwhile, who knows how long it will be before someone else ends up looking like a rag doll attacked by a rabid dog? No, to answer your question, I don't like those guys much."

"So anyway," Mike continued, feeling marginally better after venting, "Are you interested in taking a ride out to the morgue with me? You could think of it as a date. Minus the fun, of course."

Sharon whistled. "A morgue? How can I say no? You really know how to show a girl a good time."

Mike nodded, leaning back in his chair. "It's what I do. I figure it's the perfect place to take you: I can't help but look good compared to the stiffs that hang out there."

28

Alone in the Paskagankee Police Explorer, Sharon casually asked, "So, what was the deal with The Maneater?"

She kept her eyes glued to the empty pavement unwinding in front of the vehicle like it was the most fascinating thing she had ever seen.

"The...what?"

"Oh, yeah," she replied. "I forgot you're new in town. The skinny little vulture with the hair that looks like a lit match who was in your office earlier—she's known around here as 'Manheim the Maneater.'"

"Really," Mike said. "Maneater, huh? Sounds promising."

He ducked as Sharon threw a backhand his way. "You mean she wasn't really into me?"

"So you saw through her little sexpot act?"

Mike laughed. "I realize I'm extremely young-looking, but I wasn't born yesterday." He ignored the snort of derision that came from across the front seat.

"Seriously, though," Sharon said. "Watch out for her. That chick will play up to you any way she has to if she smells a story, but she'll also turn on you in about half a second if it suits her purposes."

"Thanks for the warning, but I don't think she'll be playing up to me again any time soon. We weren't compatible on a couple of very important issues, like where she gets her information and how much time she'll be spending in a holding cell if she ever enters my office again without an invitation."

"Good," Sharon sniffed. "Make sure you don't see eye to eye, or any other body part to body part, with her."

"Yes, ma'am."

29

Dr. Jan Affeldt was no more engaging inside his plush office than he had been last night standing in the freezing Maine woods. He glanced up from his paperwork when Mike and Sharon entered, looking to Mike for all the world like a man who has just bitten into a week-old tuna sandwich.

"Yes, what is it now?" he asked impatiently. "I just finished speaking with your two 'experts' from Portland less than an hour ago, and I have to tell you, if they're the people you're counting on to help you break this case open, you had better expect it to take a while."

"Finally we agree on something," Mike said, pulling two hard-backed chairs across the carpeting in front of Affeldt's desk and sitting in one without waiting to be asked. He wondered how Affeldt had convinced the county to dress his office up so nicely, or whether perhaps the doctor had done it himself, paying for the beautiful Persian rug, expensive oak desk and the crystal chandelier out of his own pocket.

Sharon took the chair next to Mike and then he said, "I have a feeling we weren't high on the priority list down there at State Police headquarters. They took the call from the AG and sent their two biggest screwups our way.

"The thing is," he added, "I'm afraid that if we don't get to the bottom of whatever the hell is going on out there, we very quickly *will* become high on the list of priorities because it seems pretty clear to me that people are going to continue to die. Whoever is doing this has targeted Paskagankee, and isn't likely to stop until he's caught."

"Agreed. Let me guess," the doctor said with a sigh. "You want me to repeat the results of the autopsy for you after I just finished going over them with your two friends."

Mike nodded sympathetically. "Life sucks sometimes. But look at the bright side. You don't have to stage the whole dog and pony show, just hit the highlights and we'll be out of your hair."

He glanced at Affeldt's balding head. "Or at least out of your office."

Sharon kicked his shin out of sight of the ME.

Affeldt sighed again, choosing to ignore the chief's attempt at humor. He seemed to sigh a lot. "What do you want to know?"

"Was Mr. Cheslo killed before his body was torn apart or was he still alive when it happened?"

"Well, you understand I can only make an educated guess," Affeldt said, "but based on the large volume of blood spilled on the road near the car, and the relatively small amount found where the body came to rest, I would say he most likely was dead when he got taken apart. He wouldn't have lasted long, in any event, given the end result."

Sharon blanched, turning in her chair and looking out the window.

Mike guessed she was feeling a little queasy. He certainly was.

The ME continued. "Even if I'm wrong and he was alive when…it happened, he was not necessarily conscious for any of it. The head trauma was extensive, and included a severe blunt-force injury. The skull had tiny bits and pieces of road pavement impacted in the bone and it had literally cracked open.

"I believe he was thrown to the ground next to his car with such force that the head trauma, if it didn't kill him, almost certainly rendered him unconscious for the short remainder of time—say anywhere from a few seconds to two or three minutes—that he was left alive."

"I guess that's a blessing," Sharon mumbled under her breath. She sat sideways, facing away from Mike and the doctor. He guessed she was embarrassed about being so affected by the gruesome scenario, but he felt exactly the same way.

"Did you find any evidence to suggest the body was cut or chopped up? Saw marks, slashes, anything?"

"Absolutely not," Affeldt said reluctantly. "I stand by my earlier statement regarding Victim Number One: the damage was done by hand—by human hand."

Mike shook his head. "That doesn't make sense, doctor. No one is strong enough to pull a body apart like a Thanksgiving turkey."

"You think I don't know that?" the doctor replied. "I know that better than anyone, but you asked for the results of my autopsy, and that's what I found."

"Okay, doctor, thank you," Mike said and stood to leave. He grabbed Sharon's elbow as she rose next to him. She appeared pale and more than a little shaky.

"There is one more thing," the medical examiner said. Mike and Sharon turned. "I found a trace of saliva on the remains of the victim that did not belong to him. Actually, it was quite a bit more than a trace."

"What does that mean?" Mike asked.

"It appears to me that you should be searching for a person who has lost control of his bodily functions, at least to the extent that he was drooling excessively."

"So there will be DNA evidence."

"Absolutely. Catch the perpetrator, and you should have little difficulty tying him to the crimes."

"Is there any evidence to suggest this was done by a group of people, perhaps some sort of cult?"

"None," the doctor answered. "It is my opinion, as impossible as this sounds, that this havoc is being wreaked by one person. And before you say it again, yes, I do realize that's impossible, but my job is to tell you what the evidence suggests."

"I understand," Mike said. "And thank you for your time. I'm sorry you had to do this twice."

"Yes, well, keep those two idiots away from me, if you don't mind," he shot back. "They didn't want to hear a word I said about a single perpetrator."

The two Paskagankee Police officers walked out of the office. By the time they closed the door behind them, Dr. Affeldt had returned his attention to his paperwork

They walked to the cruiser in silence. As Mike slid behind the wheel, he asked, "Are you all right?"

"That was hard to listen to," Sharon admitted, "but I'm okay. Please don't think poorly of me because of my reaction in there, it's just that I—"

Mike held up his hands. "First of all, I couldn't think poorly of you because of that. Anyone with a shred of humanity would feel sick hearing the things Affeldt was saying, especially after getting a firsthand view of the crime scene. I would be worried about you if you sat there and listened to all that and *didn't* have any reaction. Believe me" he said, "I felt pretty sick in there myself."

She looked at him gratefully and said, "Thank you for saying so. What now?"

"I think I need to talk to the guy I replaced, Chief Court. Maybe he can give us some insight into this mess."

30

Snow began falling in large flakes as Mike pulled the cruiser into the parking lot behind the police station. The flakes drifted lazily to the ground, slowly covering the layer of ice. It made him fear the driving conditions would deteriorate rapidly once again.

Sharon nodded at the mostly empty lot. "Looks like our State Police investigator friends aren't here. I don't see their car."

"Good," Mike said gruffly. "Maybe the Two Stooges will slide on the ice and drive into a tree and we won't have to deal with them for a while."

"That might not necessarily be a good thing. Could you imagine the shitstorm that would rain down on us if one of those two was the next to get dismembered?"

"That's a good point, but I can dream, can't I?"

They stepped out of the cruiser and slipped and slid into the station, alternately holding each other up and waving their arms for balance. The heavy winds and driving rain that marked the storm prior to this afternoon had moved on, but this snowfall could turn out to be just as dangerous. It was impossible to see the icy spots under the blanket fluffy frosting.

The station house was quiet, with most of the officers on duty in the forest performing the search mandated by Detective O'Bannon. The pair threaded their way around workstations to Mike's office at the rear of the building. He closed the door and took a seat behind his desk, looking up the contact number for the recently retired Chief Wally Court.

Mike dialed and then stared at the telephone receiver in disbelief as a recorded message told him, "The number you are calling has been disconnected or is no longer in service. Please check the number and dial again."

He activated the speaker and let Sharon listen.

She furrowed her eyebrows and he said, "Did you hear anything about Chief Court planning to leave town after his retirement?"

"Not a word, but as you might imagine, being a female officer and the new kid on the block to boot, I would probably have been the last person to find out from Chief Court or anyone else in this little Boys' Club."

"That's strange, though," Mike said. "He moves away two weeks after retiring and doesn't leave a forwarding number, or post a note in the station, or send an email, or as far as we know say anything to anyone? It doesn't make sense," he said, almost muttering to himself.

"Let's try his cell, although with the spotty coverage around here, we probably wouldn't be able to contact him even if he was sitting in the next room."

Mike dialed Court's cell number and was surprised when the call went through, although it was routed straight to voice mail. A recording in the gruff voice of the ex-Paskagankee police chief advised him to leave a message.

Mike thought it was probably an exercise in futility, since who knew how often the man checked his cell-phone voice mail but left a quick one anyway. "Hello Chief, this is Mike McMahon. As you have probably heard, we've suffered a couple of horrible murders in the last few days, and I was hoping to take a few minutes at your convenience to pick your brain. Please return my call as soon as possible."

He hung up and shook his head in frustration. "Where the hell could the guy be? I hope…"

"What?"

"I hope to hell he hasn't become a victim."

31

Professor Kenneth Dye was not the least bit surprised when the telephone rang and his caller ID displayed the number for the Paskagankee Police Department. He had known ever since the two officers walked out his front door a couple of days ago that they would contact him again. He expected it to take a little longer than it did, but perhaps the situation up there was worsening faster than even he had envisioned.

"Hello?"

"Hello, Professor Dye, this is Chief Mike McMahon of the Paskagankee Police. Officer Dupont and I visited you a couple of days ago."

"Of course," Dye answered. "How are you, Chief McMahon?"

"Well, if even a little bit of what you told us is true, then you probably already know the answer to that question. Honestly, we're not doing well, Professor. We suffered another murder last night and still have no solid leads."

A chill washed through Ken. He knew what was coming, and even though he had been expecting it, he dreaded hearing the actual words.

He took a deep breath and in as steady a voice as he could manage, said, "I'm very sorry to hear that, Chief McMahon."

"Thank you," came the reply, and then silence, as if the police chief was deciding how to continue. "Professor..."

"You want my help but can't figure out how to ask, is that about right?"

"Listen, Sir," the chief said. "I live in a world where evidence of criminal activity is that which I can see and feel and touch. The idea of some three-hundred-year-old spirit butchering people, wreaking havoc in my town, is something I'm having more than a little trouble swallowing. I don't mean it as a condemnation of you and the research you have spent your life conducting, I guess I'm just a natural skeptic."

"I understand, better than you know," Ken answered, thinking of the years of marginalization he had suffered from his supposed friends and colleagues, the educational elites who were supposed to be so open minded to new ideas and who had shunned him for his theories. "But if you're not convinced that what I told you is true, why are you calling me?"

"Well, that's the thing," came the answer. "There have been some developments in the cases that are…well…"

Again Ken took pity on the police chief. "Theses developments, they're inconsistent with the realities of life as you understand it?"

"Exactly," McMahon replied. "They are impossible."

Ken smiled despite the cold finger of fear worming its way through his intestines. "So what is it I can do for you?" he asked, knowing full well what the answer would be.

"I'd like you to come to Paskagankee."

32

Getting time off from his teaching gig at the university would not be a problem. Ken simply emailed the department head a request for a leave of absence due to a personal emergency, and that was that.

He wasn't particularly concerned about who the university would find to teach his classes. He knew the school didn't care about his work, and most of his students probably didn't give a damn either; it's not like anyone was majoring in the stuff he taught. Most people treated his lectures like a bad joke.

He threw some clean clothes into a bag, which he then tossed into the back seat of his car. Ken figured he would be in Paskagankee for less than a week, probably a lot less if his theory about what was happening up there was correct.

He turned his thermostat down to fifty—no point wasting energy, but he didn't want his pipes to freeze, either—and then sat down at the kitchen table with a pen and a couple of sheets of plain lined paper.

An hour later, Professor Dye carefully folded the letter he had written, slid it into an envelope, addressed it, and placed it on the table. He felt wrung out after putting his thoughts down on paper, exhausted, like he was getting over a bad case of the flu.

He shrugged into his heaviest winter coat, then locked up the little house and walked carefully through the ice and the now rapidly mounting snow to his car for the trip to Paskagankee.

He felt like a man going to the gallows.

33

Mike stood in the middle of an enormous windswept field engaged in a heated conversation with Warren Sprague.

Sprague was a local farmer and longtime town council member who annually held a popular bonfire on his property the Friday night before Thanksgiving. The field easily encompassed five wide-open acres, which were surrounded on all sides by the ubiquitous and massive Maine north woods. The ground, lacking any barrier to the gusty winds, had been scoured almost completely clear.

"You don't seem to appreciate the seriousness of this situation, Mr. Sprague," Mike said. "There have been two murders committed in the last three days and I've seen nothing that leads me to believe the perpetrator intends to stop."

He lifted his cap and ran his hand through his hair in frustration. A massive pile of dead trees, branches and brush loomed over the men as they argued, ready and waiting to be set ablaze tomorrow night.

A single rutted dirt track led from the road, through the forest and to the field, located a half-mile behind Sprague's centuries-old farmhouse. The woods were thick and tangled in that stretch, at times threatening to consume the Explorer whole as Mike had bounced along the narrow access road to meet with the farmer.

He couldn't imagine trying to keep the townspeople safe in this field tomorrow night, but as the event was being held on private property, he had no authority to shut it down, which is why he was standing out here in the chill wind trying to convince this stubborn New Englander to postpone the gathering.

The local volunteer fire department had issued a permit weeks ago authorizing the bonfire, and the chief of that department had told Mike in no uncertain terms that revoking the permit was out of the question.

"If I pull the permit," the man said with a scowl, "where the hell am I going to drink tomorrow night?"

Mike's only hope was to convince Sprague to reschedule the event.

The Paskagankee bonfire was traditionally one of the biggest social events of the year in the isolated village. It represented the last opportunity for people to come together and visit with neighbors before the onset of the long winter, and Mike's debating skills were getting him nowhere against the taciturn Sprague.

"I've been holding this bonfire every year for more than three decades," the man told Mike, "through good times and bad, and I'm not about to stop because some nutty bastard is running around with a knife."

The police department had of course issued a warning to the citizens of Paskagankee regarding the murders, but most of the more ghastly details about the condition of the victims' bodies had been withheld. Mike wanted to avoid panicking the public while still convincing townspeople of the gravity of the situation, but now he began to question his decision to withhold information. If everyone in Paskagankee were as cavalier in their attitudes as Sprague, he would have his hands full trying to avoid a potential bloodbath tomorrow night.

The farmer continued lecturing Mike, a threadbare green John Deere baseball cap perched atop the man's head. It looked like it had been there since the day he was born, which, for all Mike knew, maybe it had. Sprague's face was ruddy and weathered from a lifetime spent outdoors in the harsh Maine climate. Mike pegged the farmer's age at about sixty and noted with frustration that the man viewed the world with the self-reliant attitude and obstinacy for which Maine Yankees were justly noted.

"I know you think you're doing us a favor, Chief McMahon," he said, "trying to protect us. And don't get me wrong, it's not like I don't appreciate that you got a job to do. But lemme tell ya something, seeing as how you ain't from around here. This town is so isolated, we need activities like my bonfire to help hold the community together.

"Besides," he continued, "there will be hundreds of people gathered here, all talking and laughing and drinking. If some psychotic son-of-a-bitch were to attack anyone at this event, he would find himself swarmed under inside of thirty seconds by some of the toughest men you've ever seen."

Mike tried again. "I'm not questioning anyone's toughness, Mr. Sprague, and I fully recognize that I'm the outsider here. But you need to understand this situation is worse than you are aware and worse than anything this town has seen."

He thought about what Professor Dye had told him about the bloody history of Paskagankee and added, "At least recently."

The farmer nodded curtly and said, "I know you're just trying to do your job, Chief, but we'll be fine tomorrow night. Come on by and share a mug of hard cider with us. You'll see what I mean if you do.

"Besides," he leaned over and whispered conspiratorially to Mike, despite the fact they were all alone on the frozen field. "Chief Court wouldn't'a canceled."

He winked at Mike with a sly half-smile.

Mike pursed his lips and shook his head and gazed at the trees looming up from the edge of the forest in the distance. From here they looked like gigantic, slowly advancing skeletons advancing.

"I'll take you up on that visit," he said. "But I'll be working, so I'll have to take a rain check on the drink. I'll gladly enjoy a mug Saturday, though, if we get through tomorrow night with no problems."

"Fair enough," came the reply. Sprague clapped him on the back. "Everything'll be fine, Chief, you'll see."

34

Mike sat at the kitchen table helping Sharon prepare dinner. It was the first night they had managed to leave work at a reasonable hour since before the Crosker murder, and they decided to celebrate by broiling a couple of steaks.

Or, more accurately, Sharon broiled the steaks—as well as peeled the potatoes and steamed the vegetables—while Mike contributed to the dinner-making effort by enjoying her figure in her jeans and sweatshirt and admiring her effortless grace in the kitchen.

"How'd you get to be such a great chef?" he asked, amazed at her seemingly innate sense of timing. She was cooking everything perfectly even though she used no timer that Mike could see.

She laughed. The sound reminded Mike of birds singing on a sunny spring morning. "How do you know I'm a good cook, when you haven't tasted anything yet? Maybe it's all going to taste like pig slop."

"Oh, I've tasted plenty," he reminded her. "It's just that none of it has been food yet."

Sharon blushed, then jumped in surprise as Mike's cell phone chirped.

"Dammit. I should have turned that thing off," he said, despite knowing he would never consider doing that.

He answered the call and was surprised to hear Professor Ken Dye's voice on the other end of the receiver, scratchy and weak. He sounded like he had fled to the other side of the world.

"Hello, Chief McMahon?" Dye said. "I'm in the middle of Paskagankee, right in front of the police station and town hall, and I have no idea where to go now. Could you give me some directions?"

"Of course, Professor," Mike answered, "but I thought you were going to get a good night's sleep and drive up tomorrow. The weather is forecasted to finally break, and to warm up considerably."

"Yes, I know," Dye replied. "But the more I thought about it, the more I felt we just could not afford to waste another eighteen hours before trying to get control of this situation, so here I am."

Mike said, "Stay right where you are. Park your car in the police station lot and I'll be there in fifteen minutes."

He hung up and apologized to Sharon. "I've got to pick up Professor Dye. He decided to drive up tonight. The guy is really concerned, and his concern is making *me* very worried. Is there any chance we can make it a meal for three instead of two?"

"Of course," she said. "I'll throw in a couple more potatoes and some more veggies, and you'll have to make do with a normal-sized portion of steak instead of the Fred Flintstone caveman platter you bought. We'll share our steak with the professor and everyone will still have plenty to eat."

Mike grabbed her around the waist and drew her into his arms, kissing her on the lips, hard.

"No drinking while I'm gone either," he said.

Sharon smiled easily. "It's funny, but since we've gotten together, I haven't thought once about getting drunk. I guess I'm busy with more important things," she said, training her blue eyes on Mike's and squeezing his butt.

It was his turn to jump. That was the last thing he had expected out of her.

He walked out the front door and into the icy mess as Sharon pulled more potatoes out of the cloth sack in her pantry, whistling a tune he did not recognize.

35

Ice tinkled in Professor Kenneth Dye's glass as he sipped his Chivas. Mike could see Sharon eyeing Dye's drink with what looked like a sense of longing, or perhaps he was imagining it because of what he knew about her.

He and Shari were drinking coffee, and even though she cornered him when Dye wasn't paying attention and told him to share a drink with the professor, that she didn't mind, he felt good about staying non-alcoholic. For one thing, it demonstrated his support to Shari, and for another, Mike had an uneasy feeling in his gut that he should keep his wits about him, that things were somehow about to spiral out of control.

Dinner went well, with Dye and Sharon hitting it off and quickly chatting like fast friends. Mike was amazed. Sharon was easily thirty years younger than the seemingly egg-headed academic, and employed in an occupation—law enforcement—that would lead you to believe they could not possibly have anything in common, yet there it was. The three of them talked and laughed through dinner as the teacher regaled them with stories about his colleagues in academia, about amusing things his students had done over the years, and about the time he spent living among Native American tribes.

Although the professor initially had struck Mike as high-strung and stuffy, in reality he was outstanding company and the time flew as they ate and talked. After dinner Sharon served a homemade apple pie she had somehow managed to put together and bake in the time Mike was out of the house retrieving Professor Dye.

Mike was beginning to think she may have missed her calling; that although she seemed to be a fine cop, she could have earned big money as a chef in some fancy five-star restaurant in Manhattan had she chosen that career path.

Now Sharon and Ken Dye relaxed at her small kitchen table while Mike cleared away the dishes and piled them in the sink. The professor insisted on helping wash them and was only dissuaded when Mike said he was going to leave them for later. Dye raved about the meal, and Mike could tell Sharon appreciated the praise despite also being a bit embarrassed by all the attention.

"How in the world did you learn to cook so well?" the professor asked.

She related to Dye that she had been left more or less on her own after her mother died, and that she had spent hundreds of hours in the kitchen as a young teen, using the time as a way to feel close to the woman whose cooking, Sharon insisted, would have put hers to shame. Mike watched her with admiration, realizing he still had plenty left to learn about this complex young woman.

Gradually the conversation slowed. The coffee cooled and the three began to face the fact that as pleasant as the evening had been, there was a darkness bringing them together. Sinister events had taken place and were likely to continue into the foreseeable future.

Mike placed the last of the dishes in the sink, and they clattered against one another, the noise louder and more jarring than it should have been. He dried his hands and sat back down in his chair.

"I must say, professor," he said, "you didn't seem terribly surprised to hear from me when I called you earlier this afternoon."

"Oh, I wasn't surprised at all. I did think it might take you a little longer to get back in touch with me, but the moment you walked out my front door I knew we would be seeing each other again at some point."

"Really," Mike said. "And why is that?"

"Because of what I told you in my living room. You see, Chief McMahon—"

"Mike," he interrupted.

"Okay, Mike. You see, Mike and Sharon," he said, nodding to their host, "You view the story I told you as a legend, a long-ago tale of love and sex and treachery. Well it is all that, and quite a fascinating tale too, if I do say so myself. But it's much more than just a story.

"The truth is I don't view Paskagankee's tragic history as some fanciful legend that has no bearing on present-day events. I lived among the Abenaqui as well as with many other tribes for years, and I know for certain that many, if not most, of their legends are based in fact. I've seen things you would not believe if I told you. I sometimes have a hard time believing them myself, and I was there.

"Anyway," the professor said, smiling at Sharon, who stared spellbound at him as he spoke, "the upshot of all this is that I don't just *believe* that the spirit of a murdered Native American girl has taken possession of someone's body and is doing unspeakable things to the people of Paskagankee, I *know* that is the case. And as I told you at my home, the bloodshed will not stop until the spirit is neutralized. In fact, it will get much worse."

The room fell silent and then Professor Dye looked earnestly at Mike. "You found the body of the missing man, didn't you?"

Mike frowned and nodded.

"And the corpse was torn apart and horribly disfigured, wasn't it?"

He nodded again.

"And now other victims have been discovered, haven't they?"

"One," Mike answered. "It was a stranger—a salesman passing through town during the height of the storm who was unfortunate enough to run out of gas at the wrong time and in the wrong place."

"So," Professor Dye said, taking a sip of his now cold coffee. He grimaced and the three of them looked simultaneously at the clock on the wall as if unable to believe forty-five minutes had passed since Mike finished clearing the dishes.

"So," the professor repeated. "You recognized in the crimes the similarities to the legend I related, and you have nowhere else to turn."

"That's about the size of it," Mike admitted. "Except the

situation is even worse than that. A special serial murder task force has taken over the case, per order of the attorney general, who is getting his marching orders from the governor. I'm no longer involved in the official investigation, except in the most peripheral way."

Professor Dye asked, "Have you told the task force about the history of Paskagankee and its relationship to the murders?"

"Are you kidding me?" Mike said. "The task force at the moment is comprised of two State Police investigators, and they already think I'm a modern-day Barney Fife. If I mentioned any of this to them, I'm pretty sure I'd be shipped off to the nuthouse and that would be the last you'd ever hear from me.

"Besides," he added, sipping his own cold coffee, "those guys are the most by-the-book, closed-minded, hard-ass idiots I've ever met in my life, and I ran across more than a few during my years on the Revere Police Department. If you think you're having a hard time convincing *me* that what you say is true, try taking the issue up with them and let me know how that goes."

The professor smiled. "I've spent the last two decades dealing with people like the fellows on your task force. You might imagine that academics are open-minded individuals, but in many ways they are no different than anyone else. They have their own pre-conceived notions about the world and how things fit into it, and if you try to get them to look outside that carefully constructed box of expectations, they shut their minds immediately. So I think I know exactly what you're talking about.

"But here's my question," the professor said. "If you're no longer a part of the investigation, why am I sitting in this kitchen right now? I assume you didn't call me here just to chat, as pleasant as it has been."

Mike shook his head. "No, I didn't call you just to chat. I will admit to you, and I think I mentioned this before: I'm a pretty straightforward guy. In my world, crimes are committed by people in flesh and blood bodies; people who leave fingerprints and DNA and other physical evidence behind that we use to establish guilt. The idea that a series of murders are being committed by a three-hundred-year-old Native American coming back from the dead to inhabit an innocent body is not the sort of thing that I would normally put much stock in. Or any stock, for that matter."

"So you've said. But let me ask you something," Professor Dye interrupted.

"Go ahead."

"And this is directed to you, also," he said, speaking to Sharon. "Since you grew up in the area, maybe you know the answer to this question. Can either of you tell me the literal translation of the word 'Paskagankee'?"

Sharon shook her head. Mike said, "Well, it's obviously a Native American word, but beyond that, I don't have a clue."

Professor Dye said, "The name of your town—'Paskagankee'—is actually a derivative of two Abenaqui words: '*Paskigan*,' which translates from the tribal language as 'gun,' and '*Ki*,' meaning 'land' or 'place.' So, put the two words together and you have 'Paskigan-Ki,' which, translated precisely, means 'gun-place,' or 'land of the guns.'

"Of course, the men who incorporated this town hundreds of years ago rearranged the spelling to suit the conventions of the English language, ultimately settling on 'Paskagankee,' as it is known today, but the town's name is actually—and quite literally—taken from the bloody tragedy that occurred on the precise location of its original settlement, more than three hundred years ago."

"That's quite the history lesson," Mike said.

Professor Dye smiled. "Once a teacher, always a teacher, I suppose. But the point is this is not just some tale told by kids sitting around a campfire under a full moon. These events were real and they actually happened. You called me because what I'm saying resonated with you, and it's the only thing that ultimately makes sense when you consider the entirety of the evidence, am I right?"

Mike looked at Sharon and shrugged. "Yes, I suppose so. But let's say I stretch credulity to the limit and buy into your theory—"

"It's not a theory," Professor Dye insisted. "It's reality."

"Okay," Mike agreed. "Suppose for the sake of argument I buy into the reality, as you call it, of a Native American spirit seeking vengeance for the horrible death she and her baby suffered three hundred years ago. How is it physically possible? Even if she takes over a human body, that body still has finite physical limitations.

How is it possible, biomechanically speaking, that she could instruct a human being to tear a victim apart limb from limb? That's simply beyond the capability of the human body, whether inhabited by an evil spirit or not!"

"I disagree," the professor said. "The problem you are having is that you are viewing the situation from within parameters you would consider 'normal.' Let me ask you another question: Have you ever heard the stories of men or women being involved in horrific accidents and somehow receiving a rush of adrenaline so intense they are able to perform superhuman acts of strength for a few seconds? You know, an infant gets trapped under an automobile and the mother lifts the car off the baby all by herself, that sort of thing?"

Mike and Sharon both nodded their heads. "Sure, I've heard of those things happening," Mike said.

Sharon added, "I've even seen interviews on the news with people who have done exactly that. They're never able to explain how they managed it afterward."

"Under the proper circumstances," Professor Dye said, "these sorts of things *are possible* for people to accomplish, do you agree?"

Again, Mike and Sharon nodded.

"Then why is it so difficult to believe that a human could perform feats of strength that would otherwise be considered impossible in *this* situation? If you accept the premise that it is within the realm of possibility for a spirit to inhabit a human body, then it becomes not just possible, but in fact likely, that the spirit could compel that human host to do things which would otherwise be physically impossible."

Mike hesitated. "But…"

The professor continued, "You are limiting yourself with your refusal to accept the notion that the Native American girl's spirit could be lingering in this dimension, trapped here until she is able to extract some sort of retribution for the terrible loss she suffered.

"Don't feel badly about that," he added with a smile. "I don't blame you. It flies in the face of everything you've ever learned in our American culture about life on earth and about the possibility of an afterlife. But you called me here because deep down inside, you know that what is happening in Paskagankee is fundamentally different than anything you've ever seen or experienced in your years as a law enforcement professional."

"You got that right," Mike muttered.

"There is another consideration, too," Dye said. "Whoever's body has been invaded—"

"The host," Mike interrupted.

"Exactly. The host. Whoever is serving as the spirit's host is a victim as well, and completely unaware of the situation. He—or she—is either in a coma-like state or perhaps even dead by now. Once possession occurs, it is not necessary for the host to remain alive for the spirit to exert control. Therefore, if the spirit compels the host to accomplish something too physically taxing, ligaments could tear, muscles could pull, bones could even break, and that would not stop the body from performing the task the spirit commands."

The room became silent as the two police officers contemplated the professor's words. Although the house had been warm and toasty throughout dinner and dessert, it felt cold and even alien now to Mike McMahon. As difficult as it was for him to accept the professor's words, at the moment his scenario was the only one that seemed to fit the evidence.

Two apparently random murders committed miles apart, both bodies traumatized in the most gruesome manner imaginable: dismembered, possibly while the victim was still alive—at least in the beginning—with no evidence the feat was accomplished using any tools besides human hands.

Ken Dye sipped his Chivas serenely while Mike and Sharon worked through his argument. It was obvious to Mike the man was no stranger to dealing with disbelief.

Finally Mike spoke up. "You said this nightmare will continue and even worsen until the anguished spirit of this Abenaqui girl is neutralized. How do you propose we do that and why is it that you even know *how* to do it?"

The professor rubbed his hands together and appeared pleased by the question, almost as if Mike was a student finally beginning to grasp the essence of a particularly vexing problem.

"Well," he said. "First of all, I'm not certain I *do* know exactly how to rid Paskagankee of the spirit. I believe I have gained enough experience from my years of research into the Abenaqui to accomplish it, but I must stress this is unexplored territory for me as well as for you, and I am operating on theoretical concepts only."

"In English, please," Mike said. "I'm confused enough as it is."

Professor Dye smiled. "I'm sorry. It's just that for so many years not one single person has shown the slightest bit of interest into my research, so now that you two are trapped here discussing it with me, it's all bubbling out. To put it as simply as I can, the Abenaqui have a centuries-old theory about what it will take to permit the spirit of the young mother to be put to rest once and for all. I believe their theory is correct, that their methodology will work, and that in fact it is the *only* way to stop what has begun happening here."

"Okay, now I'm with you. Now we're moving from theories and concepts to the actual process of stopping a killer," Mike said. "Let's say you're right about what's going on here in Paskagankee. What do we have to do?"

"It's not 'we,' I'm afraid," Professor Dye said. "It's 'me.' Unfortunately, it is incumbent upon me to put a stop to the carnage, hopefully before anyone else is killed."

"Okay, you then," Mike said. "My question remains the same. What do *you* have to do?"

The college professor shifted uneasily in his chair. The man who had been so forthcoming, so eager to discuss his work and his controversial theories, now looked exactly like a suspect caught in a lie.

"I...uh...I really don't think I can explain it so you would understand," he said haltingly. "It involves techniques I picked up over years of living with the Abenaqui people."

Mike gazed at the man with the flat cop stare employed by law enforcement professionals everywhere and said, "I'm not buying that, Professor. Stop beating around the bush. What is it you have to do, exactly, to stop the murders in Paskagankee?"

Ken Dye's face brightened and he pushed Mike's concerns away literally with a wave of his hand. "I'm not trying to be evasive, Chief, believe me. It's just that I simply can't explain it to you in a manner that would seem logical. Please, I'm asking you to trust me. I have a very strong sense that I know how to end this. You will be with me when we confront this spirit, of that I'm quite certain, and it will become clear what must be done at the appropriate time."

Mike sat unmoving at the table, staring at Professor Dye, his fingers drumming the scarred wooden surface steadily.

He considered grilling the professor further, but Sharon finally interrupted. "It's getting late and I know I'm tired. Please tell me you'll stay here with Chief McMahon and me tonight, Professor Dye."

And that was the end of the questioning.

For the time being.

36

Eight a.m. found Mike and Sharon back at the Paskagankee Police Station, Sharon for her regular patrol shift and Mike for a meeting with Mutt and Jeff from the State Police Task Force.

He would have much preferred riding in a cruiser with Shari, but the two men investigating the brutal crimes on behalf of the attorney general had agreed to give him a briefing on their progress and he had no intention of missing it. Paskagankee was his town now, and Mike was determined to be as involved in the murder investigations as possible, even if it meant deferring to the two smug assholes who had taken over his investigation.

He thought back to last night and what Professor Dye had said. The man's tale was a wild one, there was no doubt about that, but Dye had told it calmly and rationally. He exhibited no signs of delusion and as much as Mike wanted to dismiss him as some sort of wild-eyed crackpot, he found himself giving more and more credence to Dye's bizarre theory.

What choice did he have, really? There was no alternative that Mike could conjure up that came close to fitting the meager evidence they had collected, and he was willing to bet that the two idiots here at the attorney general's behest didn't have anything more to hang their hats on, either.

He wondered, though, exactly how the professor intended to rid the town of the ancient Native American spirit if his theory was correct. Was it really possible the solution was so complicated Dye couldn't explain it to them? How the hell did the man expect to gain Mike's cooperation if he wouldn't share his plan?

He sighed. Maybe Professor Dye had just been too tired after his long day to get into it with them last night. Mike made a mental note to press Dye hard on the issue before Warren Sprague's damn bonfire tonight. That foolish and risky testament to Yankee stubbornness was scheduled to kick off at seven o'clock, and the thought of the potential danger it represented gave Mike an uneasy feeling in the pit of his stomach.

The bonfire may be a Paskagankee tradition, but it was happening at the absolute wrong time, and he was powerless to stop it.

After Sharon invited the professor to sleep at her house last night, the exhausted man had gratefully agreed. He seemed to have no desire to go back out in the cold, dark night and drive to the Maple Leaf Motel in the wee hours of the morning. Mike couldn't blame him, he wouldn't have wanted to either.

Mike had been more than a little concerned about what Professor Dye would think of the chief of police sleeping with one of his officers, but if the professor felt any sense of disapproval, he kept it to himself. He had insisted on sleeping on Sharon's living room couch, flatly refusing her offer of the bedroom, and the night had passed quickly, not surprising given the sheer exhaustion felt by everyone in the house.

Detectives O'Bannon and Shaw (the man's name *was* in fact Shaw, not Shore; Mike had faxed the attorney general's office for some background information on his two guest investigators) strolled into the police station at about quarter to nine, proceeding directly to Mike's office and entering, this time without even a courtesy knock.

O'Bannon stopped in front of Mike's desk and said, without preamble, "I'm not convinced there has even been a murder here in Paskagankee, never mind two." He was dressed, as yesterday, in a dark blue suit with maroon rep tie, exactly the same thing his mostly silent partner had chosen to wear. Mike wanted to ask if they coordinated their outfits every morning or if the blue suit thing was what homicide task force investigators in the State of Maine were expected to wear.

He swallowed his question, though—and almost his tongue— when O'Bannon's statement registered. "You're not sure those two men were murdered? So, what then? They tore themselves apart for kicks because, what the hell, they had nothing better to do in this boring little town, with Mr. Crosker tossing his own skull up in a tree as sort of a *piece de resistance?* 'Look Ma, no head'?"

"You don't need to be a wiseass," O'Bannon shot back. "Of course they didn't do it to themselves, that's not what I'm saying. I think you have an animal problem. Those two vics were unfortunate enough to wander into the path of an aggressive bear, and they paid the price."

"What?" Mike could not believe what he was hearing. "Did you talk to the ME? Did you even look at those two bodies or at least at the bits and pieces we were able to recover?"

O'Bannon's face began to redden as he struggled to control his temper but Mike didn't care. He was fighting a losing battle with *his* temper as well. This was why the investigation had been pulled out from under him? So these two dimwits could whitewash the whole thing? What was the AG thinking?

"Of course we looked at the bodies, Chief. And of course we talked to the ME. We talked to neighbors of the Crosker family as well. Know what we discovered? They've had issues with bears in that area of town for quite some time. The bears are getting more and more aggressive. I think a rabid one just happened to run across Harvey Crosker as he was working on his driveway and the animal decided poor ol' Harvey looked too delicious to pass up."

Mike stood up from behind his desk and walked over to the office door, doing his best not to slam it shut as he attempted to keep the whole building from overhearing the discussion.

"Let me get this straight," he said quietly, his voice shaking with rage. "You believe, after the one day you've spent investigating these cases, that both of those men lying in the morgue in pieces were killed by a rabid bear? What exactly are you basing that theory on? There were no teeth or claw marks on either victim, no evidence of rabies, either, for that matter. And as far as the bear situation is concerned, of course there are bears in the area of the Crosker home. There are bears all around us. You gentlemen may not have noticed, but you're in *Northern fucking Maine!*"

His voice had continued to rise as he spoke to the two men, and by the time he finished, he was nearly screaming. Dispatcher

Gordie Rheaume was staring into the office, a look of alarm on his aging features. It would have been amusing, had Mike not been so angry.

"Have you two geniuses stopped to consider how stupid you're going to look when the next person gets killed, and it's not by a bear?"

By now Detective O'Bannon was furious as well, although it looked to Mike as though Shaw wasn't even paying attention. He stood by the door examining his fingernails. Apparently people losing their temper around his partner was nothing new.

O'Bannon stepped directly in front of Mike, his face inches away, and said, "I've had about all of your insults I intend to take. I did a little research on you, Mister Big-Shot Police Chief. I know all about what happened with that hostage situation in Revere. You wanna know what I think?"

Mike was stunned. He stared at the man in disbelief as his brain tried to process O'Bannon's words.

"I think you couldn't hack it any more in the big city so you ran up here to Redneck-Land and once you got here it was too goddamn boring for you, so you took a simple animal attack and made a big deal out of it. Well it's not a big deal and it never was!"

Mike kept his clenched fists by his side, resisting the urge to take a poke at the investigator.

He had to try again. "If it was an animal attack, where were the bite marks? Or did the bear borrow the victims' hands to tear them apart with? Because the only markings that were on them were exactly those—human hands. That's it. Can you please explain to me how a bear used human hands to dismember those people?"

O'Bannon waved his hand as if brushing away a pesky mosquito. "Animal attack is the only explanation that makes sense. I'm certainly not buying into this crazy notion you've fallen in love with that another *person* ripped those guys apart like pulled pork."

Mike wondered how this "briefing" had gotten so far off track and how these two idiots could even consider themselves investigators. It was clear their only concern was closing the cases for the attorney general and motoring on back to Portland.

His plan had been to ask the two men to interview Professor Dye, just to get their take on his story, but Mike realized now that doing so would be a fool's errand, a complete waste of time. Frick and Frack would not be the least bit inclined to listen to more than a sentence or two out of the professor's mouth before they closed their minds to what he was saying and probably filed paperwork to have both Dye and Mike involuntarily committed to boot.

"So that's it then," Mike said. "You two are fully satisfied with your conclusions and you're going to close your one-day investigation and go home?"

"No, that's not it," O'Bannon told him. His face was still bright crimson but seemed to be gradually returning to its normal shade. "Detective Shaw and I know how worried you are about this bonfire that crazy farmer is hosting tonight. Although we feel sure," he glanced at Shaw who was still busy examining his fingernails— the man must have the cleanest cuticles in all of Maine, Mike thought—"that there is nothing to worry about, at least not in terms of people killing one another, we will stick around tonight to help keep an eye on things. Then, when Saturday morning comes and everyone is still alive and well, we'll head back home. Think you can live with that, Chief?"

Mike was sorely tempted to tell the men to go screw themselves, that he would secure the bonfire himself and the hell with the two of them, but managed to refrain from doing so. His sense of impending disaster regarding that evening's event had grown markedly stronger as he argued with the two investigators. Even though he detested the men, or at least O'Bannon—it was hard to have an opinion one way or the other on Shaw, since he never seemed to say much of anything—he was thankful for the presence of two additional warm bodies to watch over the festivities at the Sprague Farm.

"That's fine," he told them and reopened the office door as an indication that they were welcome to leave.

Gordie Rheaume looked away quickly. It was obvious he had been straining to hear what was going on and Mike stifled a smile. At the moment Gordie was the only other person inside the station, and Mike knew that within the hour every Paskagankee Police officer on duty would be filled in with as many juicy details as he had been able to pick up through the closed door.

O'Bannon and Shaw stalked out. They weaved through the

stationhouse and crashed through the front door. Where they were going now and how they were going to pass the time until tonight's bonfire Mike had no idea and didn't much care. It was clear to him that they couldn't investigate their way out of a paper bag, so whether they were working or not didn't make much difference, so long as they stayed out of his hair.

37

The Katahdin Diner, the only eatery in downtown Paskagankee and, therefore, normally a very crowded place, bustled with its typical barely controlled chaos at 12:45 in the afternoon. Young waitresses rushed back and forth between the kitchen and the dining room carrying trays piled high with entrees, desserts and coffee. The place was raucous with the sound of people talking, laughing, and occasionally arguing. Plates rattled, glasses clinked, and silverware banged against dishes.

Mike loved all the activity and tried to eat at the Katahdin as often as he could.

At the moment he was taking a quick lunch break with Sharon, who had rolled up in her cruiser five minutes ago as Mike took the first sip of his coffee. The brew was hot, and strong enough to strip paint. Steam rose off the surface of the mug in great waves that reminded Mike of fog rolling in off the Atlantic. He wondered absently how the hell they could possibly get their coffee so hot and whether the owners of the diner had ever been subject to a lawsuit from some unwary customer taking a big gulp and scalding the skin right off the roof of his mouth.

His coffee musings were instantly forgotten, though, as the petite officer walked through the front door. Sharon looked adorable, even dressed, as she was, like any other cop in the town's simple police blues. She removed her hat upon entering the restaurant and scanned the tables looking for Mike. Then she threaded her way through the crowd, gracefully sidestepping the

183

perpetually rushing waitresses and stopping to share a word or two with several people Mike didn't recognize.

She slid into the booth next to him and gave him a quick peck on the cheek, which surprised Mike.

She laughed when she saw his face and said, "I know what you're thinking, but I grew up in this town. Trust me on this: They're already talking about us anyway, so I figured, what the hell. Might just as well throw some gasoline on the fire."

"You're not concerned about what they might be saying about you?"

"No. Are you?"

"Nope. But on the other hand, I didn't grow up here."

Sharon laughed. The sound was big and boisterous, not what one would expect from such a tiny woman.

"I'm a drunk and this is a very small town, remember? Most of these people have seen me at my worst, sprawled across three chairs at the Ridge Runner at closing time, stumbling around trashed out of my mind. The last thing I'm worried about is that people will gossip about me seeing the handsome new stranger in town."

"Huh," Mike said with a frown. "Handsome new stranger? I thought you were only seeing me," and was rewarded with a punch on the arm.

"Do I have to sit here and starve all day or are you going to buy me some lunch?" she asked, and Mike raised a hand to get the attention of the nearest waitress.

He loved how Sharon was always surprising him. Just when he thought he was beginning to get a handle on her multifaceted personality, she would do or say something that came straight out of left field.

They placed their order and the waitress winked at Sharon as she walked away.

"I went to high school with her," Sharon explained. "I'm sure she'd be coming on to you herself if I weren't sitting here."

Then she changed gears and asked, "So how did your briefing by the big shots from Portland go?"

Mike shook his head disgustedly. "You don't want to know. It was even worse than I had expected, and I wouldn't have thought that was possible. They're going to try to whitewash the whole thing. O'Bannon's claiming there weren't any murders at all."

Anger flashed in Sharon's blue eyes and she said, "But that's ridiculous! How are they going to explain away two gruesome killings?"

"Bears," Mike replied simply.

"What?"

"I know," he said. "I know. It's frustrating. You're preaching to the choir, sister. But never mind that. Right now, I wanted to talk to you about our new friend Professor Dye."

"I like him."

"Yes, I noticed," Mike laughed. "You two were chatting away like long-lost soul mates five minutes after you met him. But that's not what I want to talk about."

"Okay, what do you want to talk about?"

"I want your take on his story."

"My take? What do you mean?"

"Come on, Shari. I know you were listening to him. Don't you think that whole Abenaqui legend thing is a little…I don't know… unusual? Strange? Insane?"

She sat for a moment gathering her thoughts. Mike waited patiently.

She reached out absently and took a sip from his coffee cup just as the waitress brought their lunch order—cheeseburger and fries for him and a salad and coffee for her.

"Here's the thing," she said, picking a crisp piece of lettuce delicately off her bowl with two fingers and plopping it into her mouth. "I'm Catholic."

Mike waited for further explanation. When none seemed forthcoming he said, "So?"

"Well, think about it," she said. "Although Catholicism and Native American religions—if you could even call them that—are radically different in many ways, in their most basic forms they *do* have some things in common. There are grand mystical elements in both that stretch the credulity of non-believers."

She did it again, Mike thought. *Once again she has surprised the hell out of me.*

"How so?" he asked.

"Well, take for example the Eucharist in the Catholic Church.

That's where the parishioner stands in line during mass to receive a small wafer of unleavened bread from the priest or a designated Eucharistic minister. The bread is blessed and has been transformed into the body of Christ."

"Yeah, I understand," Mike said. "The bread represents Christ."

"No," Sharon answered, shaking her head vigorously, her short black hair flying around her face. Mike loved it when she did that.

"That's exactly my point," she said. "If you're a Catholic, your faith tells you that the bread doesn't *represent* Christ's body, it actually *is* Christ's body. It's transformed by the priest's blessing during mass."

"I'm still not following you," Mike said, feeling like a dunce and once again remembering why he had had so much trouble in school as a kid. "What does any of this have to do with an ancient Native American spirit?"

"Well, where is the difference between a Catholic *knowing* the piece of bread he is taking into his body is a tiny bit of Jesus Christ, and a Native American *knowing* that a curse can force a restless spirit to take over a human's body? Does one require any more faith than the other? And more to the point, if one is possible and credible and accepted by millions around the world as truth, why couldn't the other be possible and credible too?"

Mike sat back in the booth, his burger temporarily forgotten. He stared unblinkingly at Sharon. "You believe him, don't you?"

Sharon smiled. She hadn't forgotten about her salad and was chewing it with gusto. "You believe him too, you just don't want to admit it to yourself yet.

"Look at it another way," she said. "Did you ever read any Sherlock Holmes stories when you were a kid?"

"Why?" he asked. "Are you planning on calling Holmes back from the grave to solve this case? You do realize he was fictional, right?"

This earned him another punch in the arm and he said, "If you're going to do that, could you at least alternate arms so I can have matching bruises?"

She laughed again, the sound full and rich and genuine. "We don't *need* Sherlock Holmes, you're just as sharp as he ever was, and you have the added advantage of being real, to boot. But you haven't answered my question. Did you ever read any Holmes?"

"Sure," he said. "What's your point?"

"Just this. In one of the stories, I can't remember which one, Holmes supposedly tells Dr. Watson, 'When you have eliminated the impossible, whatever remains, however improbable, must be the truth.'"

"So you're saying—"

"There is *no other possibility* that fits what we know," she said. "So why would I force myself to disbelieve the evidence just because it makes me uncomfortable or forces me to think outside the box?"

"But you don't even seem all that uncomfortable with it."

"I'm not," she agreed, shrugging. "Just because it involves a concept with which I'm unfamiliar, doesn't mean I'm going to discount it or dismiss it out of hand."

"Fair enough," Mike said, draining his coffee and picking up the check. "Wow."

"What?"

"My brain hurts now. Thanks a lot."

"That'll teach you to ask for my opinion."

Mike chuckled. "I think maybe I need to do that more often, not less."

They walked side by side to the cash register at the front entrance, Mike acutely aware of the townspeople watching them pass by. Sharon seemed not to notice.

After he paid the check, they strolled out the door, and Shari offered to drive him back to the station, which was located a few hundred yards down Main Street.

Mike declined. "I need to think," he said, giving her a quick kiss before she could beat him to the punch.

Sharon smiled, her face lighting up. Then she slid behind the wheel of the cruiser and drove slowly down the street.

38

The weather, which for the past week had remained stubbornly cold, windy and stormy, was finally beginning to change.

From Mike's perspective, it was not a change for the better. Clouds still churned over the town, dark and threatening as ever—he was beginning to think if he ever did see the sun again he might not recognize it—but now the temperature seemed to be moderating and was forecasted to continue doing so.

Normally, a warming trend would be good news. The snow and ice could finally begin melting off the trees, power lines and roads. Paskagankee might be able to see bare ground and make a fresh start before experiencing the truly severe weather that invariably accompanies a Northern Maine winter.

Normally.

But in this case, the rising temperatures meant fog.

Lots of fog.

Waves and waves of fog, roiling and thick, covering everyone and everything in its slick moisture and reducing visibility below even what it had been during the worst of the ice/sleet/freezing rain/snow storm that the town had just endured.

As the late-afternoon daylight began to leach away, the fog made its appearance in earnest, blanketing Paskagankee in a whitish-grey mist.

Wonderful, Mike thought. *The one thing we have going for us with this damned bonfire is the sheer vastness of the wide-open field. There is no possible way anyone or anything could approach from the forest without being seen hundreds of yards before their arrival.*

But if the fog is heavy enough, that advantage will disappear. We'll have people wandering around in the dark and the fog, most of them drinking, for good measure. They will become sitting ducks if our resident Native American expert is correct about what is happening in this town.

Mike, Sharon and Professor Dye were again seated at Sharon's kitchen table, each in the chair he or she had occupied last night. This had become the unofficial meeting place for the small group.

As he had promised himself earlier in the day he would do, Mike pressed Ken Dye hard on the question of exactly how the man planned to rid Paskagankee of the vengeful spirit.

"What are you going to do, sit down with her and have a little séance?"

That question elicited a laugh from Dye.

It was not exactly the reaction Mike had expected. He was trying to get under the man's skin, to make him so angry he would just blurt out an answer, but it wasn't working.

"A séance would be nice, probably quite informative in fact, but unfortunately in this case it wouldn't do us any good," the professor said. "In any event, if we could communicate with this woman, I doubt we would want to hear much of what she has to say."

Professor Dye continued. "Honestly, Chief, I appreciate your position, but you don't need to concern yourself with the specifics of how I intend to break the curse. It's just a bunch of things I need to say and do. A ceremony of sorts. At least that's my theory. Remember, I don't have any hard proof that this will work, although I believe strongly that it will, based on a lifetime of research and experience."

Mike shook his head and told him, "You are one tough nut to crack. Your students must view you as their toughest teacher."

At that, Dye laughed again. He seemed to have lost much of the despondency he displayed at the end of their conversation last night.

"Not hardly," he said. "Those kids knew they could push me around. After all, it's not like I could seriously affect anyone's future. None of them were exactly planning a career in Native American folklore. I think I'm living proof there isn't much of a future in that."

Sharon spoke up. "I disagree. If you're correct about this spirit murdering people in Paskagankee, then you hold the key to all of our futures, don't you think?"

"A frightening prospect," the older man said.

His voice took on a somber tone, although he had a gleam in his eye. "One might even say 'grave.'"

Sharon erupted in laughter, the sheer joy of her response causing Mike to laugh too. She had certainly taken to the professor, a man old enough to be her father. Mike wondered if that might be part of the attraction for her, if perhaps Professor Dye offered something she had never received from her real father during the critical period of her adolescence: the nurturing guidance of a male parental figure.

"So," Mike said, once again focusing his attention on the professor. "Let me rephrase my question. How do we go about doing whatever it is we need to do that you seem so certain about but are so unwilling to describe?"

In answer, Ken Dye spoke directly to Sharon. "You grew up in this town," he said. "Having spent all of your formative years here, you must be at least somewhat familiar with the original Paskagankee village, are you not?"

"Of course," she answered. "Theoretically. But like I said last night, most of what I heard as a kid were whispered stories and rumors. Nobody that I'm aware of, not even the old timers in Paskagankee, possess a whole lot of knowledge about the original village, at least none that they seem willing to share."

"I understand," Dye said, "but my question was in reference to the physical location of the old village, not the stories and legends about it. I've been there, but not in many, many years, and I really have no recollection of its location in relation to the current town of Paskagankee, other than in a very general way. I'm fairly certain it's east of here, but beyond that my memories are quite vague, and I don't have much confidence in them. It's been over thirty years."

Sharon shook her head. "I spent a lot of time in the forest surrounding Paskagankee drinking and partying when I was a kid, but even the most adventurous among us had virtually no first-hand experience with the old village. It's not that kids wouldn't have tried to explore it given the opportunity, but there weren't many people who knew how to get there, and with the thick wilderness surrounding the town, nobody ever bothered trying."

Mike looked at the professor and said, "You obviously think the original village is where we need to go."

"It makes sense, don't you think? The original town was built on the site of the massacre that took place a century before Paskagankee's settlers arrived. And that massacre is the reason the spirit of the young mother is here in the first place. If she has managed to gain possession of a human body, that's where she should be."

"Well, that's a problem then, isn't it?" Mike answered. "You've seen how dense and wild the forest is. If we don't know how to get there, we could wander around the woods for decades and never find it. And something tells me we don't have decades. We might not even have days.

"But in any event, there's nothing we can do until tomorrow at the earliest. We have to be at the Sprague bonfire tonight. A lot of people could be at risk."

"There's no 'could be' about it. A lot of people *are* at risk."

Professor Dye looked at his watch. "When do we leave?"

Mike shook his head. "I'm sorry professor. When I said 'we,' I was referring to Sharon and me. As Paskagankee Police officers, we have an obligation to keep the people safe at that bonfire. You are under no such obligation. You just hang out here, have a couple of drinks, and we'll be back as soon as that testament to foolishness ends."

"Absolutely not!" Professor Dye answered vehemently. "That is unacceptable. You said yourself the reason you're so concerned about tonight's bonfire is that you believe the killer may strike again while it is taking place. If you have any faith at all in what I've been telling you, then it is imperative that I accompany you tonight. We may not have the luxury of choosing the time and place of the confrontation with this spirit, Chief, and if it turns out to be this evening, what would be the point of me sitting here sipping Chivas when I am the only person who can stop it?"

Mike sighed heavily. He knew the man was right, and yet, given the deep-seated unease gnawing at him, he didn't feel it was appropriate to expose even one more civilian to the danger than was necessary.

"Why do I have the feeling I'm going to regret this?" he asked as Dye smiled in satisfaction.

"As I said," the professor prodded, "what time do we leave?"

39

The four-wheel-drive SUV jounced and stuttered over the trail leading through the woods to Warren Sprague's open field. The Explorer's reinforced suspension bounced the vehicle's occupants in random directions, alternately pulling them tight against their shoulder restraints and then slamming them back into their seats.

Professor Dye, who had not traveled the narrow access road before, sat in the back seat holding his breath, convinced that at any moment the truck would be tossed off the trail straight into a tree trunk.

Chief McMahon and Officer Dupont seemed prepared for the rough terrain, though, and that only made sense. The chief had come here just yesterday in his futile attempt to convince the bonfire's host to cancel the event, and Sharon had already admitted her familiarity with the woods surrounding town from her wild youth.

The nervous tension Ken had been feeling since seeing the news story about the disappearance and subsequent brutal murder of Harvey Crosker—the very real sensation of a ball of fear growing in the pit of his stomach—was now blossoming into outright terror. He had made every attempt to maintain a calm and reasonable persona, both to assure the two police officers who seemed actually to be giving him the benefit of the doubt that he wasn't a stark, raving lunatic, but also in an effort to prevent his nervous system from short-circuiting and maybe causing him to stroke out.

Ken watched the trees bounce slowly past the rear window,

their branches scraping the side of the car. All the leaves had long since fallen off the trees way up here in northern Maine, and the bare ends of the branches looked to Ken like bony skeletal fingers, reaching for him, grasping, trying to clutch him and pull him into the thick black forest.

If anyone could be prepared for the impending confrontation, it was Ken Dye. He had heard rumors of the Abenaqui legend for the first time as a young child, and shortly thereafter began the exhaustive research that would eventually consume him and become his life's mission.

Ken knew he was ready, although to say he was also scared shitless would not be an overstatement.

He almost wished he understood a little less about what they were up against, like Sharon and Mike did. But wishes were irrelevant at this point. Professor Kenneth A. Dye was the only person who could bring an end to what had been set inexorably in motion here in this isolated and remote town.

It had to be him.

He could not explain to the two police officers why that was the case without putting them and everyone else in even more danger than they already faced.

They deserved the truth, if for no other reason than the fact that now, at the exact moment in time when Ken Dye most needed someone to believe in him, he had found two people who did.

Oh, they were skeptical, of course they were—especially the chief, Mike McMahon—and why wouldn't they be? Ken had no solid proof to offer in support of his hypothesis, but the fact that the evidence in the two murders pointed to nothing the police could quantify in terms of traditional crime-solving, surely helped his case.

In any event, Ken knew he owed a debt of gratitude to the man and woman sharing the car with him tonight. It was a debt he could never repay.

He tried to clear his head. Told himself to concentrate on the task at hand. Becoming dewy-eyed and sentimental would be a mistake, one that would likely end up getting more people killed.

Focus, he told himself, *and just do your best to bring this thing to a successful conclusion.*

The vehicle crept along the rutted path. Outside the windows the fog seemed alive, writhing and dancing, thick as soup in one area and then nearly nonexistent in the next. The forecast called for temperatures continuing to moderate through the night and into tomorrow, so the likelihood of the fog lessening was slim. In fact, conditions would probably worsen.

The tension inside the Explorer was palpable. Silence reigned as each member of the little group concentrated on his or her own thoughts and, Ken assumed, fears.

At last the vehicle slid through a small opening in the forest and burst into the massive open field. The heavy fog refracted the truck's headlights unpredictably, making it even more difficult to see out here than it had been while they were driving through the forest. At least back there the trees looming on both sides of the trail had focused the light more or less straight ahead.

From the back seat, Ken could vaguely discern the shadowy, boxy shapes of vehicles ahead and to their right. Mike turned the SUV in that direction and crept along the edge of the trees. Rows of parked cars came into focus, and the chief nosed into the first available spot.

The three climbed out of the vehicle and fell in behind a cluster of teens who seemed to know where they were going. Mike clearly had no clue which direction would lead them to the big bonfire, and Sharon, although she had attended the event many times as a youth, admitted she really didn't remember enough about those visits to be able to point them in the right direction with any degree of confidence.

Ken hoped the kids in front of them were headed toward the bonfire and not out into the woods to do whatever it was teens around here did in the woods. He assumed the presence of two uniformed Paskagankee Police officers a few feet behind them would be motivation enough to move in the direction of the huge mountain of timber—at least until they could ditch the cops—and apparently it was. They slogged along for a few minutes and then he began to see the unfocused yellow haze of the gigantic pile of burning brush and trees.

The sound of voices grew louder and soon the group broke through enough of the fog to take in the impressive sight of the twenty-foot-high pile, brightly ablaze with dancing flames. The fire had clearly been lit only a few minutes ago, as the entire pile of debris had not even caught yet. Sharon had said Sprague traditionally threw the first match into his bonfire at seven p.m. sharp, and it was just a few minutes past seven now.

Ken gaped in open amazement at the number of people milling around the bonfire, here in the chill of a late-November northern Maine evening. He had no idea what the population of Paskagankee was—One thousand? Three thousand? Five thousand?—but whatever the number, it seemed clear that a large percentage of those people had decided to brave the pervading dampness of the thick fog as well as the hazardous driving conditions to come here and enjoy the community celebration.

Townspeople gathered in various-sized groups, some holding large paper cups, presumably containing generous helpings of the hard cider Warren Sprague had promised Mike McMahon. They were all chatting and gossiping amiably, occasionally breaking out in raucous laughter.

The recent murders of Harvey Crosker and the unlucky stranger passing through town during the height of the storm dominated the conversation, but if anyone felt concerned about his or her safety this evening, they weren't saying so, at least not loudly enough for Ken Dye to hear it.

Professor Dye and the two police officers stopped at the bonfire, now rapidly gaining in intensity, to warm their hands. Chief McMahon handed Ken and Sharon portable radios with explicit instructions for both of them to check in every fifteen minutes. The original plan had been for Ken to patrol with Mike, but he was able to talk the chief out of forcing them to stay together, pointing out that the professor was probably the least at risk, since he knew best what they were up against.

The fire grew bright and hot as the interior of the gigantic pile of brush and debris began to smolder and finally catch. The intense heat pushed the small group back a couple of paces as Chief McMahon gave them his final instructions.

"Make your outer perimeter the farthest group of people that you can observe. I don't want you exposing yourself when you're alone, especially considering the restricted the visibility. And DON'T forget to check in every fifteen minutes."

"How many officers do you have in the area?" Ken asked the chief.

"We have one stationed at each end of the access road, if you can call it that, as well as two officers walking around in plain clothes. I'll be in touch with them on a separate radio. Also, the two State Police investigators volunteered to help out tonight before leaving for Portland in the morning, so they're here somewhere, too."

Ken couldn't help but notice the disdain in the chief's voice as he referenced his State Police counterparts. He tried to mask it, but it was definitely there.

The chief rubbed his hands together and then slid them into a pair of fur-lined leather gloves. "Are we all set?"

Both Ken and Sharon nodded, and Mike said, "Let's get started, then," and walked away from the fire.

The thick, swirling fog enveloped his receding form almost immediately, and then he was gone.

40

Sharon Dupont had visited this place many times as a youngster, and not just to attend the annual pre-Thanksgiving bonfire.

After discovering alcohol as a teen, she and her friends had adopted Sprague's Field as their own private location in which to drink and party. The area was secluded, never patrolled by the cops and rarely by the farmer who owned it, especially after dark. And it was mysterious and a little scary to boot.

In short, for a kid looking for a place to drink or get high, it was perfect.

Sharon couldn't remember exactly how old she had been when she fell under the spell of booze and drugs, but she knew it happened pretty quickly after the death of her mother. Her slide into alcoholism roughly coincided with her father's determination that hanging out at the Ridge Runner was preferable to spending time at home with his young daughter, the child who resembled her mother so closely it was almost spooky.

In other words, she guessed, it would have been shortly after her twelfth birthday.

She immediately took to drinking and smoking, both as a way to lessen the pain of loss—her mother to death and her father to disinterest—and as means to becoming a valued member of a group. Any group would do, as long as she was allowed to belong.

The group of young drinkers and drug users in Paskagankee was a tight-knit bunch, and Sharon knew now, years later, with the benefit of age and a little life experience, that belonging to that misfit group allowed her in some small way to be part of a family, an opportunity she had lost at home the day her mother died.

Additionally, Sharon came to recognize that she had been cursed with an addictive personality, and the exposure to alcohol and drugs, especially at the very age when a young teenage girl is particularly vulnerable in trying to develop an identity, had virtually assured she would become addicted.

And addicted she had been. By the time she entered high school, Sharon was drinking almost as much as her father: virtually every day, sometimes even before or during school.

An extremely intelligent child, as a youngster Sharon had earned outstanding grades, but following the death of her mother, her schoolwork suffered, her grades plummeted, and her dad barely noticed.

She stumbled through high school, literally on many occasions, until the winter of her senior year, when, as punishment for passing out drunk in a snow bank in the middle of the school day, she had been forced to report to Paskagankee Police Chief Wally Court for a month-long public service assignment.

Those thirty days changed the course of Sharon Dupont's life forever. She was still an alcoholic and knew she always would be, but working in the police station under the watchful eye of Chief Court gave the teen an element that had been sorely lacking in her life since the death of her mother—steady, consistent discipline and the faith of another human being in her value as a worthwhile individual.

The work she performed over that life-changing month was nothing particularly exciting or challenging. In fact, as Sharon looked back on it now, it had been pretty damned boring most of the time—basic filing, sweeping floors, washing windows in the station—but her time spent with the police chief of Paskagankee gave Sharon a peek into a world she had never before seen. It was a world of responsibility and trust, a world where people did the right thing just because it was the right thing.

Chief Court displayed a plaque prominently in his office, and it had intrigued Sharon enough that she still thought about it even now. It was a simple wooden square, and on it was stamped the words, "CHARACTER IS HOW YOU ACT WHEN NO ONE IS LOOKING."

Thinking back on it, Sharon believed that in all probability she owed her life to Chief Court and the personal interest he had taken in her when she could just as easily have ended up another pathetic, used-up alkie falling off a bar stool every night at the Ridge Runner and eventually dying of liver disease or getting raped and killed by some slime ball in the Runner's parking lot.

Walking on Warren Sprague's field, the same one she had stumbled around upon drunk and stoned as a teenager, was a jarring experience. When she left town to attend the FBI Academy in Quantico, Virginia, she had been one hundred percent certain she would never return, certainly not for more than a few days at a time to visit her father. So to find herself here, of all places, on the strange and frightening mission she was engaged in with Mike McMahon and Professor Dye, seemed even more surreal than it otherwise would have.

Her radio crackled to life as Mike checked in with her. "How's it going?" he asked.

"It's cold and wet out here, so it's lots of fun," she said brightly. "But no sign of anything unusual unless you consider the fact that people coming out on a night like tonight to stand around in this weather and gab with the very folks they spend the rest of the year gossiping about is a little strange in itself."

Mike chuckled. "Don't let your guard down," he told her. "Our friend the professor is convinced something's going to happen tonight, with all these potential victims gathered in one place."

"Don't worry about me. I couldn't possibly be any more guarded."

"Good," Mike answered. "I want you back in one piece."

They signed off. Sharon assumed Mike would now contact Professor Dye who, for all she knew, might be standing right next to her. The fog was so thick they could be ten feet apart and never know it unless they tripped over each other.

Sharon was glad to hear Mike chuckle when he talked to her. He was extremely professional at work, maybe the best boss she had ever had, but the more she got to know him the clearer it became that he was haunted relentlessly by the events of that steamy summer night a year and a half ago on the streets of Revere, Massachusetts.

Knowing the little girl's death was accidental was one thing. Being able to forgive himself for pulling the trigger on the shot that took her life was another issue entirely.

He had not yet reached the point where he could let himself off the hook. Maybe he never would.

A sharp snapping noise off her left side broke Sharon out of her reverie. She tensed, angry with herself. She had just promised Mike she would stay alert and had then almost immediately fallen into a daydream.

For Christ's sake, concentrate on what you're doing.

The officer stopped dead in her tracks and peered into the heavy mist. The noise had sounded exactly like a large twig breaking, the sound a hiking boot might make stepping on a brittle branch.

It was no use. Sharon couldn't see a thing. She had been walking clockwise around the huge bonfire, remaining oriented in the fuzzy darkness by moving just far enough away from the fire that it remained a vague yellow-orange glow far off her right side.

It struck her as extremely unlikely that any townspeople would have wandered this far from the bonfire, given the thick fog. If you lost sight of the glow you could wander for hours in the shroud of misty darkness with absolutely no sense of direction. Yelling for help would be no guarantee of assistance, either, since the fog refracted sound as well as light. You might scream loud enough to be heard by someone a few hundred feet away and still not be found until morning.

The silence was nerve-wracking.

From somewhere far off to her right, Sharon could hear the low hum of the people congregated around the fire. It was nothing more than an indistinct murmuring of indecipherable words and conversation.

To the left, though, it seemed that whoever or whatever had snapped the branch was standing still just as she was doing, aware that his (its) presence had been discovered and not wanting to compound the mistake.

Taking a hesitant step or two in what she thought might be the right direction, Sharon aimed her heavy Maglite into the mist, serving only to blind herself as the refracted beam struck her in the face like the oncoming headlights of a car. She cursed under her breath and snapped off the flashlight.

Another cracking sound made her skin crawl.

This one was similar to the first but far softer. It seemed exactly like the kind of noise a person might make if he was trying to sneak quietly away but could not see the ground well enough to avoid all the downed branches.

Sharon reached for her radio to call Mike for help and then froze as the obvious problem occurred to her: she had no idea where in the hell she was. It might take forty-five minutes for backup to locate her and by then whoever was trying to sneak away would be long gone.

She took a deep breath, not liking the way it caught in her throat, and said, "Who's out there? Stop right where you are," trying to sound authoritative but feeling nothing of the sort.

Dead silence greeted her call and she took another halting step forward, then a few more, moving farther away from the bonfire than she intended. Reluctantly she reached for the service weapon at her hip, leaving it holstered for the time being with her palm resting on the grip.

She stopped and listened intently, rewarded for her efforts only with the sound of the blood rushing in her ears.

Another step forward. Still nothing but the ever-present grey-white fog filling her consciousness.

A sudden flash of movement to her left caused Sharon to whirl on the balls of her feet, simultaneously drawing her weapon and barking, "Freeze, Police!"

The movement ceased immediately and when she took another step forward, two figures materialized in front of her. A boy and a girl, neither more than sixteen years of age. Their faces registered shock and fear when they saw her gun and Sharon quickly holstered it.

"What the hell are you kids doing out here?" she demanded. It sounded stupid and lame as soon as she said it, even to her.

It was patently obvious what the kids were doing out here. It was the same thing she would have been doing on a date at that age—looking for a little privacy.

Annoyed with herself for letting her imagination run wild, Sharon spoke sharply. "Get back to the fire. Do you want to get lost out here and wander around until morning?"

She gestured in the direction of the bonfire, which was no longer visible in the distance but the light from which would become apparent again as soon as they took three steps to Sharon's left. The young couple moved off toward the fire, the boy muttering something under his breath to his girlfriend as they passed in front of Sharon.

Whatever he said caused her to giggle and then they disappeared, swallowed up again by the fog. Sharon stood quietly, angry and embarrassed. She waited a few moments and then started off in the same direction.

41

Mike checked in with Professor Dye immediately after speaking to Sharon. The professor had nothing to report, which Mike chose to interpret as good news.

The plan they had developed was to patrol the area in two concentric rings. Sharon would circle clockwise around the outer ring, remaining just within sight of the blaze's glow, and the professor would walk in the opposite direction, staying within roughly fifty feet of the fire.

The professor was unarmed and untrained, so Mike wanted to be able to keep an eye on him and be able to get to him quickly in the event of trouble. It had seemed like a decent plan when they drew it up—the best they could develop under such short notice and with severely limited manpower—but these pea-soup weather conditions had thrown a real monkey wrench into things. Mike had never seen such a thick, all-encompassing fog settle into an area, and he had spent fifteen years in Revere, Massachusetts, a city located right on the Atlantic Ocean.

He hoped he hadn't made a mistake by allowing Professor Dye to come here tonight. He wondered what his friends on the Revere Police Department would say if they knew his prime suspect in two horrific murders was a three-hundred-year-old dead Native American girl, and that he'd pinned his hopes for solving the crimes on an aging academic with zero credibility in his own professional circles.

"Well, this is a thrill a minute. No wonder you left the big city to move up to the armpit of the universe."

Mike looked to his side to see Detective O'Bannon scowling at him, holding a cup of coffee in his right hand and looking like he wanted nothing more than to throw it in Mike's face.

"Nice to see you again, too," Mike answered.

Behind them, the fire crackled and popped as its heat expanded the wet wood. Incredibly, it was still gaining in intensity. The townspeople milling around the massive brush pile had gradually been forced farther and farther away from the flames as the temperature around the pile skyrocketed.

Mike decided to push O'Bannon's buttons a little. The man had been nothing but condescending and uncooperative since arriving in Paskagankee, and Mike was still smarting over the whitewash job O'Bannon and his silent partner Shaw were giving this case, which, if Professor Dye was right, was about to explode in their faces.

"Having a good time, are you?"

O'Bannon snarled, "I can't wait to put this freaking little hell-hole in my rear view mirror. What a goddamn waste of time this whole circus has been. Jeez, a couple of people get attacked by an aggressive animal and you clowns think the world is coming to an end."

Heads turned as the people in the immediate vicinity of the two men heard the anger in O'Bannon's voice and nervously stepped away.

Mike calmly replied, "Come on, Detective, it's just you and me here. The attorney general is fast asleep in bed a hundred miles away. You can't tell me you really believe the ridiculous notion that those two poor men were ripped to pieces by a bear, right? We've gone around and around on this, and there's no evidence to support that theory. Why don't you just admit the truth: you have no idea what's going on and you just want to get the hell back to civilization? I don't blame you, and I won't share your dirty little secret with anyone, I promise."

O'Bannon sneered at him, disdain evident in his voice. "Maybe my theory's a little weak, but at least mine's plausible. The rumors I'm hearing are that you and your little girlfriend have been taken in by that egghead college teacher and you're running around hunting a ghost. That sound about right, Chief?"

Mike stared at the man, feeling his face begin to flush. He knew how silly it sounded, but yes, he finally had to admit to himself, he thought Professor Dye might actually be right.

"It's not a ghost," he said after a moment's hesitation. "It's a spirit that has gained possession of an innocent person's body. Someone, I might add, who is just as much a victim as the two murdered men. And I'm well aware of how crazy it sounds, but it fits. If you would take the time to open your mind and actually pay attention to your surroundings for a change, you might find it *plausible* too."

Grimacing in disgust, looking like he had just bitten into spoiled meat, O'Bannon said, "You're about as crazy as a loon, you know that? Killing that little girl must have really done a number on you because you're just about ready for the nuthouse. I'm leaving in the morning as planned and so is Shaw. Do us both a favor and stay out of our way until then."

O'Bannon glared at Mike, his face florid either from the chilly temperatures or his anger, Mike wasn't sure which. Then he stalked off into the darkness and the mist, muttering under his breath, as the fog swallowed him whole.

Mike stood for a few minutes, thinking about the vehemence of O'Bannon's verbal attack. It occurred to him that up until a few days ago, if confronted with a similar situation, his attitude would have been nearly identical to O'Bannon's, although he hoped he would have expressed it a little more civilly.

He chuckled to himself at the incongruity of the entire mess and began another circle of the bonfire. He took three steps and ran headlong into a woman, almost knocking her off her feet.

He reached out to steady her and said, "Excuse me, Miss, I'm sorry."

She smiled at him and he realized it was the reporter he had clashed with yesterday at the police station, the one he chased out with threats of jail time.

"Well," she purred, seeming not to notice—or choosing to ignore—that she had nearly been dumped onto the muddy ground. "If it isn't Chief McMahon. Destiny seems determined to bring us together, don't you agree?"

Mike let go of her arm, saying, "Hello again, Ms. Manheim.

I'm sorry for almost knocking you over, but I really don't think destiny has anything to do with it. You just refuse to go away. Now, if you'll excuse me—"

"Oh, don't worry," she interrupted, her tongue tracing her red lips suggestively as a lascivious smile played across her face, "I understand you're taken. Off the market, as it were. I wouldn't dream of trying to get between you and that little girl you've recently become involved with. But really, Chief, come on. Don't you think she's a tad…oh, how do I put this delicately…*fresh-faced* for you?"

Mike had already begun walking away from the reporter and he froze in mid-stride. He swiveled his head and gave her a stony stare. "How do you know…?"

Melissa Manheim smiled triumphantly, moving in for the kill. "How do I know about what, Chief? The fact that you're screwing a girl nearly young enough to be your daughter? Please, give me at least a modicum of credit. Knowing things is my job, after all."

"Really, and what is your job, exactly? Harassing people who're trying to do *their* jobs?"

"Come now, Chief McMahon, don't be so touchy. Everyone has needs. I, of all people, understand that. I just wonder if the Paskagankee Town Council would be as understanding if they were to discover that their brand-new police chief—a man who's been in town all of three weeks—is *already* sleeping with one of his subordinates, and the most junior member of the force, no less? Hmm, I wonder."

"Let me guess," Mike responded, trying but mostly failing to keep the anger out of his voice. "If I agree to pass information regarding these murder investigations along to you exclusively, you'll keep the information about my personal life to yourself, is that about the size of it?"

The tall, willowy reporter said nothing. Instead she smiled and returned Mike's gaze steadily.

"I told you before, and I'll say it again," he continued. "Stay out of my way. Maybe this is all just a big game to you, but two people are dead in this town, and that amounts to two more murders than have taken place here in the last thirty years. I know, because I looked it up.

"Something is very wrong in Paskagankee, and I intend to find out what it is. Your thinly veiled threats are doing nothing to help me accomplish that goal. If you want to spill my personal life to the people who brought me here, please, feel free to do so, because it isn't any more their business than it is yours, and I've been kicked out of better places than this, anyway. So you go ahead and do whatever you think you have to do, and I'll do the same. Do we understand each other?"

Mike finally took a breath, amazed that Manheim the Maneater had allowed him to finish his rant uninterrupted. He wondered whether that was a good thing or a bad thing.

The suggestively sexual look she had adopted was gone, in its place a flat stare. It was as if the first Melissa Manheim had been replaced by an identical twin, one who had lived a very hard life.

"No problem," she spat. "I don't need you anyway, I was just trying to let you feel like a part of the team. I have plenty of sources more than happy to pass along information to me. For example, I know you believe a *ghost* committed these murders." Her eyebrows rose in emphasis.

"I don't need to tattle to the council about you and Little Miss Patrolwoman," she continued. "Once I splash the story all over the Journal about you wasting time and resources chasing ghosts while a killer stalks Paskagankee, you'll never work in law enforcement again, here or anywhere else."

The two stared each other down. Their voices were filled with venom, but the conversation had been a quiet one, so Mike didn't think anyone else had heard the exchange. He knew Melissa Manheim could do serious damage to his career if she chose to, maybe even scuttle it permanently, but was coming to the realization he didn't much care. He was committed to his current course of action and would deal with the consequences, whatever they might be, when the time came.

"I really feel sorry for you," Mike muttered, shaking his head as the furious woman strode away into the fog. He hoped he didn't run into anyone else he knew. The last ten minutes had consisted of verbal battles with O'Bannon and then Manheim. He didn't have the energy to spar with anyone else right now.

42

The night was dragging.

It was nearly midnight and Sharon was cold and tired. Even though the temperature was much warmer tonight than it had been for days, it was still only in the low forties and the moisture permeating the air made being outside for any length of time extremely uncomfortable. She had worn several layers of clothing in a mostly unsuccessful attempt to keep warm, and to Sharon it felt as though the dampness had managed to work its way through every last stitch of fabric. Her clothes felt heavy and wet.

On top of that, the night had been uneventful and mostly boring, the sole exception being the fiasco with the two high school kids.

Not exactly her proudest moment, professionally-speaking.

And as much as that boredom meant the townspeople were all safe—at least for now—maintaining her alertness became more and more difficult as the night dragged on. She tried counting the number of times she circled the big bonfire, but eventually lost track somewhere north of twenty.

The three of them—herself, Mike and Professor Dye—had taken a break around ten o'clock, rendezvousing close to the fire in a mostly futile attempt to absorb some warmth.

They resumed their separate positions, though, after only a few minutes, with Mike alternating between Professor Dye's patrol area and hers. They had had a couple of minutes by themselves to chat when their paths crossed a little while ago, but for the most part, the night had been an exercise in solitude.

Now, feeling like a zombie as she circled the outer perimeter of the bonfire for the umpteenth time, Sharon found her mind wandering to her burgeoning relationship with Mike McMahon. She didn't know where things were going, or even whether they were going anywhere at all. He was her boss and once the rumors about the two of them started being confirmed he likely would be forced either to give up his job or his girl.

But for now, she felt happy and excited, while at the same time marveling at how life sometimes takes the strangest twists and turns. Returning to Paskagankee was the last thing Sharon had ever wanted to do. Now, after being back in town just a few months, along came this slightly older, handsome, world-weary divorced man who seemed to think she was a prize worth pursuing.

She wondered what Mike had heard about her, if anything. Her past was checkered, even beyond the history of drinking and partying she had confessed to Mike. The drinking and partying was true, of course, but the rest was simply too humiliating to admit to her new lover.

The real reason for her silence when they drove Earl Manning to jail a few days ago was because she had been scared witless he would spill the sordid details of their past right in front of Mike. "Their past" had been a one-time thing, and Sharon was drunk off her ass when it happened—a condition only too familiar to her back then—but she would never get over the fact she had sunk so low, spending a night with the slimy, drunken bastard Earl Manning while still a senior in high school.

Earl was two years out of school by then and had showed up at one of the teen partying spots with a case of beer, cans of which he'd begun passing around to Sharon and her three girlfriends. It was obvious to all of them he was doing his best to get them drunk, and for the same reason young men have been getting young women drunk for centuries.

But Sharon hadn't cared about his reasons. She wanted to drink and Earl Manning represented free beer. Later, as her friends prepared to drive home, she declined their pleas to get in the car and leave. There was still cold beer to be had and Sharon, at that point in her young life, was unwilling to see it go to waste.

So she had jumped into Earl's pickup, maybe even the same

one he was driving so erratically when she and Mike pulled him over a few days ago. She really couldn't remember, although the likelihood that Earl had scraped together enough cash to buy a new one seemed slim. They had driven to the Ridge Runner parking lot where they finished off the rest of Earl's beer, sitting outside the bar getting trashed while her father was doing the very same thing inside it.

Sharon wasn't worried about her dad walking out and catching her, either. For one thing, by that time she was too drunk to care, and for another, her father was undoubtedly by then too drunk to notice. He could have stumbled right past the rusting, beat-up piece of shit truck on the way to his rusting, beat-up piece of shit car while she sat in the passenger seat of Earl's cab shotgunning a PBR and he would never even have noticed.

It was the same story a little later in the night when Earl did her in the truck, right there in the middle of the Ridge Runner lot. Good old daddy dearest would never have noticed.

Even more horrifying, she didn't think he would have cared.

The frightening thing to Sharon—at least, looking back now it was frightening—was that at the time she thought that sort of behavior was normal. You wanted to get drunk, you slept with the dude supplying the alcohol, even if he was sort of gross and clumsy and had bad breath and his body smelled a little bit like overripe cabbage.

The hookup with Earl Manning had been a one-off—so to speak—but only because he had never brought beer around the party spot again when Sharon and her friends were there. She knew she would have slept with him again had the opportunity arisen and, indeed, there were other alcohol and drug suppliers she had been more than willing to have sex with in exchange for the proper party supplies.

So when Manning began taunting her from the back of the Paskagankee Police cruiser while Mike sat next to her, she had frozen in fear that he would blurt out the wrong thing and Mike would think the worst of her.

Freezing up like that was out of character for her. Normally she could handle losers like Manning without even breaking a sweat— like nothing more than swatting a pesky mosquito—but when he started babbling in front of Mike her insides had clenched up like she was going to hurl right there in the cruiser.

She had no idea whether Manning even remembered screwing her in the cab of his pickup, although she figured he probably did. Even though he had been as drunk as she was that night, maybe more so, she doubted he had been able to coax many girls into that piece of shit truck. He probably had every last detail of his few successful conquests etched indelibly in his filthy, slimy, cockroach brain.

Mike had sensed how upset she was when Earl Manning began playing his little game and had put a stop to it immediately, something Sharon knew *she* should have been the one to do but had been unable to manage. To his credit, even though he must have suspected there was more to the story than what she told him, Mike hadn't brought it up again. It was just one more thing about the man that intrigued her and set him apart from any of the others she had known.

A loud snapping noise came from somewhere off her left and brought Sharon forcefully back to the present. It was similar to the branch-breaking sounds the two high school kids had made earlier.

She realized two things simultaneously: she had no idea how long she'd been daydreaming, and much more importantly, *she had no idea where she was.* While she was busily watching her little mental movie about Earl Manning she had unknowingly wandered out of the perimeter of the bonfire, beyond the area where the orange glow remained visible through the fog and mist.

Turning a full three hundred sixty degrees in an attempt to get her bearings, Sharon thought she heard another furtive snapping noise. This one was quieter, less obvious. She wondered if it might be the two young lovers she had interrupted before or whether another couple of kids had decided to brave the cold and the fog and the mist to get a little time away from the prying eyes of the adults.

The problem was she couldn't tell exactly where the noise was coming from. The heavy shroud of moisture hanging over the field permeated everything and had the effect of masking the sound, making it seem like it was coming from the left one minute and from the right the next.

It was loud and then it was soft.

It was everywhere and it was nowhere.

It was terrifying.

Sharon pulled out her heavy cop Maglite, with the long steel handle that could double as a weapon, knowing it would be fruitless to shine the bright beam into the mist but trying anyway. As expected, the light refracted in a thousand different directions, accomplishing nothing but blinding her and pissing her off in the process.

"Where are you?" she said, her voice booming out louder than she had expected it to. "You kids have got to stay closer to the fire. It'd be really easy to get lost out here."

Yeah, she thought to herself, *it'd be really easy to get as lost as I am right now.*

No answer.

She decided to try again, a little more forcefully. "Come on kids, let's go. It's time to get back to the bonfire. I mean right now."

Still nothing, not even the snapping sound that had drawn her attention in the first place.

She began to question whether the noise had even been made by a person. Maybe an animal *was* wandering around out here. Sharon flashed on Detective O'Bannon's theory about a hungry bear and shuddered involuntarily.

She stopped moving and took stock of the situation. Her options were limited. She had no idea where she was in relation to the bonfire and wasn't sure any kids were out here at all. She should get on the radio to Mike and let him know what was going on but didn't want to look foolish. He had given her one simple job—walk around the fire and keep an eye on things—and she had screwed it up.

She took a deep breath and struck out boldly in the direction she thought (hoped) the fire should be. Since she couldn't remember how long she had been walking while in her self-induced daze—who wouldn't lose track of time reliving those pleasant high school memories of Earl Manning?—Sharon realized she didn't know how far she should walk before determining she was traveling in the wrong direction.

Her feet were cold, despite being encased in high-quality winter hiking boots and heavy wool socks, and she was getting sleepy. The gradually melting snow and ice on the ground was alternately slippery and slushy, making it difficult and energy sapping to navigate.

Something touched her face.

A skeletal finger ran across her cheek.

Sharon cried out. She stumbled to the side in an attempt to escape the awful, bony touch and tripped over a downed log. As she was falling she realized it hadn't been a bony finger on her face at all, just the end of a bare tree branch.

She smashed to the ground and barely noticed; her brain was spinning out of control. How could it have been a branch? The edge of the forest was a good quarter-mile from the location of the bonfire. Could she have gotten that far off course while wallowing in her bad memories?

Sharon didn't see how, but it was an incontrovertible fact that she had fallen at the edge of the thick forest surrounding Warren Sprague's out-of-the-way field. That was the only explanation for the scrape on her face.

Now she began to get concerned. It could take hours for Mike to locate her if he had to circle the gigantic field on foot. She cursed and finally admitted to herself that she was going to have to radio him and ask for help. It was the last thing she wanted to do, but there was no way around it.

Disgusted with herself for making such a careless rookie mistake, Sharon reached down to the wet ground to push herself up and her right hand fell on the log she had tripped over. The end of it felt slimy to the touch, even more so than what you would expect from a thick piece of wood lying on the ground during a snow/ice storm and then a heavy fog.

Sharon snapped her flashlight on once more and screamed reflexively.

It wasn't a tree branch she had tripped over. It was a human arm, pulled free from its shirt and the shoulder to which it had until recently been attached. Bone fragments and ligaments and muscles and other gooey parts trailed from the open shoulder end. The slickness she felt when she put her hand down was human blood.

A lot of human blood.

Sharon tried to get herself under control. She was panting heavily and her temples pounded like they were being attacked by a lunatic with a jackhammer.

Of course there's lots of blood, stupid. It's a human minus the rest of the body, what else would there be?

Hands shaking badly, she grabbed for her radio to call Mike, but her hands were slick from all that blood and the radio slipped out of her grasp and dropped to the ground.

Sharon didn't want to reach down to search for it. What if she touched the arm again? She retched and questioned her decision to enter the law enforcement profession as she grabbed her flashlight and clutched it fiercely with both hands like a Titanic survivor clinging to the last life vest.

Her hands were shaking so badly now that she was afraid she would drop the flashlight, too. Hell, she *knew* she was going to drop the flashlight, of course she was, it would happen any second now, and what would she do then?

She would have to reach down in the pitch dark and the awful fog and feel around blindly to try to locate it, and then the human arm, with a hand at the end, a still-working hand, would clutch her by her own arm and pull her with inexorable pressure, it would be incredibly strong, and it would pull her into the forest and—

But she didn't drop the flashlight.

She hung on for all she was worth and snapped the beam on and the light, the blessed light, the beautiful yellow artificial sun, flooded the area, merrily refracting away in its thousand different directions and Sharon didn't care, no she didn't, not even a little bit.

She was shaking and breathing heavily through her mouth and nose, and she knew she had to get herself under control or she would hyperventilate. She couldn't do that, not here. She couldn't allow herself to hyperventilate and pass out on top of that awful severed arm.

She stood and concentrated on breathing normally, on getting control of her racing thoughts and her panicked body. The radio could wait, as could the report of the disembodied arm she had found. After all, it wasn't like the person it belonged to was standing here complaining, demanding immediate action, right?

In fact, it wasn't like the person was even still alive, was it?

Of course not.

A minute passed. Two. Finally Sharon felt she might actually be able to talk to Mike without her voice betraying her sheer terror.

Then she literally jumped straight into the air as two events occurred in rapid succession. The radio crackled to life, loudly, as Mike called for her to check in. *The volume knob must have twisted as the radio fell*, she thought, *turning the stupid thing all the way up, because that's about as loud as I've ever heard a police radio.*

Before she had a chance even to react to the call, she heard another loud snapping noise immediately behind her.

This time, the noise sounded much closer than before, and as she turned her head in an instinctive reaction, Sharon glimpsed a flash of dull red and saw a large, misshapen figure approaching fast. Then the air exploded out of her lungs with an audible *whoosh* as the impossibly large entity blasted her in the gut with one powerful blow.

With a second of agonizing clarity, she thought to herself, *what the hell was that?* And then the huge figure struck again, flinging her small body effortlessly into the tangled branches of a stout oak tree with just a flip of an arm.

Sharon heard the bones break before feeling any pain, but the gruesome sound of the shattering bones ended almost before it began, whereas the pain kept building, growing and mushrooming until it constituted her whole world, her entire existence.

The pain was white-hot and intense, and eventually it enveloped her, pulling her down and down into a black hole that Sharon welcomed wholeheartedly because it put an end to the fear and the pain.

Oh, God, the pain.

43

Mike McMahon punched the radio's transmit button with an insistence born of frustration.

"Come in, Sharon," he called for the dozenth time. Ten minutes had passed since she was due to check in and he hadn't noticed she was late until just now. He'd been caught up in a conversation with Detective Shaw (surprise, surprise, the man actually *could* talk), who had lost track of his partner, the asshole O'Bannon.

Mike told Shaw the man was probably halfway to Portland by now and that if Shaw was so in awe of his partner that he wouldn't speak up about the obvious dereliction of duty on O'Bannon's part, he should probably just hop into his car and follow him on down the road.

"Can't," Shaw replied simply and with his characteristic lack of emotion. "He's got the only set of keys to the Caprice."

Mike shook his head and laughed out loud. How could he respond to that? Shaw refused to be baited into an argument, which, Mike decided, was probably a good thing. Getting into it out here in the middle of the night with one of the guys hand-picked by the attorney general (read: the governor) to come up here and white-wash this entire bizarre affair was probably not any kind of winning strategy for the new Paskagankee Police Chief, anyway.

Mike simply held his tongue and told Shaw that if he ran across O'Bannon, he would let the man know his partner was looking for him.

"But don't hold your breath," he said. "I don't think O'Bannon and I will be exchanging Christmas cards any time soon. If he sees me coming, he'll probably head off in another direction. Of course with this fog, I suppose I might stumble over him without even seeing him until it's too late. For both of us."

Following the testy exchange, Mike checked his watch and began calling Officer Dupont's radio. He then contacted Professor Dye to be sure his transmitter was working properly and heard it squawk to life right next to him, as the two men were in the process of walking together around the fire for what felt like about the hundredth time of the evening.

"What the hell," he muttered. "She knows she's supposed to check in with me.

"Sharon, come in," he called again.

"Perhaps her receiver has gone on the blink," Dye suggested.

"Maybe," Mike answered, although he allowed his tone of voice to indicate his opinion regarding the likelihood of that scenario.

The big bonfire was finally starting to wane, although it would continue to burn through the night and well into tomorrow. The number of people clustered around it had declined noticeably over the last thirty minutes or so, as most townspeople succumbed to the miserable weather conditions and called it quits.

Mike's sense of unease began blossoming again the moment Shaw mentioned he had lost track of his partner. Mike's response notwithstanding, he knew there was no way the detective would take off for Portland without gathering Shaw first.

Now, with two unexplained disappearances in the last two minutes, Mike's senses were telling him things were going horribly wrong. A look into the worried face of Ken Dye told him that the professor was thinking the same thing.

"What do we do?" Dye asked.

"Good question," was the best Mike could come up with. He knew as Paskagankee Chief of Police and a man with fifteen years of law enforcement experience under his belt he should be able to manage something better, but he was well and truly stumped.

"Searching the woods in this fog would be suicide, not to mention we could walk within five feet of seeing…something, and completely miss it the way the mist is playing havoc with the flashlight beams."

The two men stood shoulder to shoulder, staring out into the murky night. The grey mist shifted and danced in front of them, seemingly alive with malevolent intent.

"Let's take a walk around Sharon's perimeter," Mike suggested. He knew it was probably pointless and a waste of time, but at least they would feel like they were doing something productive.

Professor Dye agreed immediately.

The night's pervading blackness enveloped the two men as they trudged along the outer ring. As expected, the heavy shroud of fog served to prevent them from gaining any insight into what had happened to Sharon or where she might have gone.

Mike cursed himself for allowing the rookie officer to walk the outermost perimeter. Obviously, Professor Dye had to stay close to the fire, but why hadn't Mike reserved the more remote outer ring for himself?

The search for Officer Dupont was conducted mostly in silence, the two men lost in their own thoughts. Mike could see tracks in the muddy snow, presumably made by Sharon as she had traipsed around and around, but there was also a confusing array of additional footprints, with no indication of whom they might belong to or what they were doing there.

After nearly an hour of searching, creeping forward at a snail's pace and searching desperately for evidence that might explain Sharon's disappearance, the pair arrived back at their starting point. They were cold, wet, tired and discouraged. Mike glanced at the professor and saw a bleak look in the man's eyes that he knew must have shown in his as well.

By now it appeared everyone had departed. It was nearly two o'clock in the morning and even the hardiest of partiers had finally succumbed to the miserable conditions. There was no sign even of Warren Sprague, and Mike assumed the farmer had retreated to his home after bidding the last of the revelers goodnight.

The once-raging bonfire had burned down to a massive pile of red-hot glowing embers. Waves of thick black smoke curled off the top of the pile and disappeared into the fog.

Mike and Ken started off to the Paskagankee Police Explorer without a word. What was there to say? They had come to the gathering to protect the townspeople, and now one of the supposed protectors was missing.

Two if you included the possibility that O'Bannon had vanished as well.

Mike was determined not to assume Sharon's disappearance was related to the string of bizarre and deadly occurrences of the last week until he saw evidence to the contrary, but he knew deep down inside that the likelihood of the events being unrelated was practically nil.

He was angry and frustrated and exhausted. He could barely stand the thought of having to wait for sunrise to begin looking for Sharon in earnest.

44

Mike sat at his desk and studied Professor Dye, who was engrossed in his work on a computer in the otherwise empty squad room. It was a few minutes after six in the morning, and the day shift officers wouldn't begin arriving for almost another hour.

Mike still had the feeling there was something Dye wasn't telling him, that there was more to his story about dead Native American mothers, and spirits inhabiting human host bodies, but he couldn't imagine what the professor might be hiding.

It seemed clear he was trying his best to help. He was genuinely stricken that Sharon Dupont had disappeared right from under their noses. The moment they arrived at the empty municipal building this morning, the professor had asked to work at a computer terminal with Internet access. Mike had guided him to a desk and he'd immediately lost himself in his work.

The two men had ridden in near-total silence, exhausted and depressed, to Mike's apartment after leaving the site of the bonfire. They stopped for a moment at Warren Sprague's home, finding him still awake, sitting at his kitchen table sipping a cup of tea before bed.

Sprague had invited them in, but they declined. Mike wanted only to ease his growing paranoia and ensure the farmer was not missing too, as well as receive the landowner's permission to search the field early the next morning. Sprague readily gave it, even volunteering his assistance, but Mike told him he didn't want one single person in that field who didn't have to be there.

ALLAN LEVERONE

The pair fell asleep almost immediately upon arriving at Mike's apartment, the professor dropping onto Mike's couch and, as he had done at Sharon's house, steadfastly refusing to consider taking Mike's bed.

"Let me take the couch," Mike said. "It's the least I can do, considering all the help you're giving me."

But Dye wouldn't consider it, and Mike was just too damned tired to do more than put up a perfunctory protest.

For Mike's part, rest was difficult to achieve even though sleep came quickly. He found himself tossing and turning, suffering strange, terrifying dreams. The reason for the nightmares was obvious: they were born out of well-deserved feelings of guilt for having failed to protect Sharon.

By five a.m. he finally gave up on the idea of getting any real rest and rose for the day. He padded into the kitchen and put on some coffee, then jumped into the shower to try to scrub away the exhaustion, frustration and fear.

It didn't work.

After dressing, Mike sat quietly at the kitchen table sipping his coffee. Eventually a stirring in the living room told him Professor Dye had awakened as well.

A few minutes later the man stumbled into the kitchen and sloshed coffee into a cup. His hair protruded at odd angles from his head, making him look vaguely like a scarecrow and drawing a smile from Mike, despite the circumstances.

The professor sipped his steaming coffee and turned to face Mike with eyes red-rimmed and bleary. "When do we go to work?"

Mike did manage another weak smile. "Not until after you finish that coffee," he said. "You look like shit."

"Thanks," the professor said with a grimace. "And this coffee tastes like shit. What do you use to brew it, squirrel droppings?"

"Nah, too bitter. I use cow pies."

Ken Dye dumped the coffee down the sink. "Then I guess it's time to leave. Could we maybe stop by the diner on the way to the station?"

Now, the man was engrossed in his work on the computer, sipping his Katahdin Diner coffee and holding it reverently in two hands like it contained the secret of life. At this point, Mike

226

figured, after just a couple of hours of fitful sleep, maybe it did.

Dawn would break in a few minutes, at which time Mike intended to pull the professor away from his research—or whatever the hell he was doing—and move the party back to Warren Sprague's field. The fog this morning looked just as thick as it had been last night, perhaps even more so, but Mike hoped the watery daylight attempting to fight its way through the low overcast ceilings would allow them to see at least enough to complete a more thorough search.

Sharon didn't just disappear into thin air, he thought. *Even a disgruntled Native American spirit can't make someone vanish, so there has to be evidence out there that will point me in the right direction.*

He refused to acknowledge the worm of fear twisting its way through his belly or listen to the voice whispering relentlessly in his ear that Sharon was dead, that she must be dead and probably torn into a dozen pieces by now for good measure. The spirit or whatever the hell it was had snatched her right out from under Mike's nose, and now she was gone, slaughtered, but not before suffering a terrifying and incomprehensibly painful death.

"NO," he whispered fiercely, pounding one hand on his desk in frustration before realizing, too late, that he was no longer alone in his office. Professor Dye stood awkwardly in front of him, clutching a sheaf of printer paper tightly in his hand.

"I'm sorry for intruding," he said, "but I think you will want to see this."

45

Sharon groaned and tried to roll over.

She failed.

She was lying on her belly with her arms pinned beneath her and she was freezing her ass off. The surface was cold and hard. A cement floor maybe? Hard-packed dirt?

She couldn't tell because she couldn't see the floor. She couldn't see anything. It was pitch-dark. In fact, when she had first awoken, just a couple of minutes ago, she felt a sharp pang of sheer terror that maybe she was blind or even dead.

Then she realized she couldn't be dead, not unless a dead body could feel pain in at least twenty places and debilitating cold as well.

She gave up on the idea of rolling over after trying to move her arms and being rewarded for her efforts with shooting pain up her right forearm and an agonizing, bright-white explosion in her left elbow followed by nausea so intense she feared she was going to puke all over herself and then pass out in the resulting mess.

I guess I'm okay just the way I'm positioned, she thought to herself when she had regained her senses. *This moving around thing is overrated anyway.*

A tiny sliver of washed-out light made its way into her prison. She could see it now after being awake for a few minutes as her eyes began to adjust to the darkness. Her range of vision was limited by her immobility and her position on the floor, but she turned her head inch by painful inch in an attempt to learn as much as possible about her surroundings.

The light was insufficient to make out much of anything beyond a few lumpy grey, amorphous shapes littered around her. But it was enough to make Sharon believe she was likely lying in some kind of large storage room or closet.

The stillness seemed unbroken and she felt fairly certain she was alone.

A headache throbbed inside her skull, which did nothing to quell her nausea. Sharon swallowed hard and tried to recall what had happened to her. She was patrolling the big bonfire last night, or at least she assumed it was last night—who really knew how long she had been unconscious?—and something had gone wrong.

What was it? The night had been long and cold and boring, that much she remembered.

She had gotten lost, that was it. She recalled her embarrassment at walking out of range of the bonfire's orienting glow and becoming confused about which way to turn.

But how had she ended up here, lying alone in the cold with what she feared were two broken arms among other assorted injuries?

Sharon concentrated hard, willing herself to remember. There must have been some kind of accident. But no matter how hard she tried to force herself to recall the events that had led her here, she simply could not. Her head pounded and swam, and she felt a hot sweat break out on her body as the nausea threatened to overwhelm her.

Fear marched through her like a conquering army as she took stock of her situation. She was alone and helpless, lying face down in some sort of big room. She had no idea where she was. Mike would be searching for her, she didn't doubt that, but how would he even begin to know where to look?

She didn't consider herself a religious person, not by a long shot, but Sharon began fervently praying that whoever had taken her had left some evidence behind, something for Mike McMahon to follow that might lead him here.

By now Sharon's head felt like a freight train was rolling through her skull. The fact that her arms were pinned beneath her body and she was unable to move them concerned her, but she was oddly reassured by the fact that both of them were at the moment causing her extreme pain. A loss of all sensation in them would have been much worse.

Feeling alone and sick and scared, Sharon lowered her head to the floor and sobbed once, regretting it instantly as the pain in her head exploded. It screamed at her, taunting her, reminding her of her vulnerability.

She closed her eyes, thinking of Mike, remembering how good it had felt holding his warm body against hers, sharing her bed with him two nights ago.

It was pointless and juvenile to wonder how he felt about her now, trapped as she was in some unknown location, essentially paralyzed and possibly dying, but thinking about him calmed her and took her mind off the present and all of its unthinkable possibilities.

She closed her eyes, remaining perfectly still, and the pain in her skull receded slightly. It was still there, she didn't even try to convince herself otherwise, but it thankfully had moved into the background.

For now.

Without realizing she was doing so, Sharon drifted back into unconsciousness.

46

"What have you got?" Mike looked up at Professor Dye. He held a sheaf of papers in his right hand and seemed anxious and excited at the same time.

"I know where the old settlement is," the professor announced. He was shaking and Mike wondered if it was with excitement at his discovery or something else.

"How did you find it?" Mike asked. "I thought we were going to have to hunt down the old-timers down at the Moose Lodge and try to find someone who might be able to point us in the right direction."

Dye shook his head. "Aerial surveys," he said cryptically.

"Excuse me?"

"Sorry," the professor said. "Sometimes I get a little ahead of myself. No wonder my students call me the absent-minded professor.

"Anyway," he said, waving the crumpled papers triumphantly in front of Mike, "the state pays engineering firms to do survey work by air. The engineers go up in small planes. They fly back and forth over predetermined areas, covering grids, mapping out whole sections of land. Running lines, they call it."

Mike nodded, starting to get the picture. "And you've accessed the maps?"

"That's right," Ken said. "But it's even better than that. They don't draw maps by hand like they used to. They actually take digital photographs and then splice them together to form images, sometimes of areas miles wide."

"And you found the photographs of the area surrounding Paskagankee," Mike said. Excitement began to ripple through his body like a thousand tiny bolts of lightning.

"Exactly," replied Professor Dye, "but it's not all good news."

"It never is. Go ahead, hit me."

"Well," Dye said hesitantly, "the old settlement is relatively close to the farmer's field from which Sharon disappeared last night. If, as I suspect, the spirit's body is using the old settlement as a base of operations, so to speak, it is entirely possible, perhaps even likely, that she was taken."

Mike lowered his gaze to the desk, not even seeing the clutter. "So that means she's dead."

"Not necessarily," the professor answered, shaking his head for emphasis.

"Listen," Mike said, exasperated. "You've seen, like I have, what happened to the other two people this…*thing*…attacked. The other two we know about, that is," he corrected himself. "It's entirely possible there are more victims we haven't discovered yet. But are you trying to tell me you think Sharon could have survived dismemberment? Is that what you want me to believe, Professor Dye?"

"No, no, of course not." The professor waved his hands like he was trying to ward off Mike's anger and pain. The wrinkled papers he held in his left hand crackled and swished through the air. "I have a theory that, if it's correct, might mean there is at least a small chance Sharon is still alive."

Mike stared at Ken Dye, then shook his head and sighed.

"Okay," he said. "In for a penny and all that. What's your theory?"

The professor sat on the edge of Mike's desk and stared at him with an almost feverish intensity. "I've studied this legend, this *phenomenon*, if you will, for decades. I've made it my life's work, and I've suffered enormous personal and professional ridicule for it. I believe there is every chance I am the most knowledgeable person alive concerning this Abenaqui legend."

"I believe you," Mike told him kindly. "And I'm sorry for jumping down your throat. I just feel…"

"Helpless," the professor finished.

Mike paused for a moment, reflecting. "Yes," he said simply.

"I understand. It's how I feel, too. But I'm not telling you this because I'm fishing for an apology. Here's my point: I don't believe the spirit's reign of death and destruction is entirely random."

Mike shook his head. "Why *wouldn't* you think that? Random death and destruction is all it's managed so far."

"Perhaps not," Dye corrected. "So far the victims have been men."

"What difference does that make?"

"Think about it. If my hypothesis is correct, and as you know I'm certain it is, the essence of this spirit is the energy of an agonized young woman, built from hopelessness and despair, which has been trapped on Earth for hundreds of years due to a curse resulting from a brutal murder committed by men—I repeat, by *men*—against her baby daughter. Despite her seemingly limitless rage against the males she has encountered, she would have no reason to harm a female, or at least no motivation to kill her."

"Then why would she have taken Sharon in the first place?"

"That I couldn't tell you," answered the professor, "I'm flying by the seat of my pants here. Maybe I'm completely off base. But it would make sense based on the Abenaqui legend, and it provides us with at least a thread of hope to hang on to. Isn't that better than nothing?"

Mike nodded, almost to himself. The man had a point, as crazy as it sounded. He absolutely had to believe Sharon was still alive. He needed that slim possibility to hang on to, like a drowning man clinging to the floating wreckage of his ship. He couldn't bear the thought that he had been responsible for the death of another innocent human being, not after the tragedy in Revere.

That had been an accident, sure. He had been cleared of any wrongdoing, sure. It was a crazy ricochet they said, an absurd one-in-a-million accidental tragedy, sure.

To Mike McMahon, though, none of that mattered. He had fired his gun and a little girl had died.

End of story.

Except it wasn't really the end, was it? Now he had made another bad decision, and there was a pretty goddamned good chance another person was dead. It didn't matter that she was a full-grown adult and a cop, too. It didn't matter that she had known the risks of the job when she signed on. The fact, as Mike McMahon saw it, was that his poor judgment had resulted in the current situation—one in which Sharon Dupont was in grave danger or already dead.

Mike looked out his office window at a parking lot. It was beginning to fill with arriving day-shift officers. The daylight was weak and barely winning the battle against the night's darkness and fog, but the conditions were likely as good as they were going to get.

"We've got work to do," he said to Professor Dye. "Let's get moving."

47

Sharon wondered if she might be hallucinating from the pain. Lightning bolts of it flashed continuously through her head, and she was certain now that her arms were broken. Probably at least one rib, too, considering how agonizingly difficult it was to breathe.

She wondered, almost as an aside, whether she was suffering from internal bleeding and if so, how extensive it was and how long she could survive it.

She lifted her head carefully and took a long look around her prison which, oddly, was now well lit and into which she could see fairly clearly, given her poor perspective from the floor.

She lay in a dirty and dingy room—perhaps a living room that had once been tastefully decorated but which had gone quickly and completely to seed. A filthy carpet covered part of the floor. At one time it may have been a rich maroon color with dark gold trim, but ground-in dirt and grime and who knew what else had reduced it to little more than the hard-packed dirt Sharon had originally suspected she was lying on.

She couldn't see the entire room, but even from her poor vantage point and through a haze of constant, almost crippling pain, what she could see made her sick with fear and disgust.

Human bodies were scattered everywhere, or at least *parts* of human bodies. They looked as though they had been fed through a shredder, with bits and pieces of clothing still attached. An arm here, a portion of a leg there, a bone that may have been part of a sternum or perhaps a shin, still with a bloody flap of torn skin hanging off it.

Sharon felt bile rising in her gullet and forced herself to swallow hard to avoid puking all over herself. *It would be a shame to ruin my lovely outfit,* she thought as she contemplated her filthy jeans and sweatshirt.

She almost giggled but instead choked back a wrenching sob.

One pile of body parts in particular nagged at Sharon's consciousness, and in her pain and general fuzzy confusion it took her awhile to figure out why. Then the answer struck her as surely and as violently as if she had been hit with a baseball bat.

That particular pile of human remains was different from the others: it was the only one in the room that seemed to be more or less in one piece. The only one besides herself, of course, and she wasn't entirely convinced all her parts *were* still intact.

Whereas the other remains were grisly reminders of the unearthly horror stalking Paskagankee—ripped, torn and shredded pieces of skin, bone, ligaments and muscle that appeared barely human—the body slumped across the room on the floor in an opposite corner seemed to be whole.

Sharon guessed it was a woman, and that she was dressed in a long gray wool skirt, although it was hard to be certain. Whether that person was alive or dead she had no way of knowing.

What she *did* know was that the body wasn't moving.

A door opened loudly behind Sharon. It was yanked back with more force than necessary and then slammed shut.

She closed her eyes and lay completely still, not that she had much choice in the matter with two useless arms and quite possibly extensive internal injuries.

After a few seconds, her innate cop curiosity overcame her fear and she opened her eyes just enough to peer across the room toward the door without revealing—she hoped—that she was alive. Her entire body was shaking from fear and shock, and she prayed whomever or whatever had just entered the wrecked interior of this prison would be too preoccupied to notice.

Shambling into the room, moving in a manner that appeared almost but not quite aimless, was the most frightening sight Sharon Dupont had ever experienced. Her bowels loosened and she nearly screamed but somehow managed to keep herself quiet by biting hard on the inside of her cheek. The coppery taste of blood filled her mouth but she barely noticed.

It was ex-Paskagankee Police Chief Wally Court, and he was moving with all the grace of a three-legged cow.

Or, more accurately, it was some abomination that at one time had been Wally Court, for this present version resembled Chief Court in only the vaguest general sense. The size was right—huge, he had always been a very large man—but nothing else even came close to resembling the person Sharon had come to know as a mentor and friend.

The Wally Court who had mentored Sharon as a troubled teen and saved her from her darkest tendencies was a disciplined dresser. He wasn't flashy in any way but would never dream of being seen without sharply-creased trousers and a meticulously ironed button-down dress shirt.

This man, or rather, this Wally Court-*thing*, appeared not to have bathed in days, maybe not in weeks. Muddy grass, twigs and straw were matted into tangled and greasy hair. A red-checked wool hunting coat hung loosely off a skeletal frame, covering a shirt haphazardly buttoned. The breast pocket was torn almost completely off the shirt and hung by a few threads. Both knees of the thing's pants were ripped open and dried blood crusted the fabric surrounding the right knee.

A stench filled the room as this Court-thing moved across the room, without so much as a glance at Sharon, and stumbled out of her sight.

The shock of this utterly unexpected arrival almost caused Sharon to forget the intense pain of her injuries. There was no question in her mind that what she had just seen was Chief Wally Court. She had known the man for years, and he had been more of a father to her than her real one ever thought of being.

It was him.

At the same time, though, it wasn't Wally Court. That man had moved with a grace and an economy of motion hard to imagine from such a large man. This shambling creature barely seemed able to remain upright, slouching and sliding rather than walking with a normal gait and actually slamming into the door-jamb before falling/crashing into the next room.

It's true, she though feverishly to herself. *It's all true.*

Professor Dye's story, which she had believed on one level but not fully understood or appreciated, was one hundred percent accurate. Because, really, what other explanation could there be for what she had just seen?

She hadn't been able to look directly into the Chief Court-thing's face, but she knew that the bright spark of life shining in the old Wally Court's eyes would have been gone, replaced by what she could not imagine, and did not want to think about.

Loud crashing noises exploded out of the room the thing had entered only a few seconds ago, and Shari's excruciating pain returned with a vengeance. Had she not already been lying crumpled on the floor, the severity of the pain would have knocked her down.

Nausea flooded through her again, and she felt lightheaded and woozy. Blackness crowded the edges of her eyesight in what was becoming a dependable ritual, rapidly covering more and more of her already limited field of vision.

Her last thought before losing consciousness again was that she had to figure out some way to warn Mike and Professor Dye about what she had just seen.

Then there was nothing.

48

The fog hung over Warren Sprague's empty field like a death shroud, cloaking the countryside in a damp grey mist that writhed and twisted on unseen breezes as if possessed.

As Mike McMahon parked the Explorer, the hulk of burned brush, limbs and small trees—remnants of last night's bonfire— loomed out of the mist, thick smoke still curling off the blackened top.

The silence was oppressive, broken only by the sucking/crunching sound of the two men's boots as they walked over the partially frozen ground in the early morning stillness.

"How do you want to do this?" Professor Dye asked, his voice sounding thin and reedy, as if being absorbed by the mist.

"Well, splitting up would allow us to cover more ground and to do it faster, but under the circumstances I don't see how we can take that chance," Mike replied.

They stopped and warmed their hands at the still-hot remains of the bonfire. "I guess we just start on the western edge of the field and work our way clockwise along the boundary between the field and the woods. Hopefully we'll uncover evidence of what went down here last night. There has to be something, we just need to find it."

Mike started off slowly toward the edge of the clearing, the forest still pitch-dark beyond the ten feet or so adjoining the field. The steam rising from their Styrofoam coffee cups mixed with the cool, damp air, trailing behind them as they moved like smoke from an old-time steam engine.

"I feel completely useless," the professor said softly. "I don't even know what I'm looking for."

"Anything," Mike replied. "You're looking for anything out of the ordinary. It might be a piece of cloth torn off a jacket or a shirt and left hanging on a branch. Or it could be something as obvious as footprints leading into the woods or maybe blood or some other sign of a struggle. I can't say for sure what it might be, but I guarantee you'll recognize it if you see it."

They approached the edge of the clearing, massive Douglas firs towering majestically in front of them. They materialized out of the gloom like gigantic sentries protecting some unknown treasure hidden inside the forest.

Mike shivered, not only from the damp cold but from a rising sense of disquiet, from the feeling that Sharon was somewhere close by. She was probably dead thanks to his miscalculation but maybe, just maybe, she was still breathing, injured and in desperate need of help.

He reached the edge of the forest and turned south. Began inching his way along the vague demarcation between plowed field and virgin forest, saying nothing, his concentration intensely focused on the task at hand.

Professor Dye followed close behind. Mike knew the older man still felt like a useless appendage, but he had other things to worry about at.

* * *

Forty minutes into the search, Ken Dye began to gain a sense of appreciation for real police work. Unlike on television shows and movies, in which the good guys seem to spend the majority of their time shooting it out with the forces of evil or speeding through congested cities locked in thrilling car chases, the bulk of real-life police work seemed to consist of the patient examination of often uncomfortable crime scenes and the search for evidence based on nothing more than blind faith that there might be some to find.

He had passed Mike and was methodically working his way down the line of trees thirty feet or so in front of the chief. Whether because he was naturally more impatient than the trained law enforcement officer or simply because he didn't know what to look for, the professor found himself moving more rapidly than Mike and had tired of cooling his heels behind him. The lack of intellectual stimulation had given him too much time to think and the resulting images filling his head were less than reassuring.

By midmorning the daylight was not much more prevalent than it had been at dawn. Professor Dye wondered absently if he would ever see the sun again. The real sun, not this pseudo-sunlight, which felt more like dusk and didn't really get the job done. He wanted strong, warming, good-cheer-inducing solar activity. His eyes were beginning to tire from the constant strain of searching and he found his mind wandering.

He picked his way a few feet into a small break in the trees—perhaps six feet across and slightly less overgrown than the rest of the tangled mass of brush and uncontrolled undergrowth—and tripped over a fallen tree branch. He stumbled to his knees and swore under his breath, annoyed and now wet and cold as well.

Without a conscious thought, the professor reached back and grabbed the branch to toss it into the woods and out of his way. The texture of the branch was spongy and for the first time Professor Dye actually gave it a look. Seconds later his coffee came up, gushing out of him in a rush of stomach acid and partially digested food, splashing onto the frozen ground as Ken Dye retched and vomited. The acid burned in his gullet and he fought another round of nausea.

He didn't want to look at it again.

He refused to look at it again.

He couldn't stop himself from looking at it again as he glanced down in horrified fascination. This time, in an unexpected display of self-control, he managed to avoid puking up anything else, not that there was much left in his stomach, anyway.

Lying on the dirty snow, where he had dropped it in his initial burst of panic and fear, was a severed human arm.

49

Mike knew right away it was bad.

He hadn't known Professor Dye very long, but it had been enough time that he could easily detect the barely contained panic in the man's voice. It sounded unnaturally loud as he called out, and Mike thought the professor might be on the verge of bursting into tears.

Icy fingers of dread clamped onto Mike's internal organs as he walked into the woods. Ken Dye was bent over, hands on his knees, a string of yellowish gunk hanging from his open mouth and stretching elastically toward the ground. It was a pose eerily similar to Harley Tanguay's from a couple of days ago.

Mike tried to imagine how he would react to the sight of Sharon's lifeless body, battered and torn apart, lying on the forest floor.

This feeling was identical to the despair that had gripped Mike on that fateful Revere evening eighteen months ago. The weather then had been the complete opposite of today—a sweltering afternoon under a relentlessly blazing sun—but he had felt the same frozen lump in his gut he could feel forming right now.

He steeled himself for the worst and shouldered past Professor Dye, looking down onto the dirty snow.

It wasn't Sharon.

In fact, it wasn't a body at all. At least not a complete body.

Rust-colored dried blood speckled the snow and mud a few feet from Professor Dye. A lot of rust-colored dried blood. Lying in the middle of all the blood, looking small and incongruously out of place, was a human arm. Or what was left of a human arm.

Mike breathed deeply. He hadn't even realized until now that he was holding his breath. The sense of relief he felt from not discovering Sharon Dupont's corpse in the forest was tempered with the knowledge that there was now at least one more victim to add to this awful killing spree. It was technically possible, of course, that the person to whom this arm belonged was still alive, but that was unlikely in the extreme and Mike knew in his heart it was not the case.

He kneeled in the muddy, bloody snow to take a closer look, careful not to disturb the scene. The arm had been torn out of its shoulder; the ball-like portion of the humerus wrenched free, with stringy muscles and stretched-and-torn ligaments trailing on the ground, serving as grisly testimony to its owner's last agonizing moments.

Covering the appendage—more or less—was a light blue shirt-sleeve and the sleeve of a heavy winter coat that had been torn off its owner along with the arm. The sleeve looked familiar, and Mike began to feel queasier. He looked up to see Professor Ken Dye standing alongside him, apparently done puking. Mike had to give the man credit for not taking the easy way out and abandoning the mess here in the forest for the open spaces of Warren Sprague's field.

"You know who it is, don't you?" the professor asked.

Mike nodded, swallowing hard. He was determined not to let his stomach get the best of him. He was a law enforcement professional, for crying out loud.

"It's Detective O'Bannon."

"O'Bannon? But he left for Portland last night."

"No," Mike reminded him. "You assumed he left for Portland when we didn't see him after that first meeting at the bonfire around seven p.m."

He looked back down at the gruesome evidence. "Obviously, that was an incorrect assumption."

Ken Dye was silent for a moment, then said, "But that means—"

"Yes, I know," Mike interrupted. He couldn't bear to hear the professor say it. "Shaw must be here somewhere, too. If something had happened to O'Bannon and Shaw was uninjured, he would have contacted us by now. He would have let us know something was wrong. Obviously, he was unable to do that."

Mike stood, his knees cracking and popping. He felt like he had aged fifty years in the past week. "We need to search the area. Now. These two men could still be alive," he said without much conviction, knowing it was not true.

Professor Dye shook his head. "They were men, not women. They're not still alive, Chief."

"We can't assume that," Mike snapped. "We owe it to them to at least canvass the surrounding area." He looked deeper into the tangle of thickly forested woods where a narrow path had been beaten down, presumably by the lethal monster that had caused the devastation.

Ignoring the path for the time being, he told the professor, "We stick together. Don't wander more than five feet from me."

The older man chuckled. The sound came out thick and raspy. "Don't worry," he said. "I have no intention of wandering off into this haunted forest by myself."

50

Two hours later, sweating and exhausted, Mike abandoned the search of the area surrounding the severed arm. The men had worked in a steadily enlarging concentric circle around the gruesome discovery. They found broken tree branches and evidence of a violent struggle nearby, along with more blood, plenty of blood, but nothing else in the way of immediately useful evidence.

Mike knew a more thorough search was called for, with teams of police investigators as well as dogs, but that would have to wait until he could get his men here. In his heart he knew what Professor Dye said was true, that both O'Bannon and Shaw were dead, victims of another violent and horrific attack.

His priority now was to find Sharon. If there was any chance whatsoever she might still be alive, as Dye seemed to believe, then Mike was determined not to rest until he found her and rescued her.

He would not be responsible for the death of another innocent human being, as he had been that terrible day in Revere. Mike knew he was damaged goods and had been since the moment he fired the bullet that killed that little girl.

His ex-wife had known it too, which was why she eventually moved on, unable to continue living with a brooding man, a man filled with darkness where once there had been light.

Mike didn't think he could survive if Sharon died because of him. He wasn't sure he wanted to.

* * *

The two men trooped out of the woods and back into the enormous clearing, perspiration soaking their clothes. The day was cool and damp but the physical exertion of fighting their way through the thickly tangled overgrowth had caused their bodies to overheat. Sweat covered their red faces, dripping off their noses onto the snow.

They sat on their waterproof packs and rested as Mike pulled a thermos and two small cups out and poured still-steaming coffee into them. Their breath rose into the moist air, floating away on the light breeze. Professor Dye reached into his pack and grabbed two ham and cheese sandwiches, passing one to Mike and biting greedily into the second.

As a professional educator, Ken Dye led what was essentially a sedentary existence and hadn't had this much physical activity in years, maybe decades. In a strange way it felt good to be moving and doing instead of sitting and thinking, theorizing about a problem and considering it in the abstract. It brought him back to his days in the field living with the Native Americans he had come to love so much, in the years before he wrote his book and became a pariah in the academic community.

Then Ken remembered why they were here, the utter destruction and devastation that had led to this moment and the horrors that likely lay ahead, and he no longer felt quite so invigorated.

Rather, he felt exactly like what he was—an aging academic risking his life and the life of Mike McMahon, as well as the lives of all the citizens of Paskagankee on his theory, on a hypothesis in which he had felt much more confident while sitting in his living room sipping from a glass of Chivas.

Now that they were getting close—and they *were* getting close, Ken could feel it—he found himself wondering how accurate his theory really was, and whether he would be able to summon the courage to face down the monster when the time came.

If he was wrong or if he found himself unable to do what must be done, the tragedy that had already begun unfolding in this tiny town was just the beginning and would seem like child's play compared to what would follow.

Professor Dye found himself staring at his reflection in the small amount of liquid left at the bottom of the Styrofoam cup. The face looking back up at him was lined and haunted, barely recognizable as his own. He splashed the remainder of the now-cold black coffee onto the muddy ground and looked up to see Mike McMahon gazing at him thoughtfully.

"Well," Dye said weakly. "This isn't getting us anywhere, is it?"

Mike smiled sadly and shook his head. Together the men stowed their supplies into their packs without another word and prepared to make their way back into the dark and foreboding forest.

Neither spoke.

There was nothing to say.

51

Mike sat next to Professor Dye on a fallen log deep in the forest and shook his head in amazement at the scene just a hundred yards in front of them.

In the diffuse, failing light of the late-November afternoon, a light made even more unreliable by the ever-present fog and the thickness of the trees and vegetation, they could see a log cabin. It was obviously of recent construction, with a thin plume of smoke rising from the red brick chimney on the northern side of the home.

"Is it possible someone is actually living there?" the professor whispered.

Mike shrugged. "As unlikely as that seems, I don't know what other explanation there could be." He tried to reconcile the Currier and Ives scene with the remote location and the horrific events of the past few days. The contrast was jarring.

It had taken more than two hours of hiking to reach this area. Progress had been slowed by Professor Dye's age and general immobility in the thick brush, but Mike knew he would not have been able to make much better time even if he had been alone. The terrain was simply too rugged to allow for anything more than a plodding, deliberate pace unless you were willing to risk a broken ankle or worse.

Following the trail had been easy, even for an unskilled tracker like Mike. The monster, or whatever the hell it was, had smashed its way through the woods, presumably carrying at least one body and likely making multiple trips. It had made no effort to cover its tracks.

Whether the lack of stealth was intentional or not Mike had no way of knowing, but it would have been a simple matter for them to find this location even without the aerial photographs Professor Dye had obtained through his research earlier this morning.

Now, sitting in the forest under what Mike hoped was sufficient cover to prevent detection, the two men studied the original village of Paskagankee, which was spread out before them in a huge clearing. He could see crumbled remains of stone and granite foundations that had supported the homes and outbuildings that made up the tiny village more than four hundred years ago. Looking through high-powered binoculars, the layout of the village was clear.

The new house, the one that had taken them quite by surprise when they first glimpsed it, had been built only within the last few years, that much was obvious. The cabin had been constructed on the eastern edge of the ancient village proper, built from native timber felled almost right on the spot where the home stood. Huge slabs of granite formed the foundation, just as they had with the original buildings.

Atop the granite lay a small but seemingly well-constructed single-story home, perhaps fifty feet long by twenty feet wide. Mike wondered how many people were living here—probably no more than two in a home this size, but there was no way to know for sure.

The front door had been constructed precisely in the center of the home and was accessible by a short stairway leading to a farmer's porch spanning the length of the house. On either side of the door was a double-hung window. Ratty-looking mismatched curtains had been pulled across each window and blocked any view of the cabin's interior. The side of the house featuring the fieldstone chimney faced Mike and Professor Dye and was windowless.

Mike could see Ken studying the building as well. The professor looked pale and wan, even more so than usual, and Mike hoped he was feeling all right. It had been a grueling hike out here after a difficult morning, and it was plain the man wasn't used to a lot of physical activity.

Now, sitting in the failing light staring at an incongruously modern-looking cabin constructed in the middle of nowhere, Mike considered how to proceed.

He had his service weapon and a spare, tucked into a holster above his right ankle. Professor Dye was unarmed. Mike suspected two weapons would be no match against whatever had unleashed the onslaught of death and destruction on his little town.

The temptation to retreat and return tomorrow with more personnel—bringing the entire Paskagankee Police Department roster, along with as many State Police reinforcements as he could wheedle out of Portland—was strong. An early-morning return would allow them the luxury of time to formulate a plan of attack, whereas anything he decided to do now would be hurried and ill-conceived.

And nightfall was approaching rapidly.

Working against a return tomorrow, though, were two factors. First, the professor had told him that adding more bodies to the pending confrontation would only succeed in putting more people at risk. The professor seemed to be one hundred percent certain he could put a stop to whatever was happening in Paskagankee, and—for better or for worse—he had convinced Mike to let him try.

Secondly, and much more importantly, Sharon might be here somewhere. Maybe she was inside that log cabin just a hundred yards away, possibly alive and probably injured, most likely gravely injured. He knew that if she *was* now still alive, she probably would not be by tomorrow morning.

He couldn't risk it. He couldn't take the chance that Sharon Dupont would die overnight while he dotted his I's and crossed his T's and waited for the perfect conditions to attempt a rescue.

So waiting was out of the question. Whatever was going to happen here was going to happen tonight, within the next couple of hours. Mike wondered if he would survive to see another sunrise and found he didn't really care. The only thing that would make tomorrow worth seeing would be finding and rescuing Sharon.

He tried to convince himself he needed to rescue the rookie officer because she was his responsibility, and although he knew that to be true, he also knew he was lying to himself if he thought that was the only reason.

He was falling in love with the young woman, and he strongly suspected she felt the same way about him. Love was an emotion Mike had given up on ever feeling again after Kate packed up her things and left, and the fact that he had found a spark with this beautiful girl—who was as damaged as he, just in a different way—made it that much harder to accept that she could be dead.

And if Sharon was dead it didn't matter whether he lived or died, either.

Mike's mind was racing. He wondered whether the search team he called in to canvass Warren Sprague's field had found any evidence regarding the O'Bannon and Shaw situation. He had radioed back to dispatch just before beginning the long hike into the forest, requesting as many officers as possible for a thorough search of the area surrounding the severed arm. Hopefully there were no more gruesome surprises awaiting the team.

He shook his head to clear his mind. Time was running out, and daydreaming about the scene at Sprague's farm wasn't going to get anything accomplished. He had to stay focused.

He scanned the area and realized the clearing seemed noticeably darker than it had been just a couple of minutes ago. He glanced at Ken Dye and found the professor gazing back at him unblinkingly, waiting for guidance.

"Wait for me right here," Mike told the professor. "I'm going to get a closer look at that house and when I do, hopefully we'll find out exactly what we're up against." He waited for the professor to argue, to say that he needed to approach the house as well, in order to do whatever mysterious thing he needed to do.

Instead of a protestation from the professor, though, Mike saw Ken's eyes widen in terror.

Then he moaned.

Mike turned quickly back toward the cabin and froze in utter astonishment.

His jaw dropped as his brain attempted to process what he was seeing.

It was simultaneously horrifying and exhilarating.

52

Candles were floating in front of Sharon's face.

Candles.

Simple white three-inch tapered candles with brightly burning wicks.

And they were floating.

She knew what she was seeing was impossible, that candles didn't float in the air. But the evidence was hard to ignore, suspended as it was above the floor a few inches in front of her.

She blinked her eyes rapidly and the candles disappeared, replaced by a decapitated human skull, its skin torn away to reveal a bone-white death mask. The terrifying rictus was suspended inches in front of her face in the same space the candles had occupied until seconds ago.

She tried to scream and found she could not. Her throat was parched and sore and she was unable to produce even a squeak.

Sharon blinked again, now close to panic, desperate to make the awful grinning skull disappear.

When she re-focused her eyes she was relieved to discover the death mask had vanished. In its place was a hazy near-darkness, a tantalizing sensation of movement just beyond the edge of her vision. She strained to hear the sound of footsteps to correlate with the perceived motion and could hear nothing.

With a supreme effort, Sharon cleared her head of some of the haziness and confusion. The shadowy darkness remained, lurking at the edges of her vision like a menacing stalker. She knew the candles and the skull she had seen were hallucinations, figments of her fevered imagination.

She was dying. She sensed death's stealthy approach and was mildly surprised to discover that the notion didn't bother her all that much.

There was a pang of regret that she would so quickly lose what she had just started to discover with Mike McMahon—his tenderness, humor, passion, and a sensitivity she had never before experienced—but otherwise Sharon Dupont viewed her injuries and impending death with an almost clinical detachment: her arms were broken and useless, she assumed at least one rib was broken and probably more, and she suspected that one or more of those broken ribs had punctured a lung. Undoubtedly she was bleeding internally.

It was becoming harder and harder to remain lucid, as evidenced by the strange hallucinations she had suffered upon regaining consciousness moments ago. She recalled her determination to warn Mike of the danger inside this house of horrors and almost laughed. She would have laughed, actually, were it not for the intense pain such foolishness would engender.

The idea of warning *anyone* about *anything* was ludicrous. She was lying face down and helpless on a filthy floor in a room littered with who knew what sorts of atrocities and she was going to—what? Jump up and charge into Paskagankee to warn Mike McMahon and save the day? She couldn't even walk a perimeter around a raging bonfire without getting lost.

Sharon shook her head and a woozy nausea rolled up her gullet. She concentrated on not throwing up, knowing instinctively that to puke right now would be a very bad idea, given her internal injuries. She realized she'd been drooling while she was unconscious and glanced down at the dirty carpet to discover blood had been leaking out of her mouth.

It was bright red and terrifying.

Again the perceived sensation of movement tantalized her, just beyond the edge of her vision, felt rather than seen. Ignoring the pain and nausea and fear, she willed herself to turn her head, accomplishing maybe half an inch of movement. It was just enough to bring the object she had sensed into her line of sight.

The object was a man, a very familiar-looking man, wearing a red plaid hunting jacket. But something was not right. His jacket was ripped and torn, almost in tatters. It hung off the man in long, stringy cloth strips.

Then she remembered.

The man was former Paskagankee Police Chief Wally Court, and she had glimpsed him a few hours previously, stumbling around inside this filthy house.

His left arm hung askew, bent a full ninety degrees between his wrist and elbow. Sharon couldn't be sure, but it looked like a fragment of bone had pierced the man's skin near his elbow. The arm was clearly broken, shattered really.

Court should have been in agony, and yet he moved silently and smoothly. Too smoothly, almost as if he were gliding instead of walking.

And his hair. His hair looked greasy and matted, with leaves and twigs and something that looked suspiciously like animal excrement smeared throughout it.

Sharon decided she must be suffering another hallucination. She couldn't imagine how, because everything seemed so vivid and real. It was not possible that Chief Court—if it really even was Wally Court sharing this nightmare scenario with her—could be gliding around this house, a few feet away, moving in eerie silence with a shattered left arm and cow shit and matted straw inhabiting his thinning gray hair. That was simply impossible and about as ridiculous as floating candles and grinning skulls.

And yet there he was.

An overwhelming sense of sadness and confusion overtook her like fog rolling in off the ocean. Sadness for what she had lost and would never regain with Wally Court, the father figure who had meant so much to her in her formative years. Confusion because she was not entirely convinced that this sight was even real and not just a product of some bizarre and random synapse misfirings occurring in her brain thanks to the severity of her injuries.

Sharon Dupont slid smoothly and completely back into her cocoon of darkness. She felt it coming and wondered for a half-second if she would ever reawaken.

Then she was gone.

53

Mike turned to see what had caused Professor Dye's eyes to widen in fear. In other circumstances, the professor's face would have been comical, eyes huge and mouth agape.

In the distance, on the front porch of the log cabin, former Paskagankee Police Chief Wally Court had appeared. The recently retired chief, whose last official act had been to hire Mike as his replacement, was a mess. He was barely recognizable.

What he was doing on the porch was a mystery, but whatever it was, he did it in utter silence, gliding inches above the structure like some demon figure skater from hell.

Ken moaned again, staring in abject terror at the...thing...a hundred yards away.

Mike swiveled as quickly and silently as he could and clapped a hand over the professor's mouth. Then he pulled him down behind a mammoth boulder, which was next to the fallen log they had chosen as their reconnaissance point.

"Ssh!" he whispered fiercely.

Professor Dye blinked and nodded. Mike pulled his hand off the older man's mouth, relieved to see some of the alertness returning to his eyes, the look of sheer panic fading but not disappearing entirely.

"What the hell is going on here?" Mike asked quietly, peering around the jagged edge of the boulder to discover the Wally Court–thing was nowhere to be seen. He assumed it had retreated back inside the house and hoped it hadn't heard or sensed their presence and was not even now moving silently toward the boulder to tear them limb from limb.

"It's the spirit," Dye told him, no longer bothering to add the disclaimer, "If my theory is correct."

It was no longer necessary. That one terrifying glimpse of Chief Court was enough to convince Mike that the professor had been right all along, that what he chose to believe or disbelieve was irrelevant to the reality of the situation.

"How the hell is it walking?" Mike asked, more out of a sense of wonderment than any real notion the professor might be able to answer the question.

But Professor Dye seemed ready for it. "The body the spirit has possessed is dead and has begun decomposing. Did you notice the stench when it came out of the house?"

Mike said, "Notice it, how could I miss it?"

Dye nodded. "Exactly. Since the flesh and muscles are decomposing, the ankles and legs are probably no longer strong enough to support the rest of the body. The human host is merely a vessel, which allows the spirit to maintain physical contact with this world. So rather than actually walking on the ground, the spirit is simply levitating the corpse and moving it at will."

Mike shook his head and grimaced. "Okay, it's the spirit, and it can levitate. I can't believe I just said that."

Professor Dye smiled nervously and remained silent.

Mike continued, "But it doesn't change anything. I still need to get a look inside that house to see if Sharon or anyone else is alive in there."

He was shocked at the sense of calmness he felt. Whatever was going to happen was going to happen soon, and there were only three possible outcomes: he would find Sharon alive and rescue her, or he would find her alive and die trying to rescue her, or he would discover Sharon already dead, in which case he didn't care what happened to him.

"Here's what we're going to do," Mike said, still speaking softly, although he assumed since they were still alive the spirit had not heard them and must have gone back inside the house. "I'm going to circle the cabin at a distance of about twenty feet. If it seems feasible, I'm then going to make my way from window to window until I find one where I can get a look inside. If you see anything I need to know about, use the walkie and warn me, then get the hell out of here if things start going sideways. Do you understand?"

Professor Dye nodded, leaning to his right and looking around the edge of the boulder to check the cabin again. Mike saw him freeze stock-still for a moment, the color draining out of his face so completely he looked exactly like the Chief Court–thing they had glimpsed moments ago.

Then the professor abruptly stood and began walking around the gigantic rock toward the cabin.

Mike leapt to his feet, and as he rounded the boulder behind Professor Dye he saw he had been wrong about the spirit. If it had gone back into the cabin at all it had done so only momentarily. The thing had heard them or somehow sensed their presence and was even now gliding toward them, moving rapidly, suspended over the ground like some hovercraft from hell.

Its feet moved like a normal person's but did not contact the ground as they swung back and forth. Instead they simply passed inches over the forest floor as the figure of the former Paskagankee Police Chief moved in their direction. He (it?) was now no more than fifty feet away, closing on them rapidly.

In front of Mike, Professor Dye stopped abruptly and spread his arms, as if surrendering to the thing. His breath came heavily and erratically, Mike could hear his ragged respiration from behind. He was almost panting, but he appeared—incredibly—calm and collected.

"What the hell are you doing?" Mike hissed, reaching out to grab the professor's right shoulder.

"This is how it has to be," Professor Dye said, staring resolutely at the terrifying apparition, which had picked up speed and was now advancing on them like an avenging angel.

"Bullshit," answered Mike as he spun the older man around and down behind him. He shoved hard and winced at the sound of the professor's head striking the boulder.

Again Professor Dye moaned, this time as he lost consciousness, slumping to the cold ground next to the big grey rock. A bright crimson splash of blood dripped down the surface and disappeared into a thin patch of moss.

Mike wondered distractedly if he had just killed the man he was trying to protect. *Just my luck,* he thought crazily and then turned to face the nightmare spirit. It was still approaching and now almost upon him.

He drew his Glock and aimed at the center of mass of the rotting corpse. The stench was nauseating, even to a man who had experienced dozens of dead bodies in his career.

"Freeze, Police!" he barked, more out of habit than any sense that the thing would actually stop. For all he knew, it couldn't even understand him. His eyes began to water from the awful odor of corruption surrounding the body.

A detached part of Mike's brain took in some of the horrific details as the thing approached. Bodily fluids seeped from every orifice as the process of decomposition proceeded according to the laws of nature. Not even a wayward Native American spirit could change some things, it appeared. What was left of Wally Court's plaid hunting jacket fluttered in the breeze, trailing the corpse as it advanced on Mike.

The thing gave no indication it understood Mike's warning to stop, gave no indication it even heard him. It was now close enough that Mike could see into its eyes, or what was left of them. They were milky-white, covered in some sort of glaze, not seeming to focus on him or anything else.

Mike fired.

Once.

Twice.

Three times.

The body of Chief Court jerked backward three times from the incredible kinetic energy of the high-velocity rounds. Three direct hits—center-mass, right in the chest, as trained—put the thing down, ripping violently into the ruined flesh and bone.

The corpse fell backward, smashing into a dead birch tree and spinning to the ground. A broken branch impaled the body in its side, sinking a good eight inches into the rotting flesh.

The smell of gunpowder filled the damp forest air, and Mike was grateful for the momentary respite from the overwhelming stench of death and corruption and decay.

He stood holding his gun in both hands. His knuckles were

white and his hands were shaking badly from adrenaline. He relaxed his grip and turned to check on Professor Dye.

Mike dropped to the cold ground and felt for the unconscious man's carotid artery. The pulse was steady and strong, and he breathed a sigh of relief. He turned his attention to the man's head and examined the wound, grateful that it seemed already to be clotting. It would have to be cleaned, of course, but after disinfection and maybe a few sutures, he should be good as new.

Professor Dye twitched and groaned. His eyelids fluttered and his head shook. Mike held the man's head off the ground with one hand and gently tapped his cheek with the other, hoping to ease him back to consciousness, slowly enough to—

SNAP!

Mike whipped his head around at the sound, loud as a gunshot in the empty forest, and saw the form of the spirit—impossibly—rising off the ground and starting for him again. The thick branch that had plunged into the thing's side as it fell broke off against a tree as it began levitating, giving Mike a two or three second warning.

He scrambled to his feet, again raising his weapon. He recalled Professor Dye's statement that bullets would be useless against the spirit, that they would simply embed themselves inside the host's body. The apparition would be unaffected and would keep coming.

How do you stop an ethereal presence that wasn't meant to exist in this world to begin with?

Mike fired anyway, not knowing what else to do. Maybe if he could put the thing down again, he could use the few seconds he would gain to come up with some other option.

It wasn't much of a plan—hell, it wasn't a plan at all—but it was all he had. The shot missed everything and Mike realized his hands were shaking so badly he was unlikely to even hit the damned thing if he couldn't get himself under control.

But by now it was almost upon him. He fired again and hit paydirt as the body slammed back against another tree trunk. Mike fired again and again, emptying his weapon into the thing, and the body tumbled face-first onto the ground with a slick, wet squishing sound.

He spotted a good-sized branch that had been knocked from a

nearby tree during the recent ice storm and hefted it. The branch was heavy and shaped like a club, maybe five feet long and six inches wide at its thickest point, then tapering down to about an inch-and-a-half at one end.

It felt solid and brutal in Mike's hands.

The Court–thing again rose silently off the ground and Mike approached it, wielding the makeshift weapon like Ted Williams turning on a fastball. He swung from the heels and connected solidly with the host's ribcage. He was rewarded with a sharp cracking sound and the thing went down again.

But only for a moment. Then it almost immediately began to rise again.

Mike's arms were already tiring and he knew he could not continue beating the thing like a piñata much longer. Once he lost the strength to keep knocking the entity to the ground, it would be all over him.

He smacked the makeshift club into the dead body and the thing fell again with a hollow thud. It had still not made a sound during the entire confrontation. The only noise came from Mike, his labored breathing sounding loud and harsh in his ears. He was just about spent.

Again the thing started to rise and again Mike clubbed it and again it went down

His arms burned and felt heavy and rubbery. Tears streamed from his eyes as the stench of death assaulted him. He felt sick.

He clubbed the thing again, and again he heard/felt ribs break, not that it made any damned difference. He tried to catch his breath and was unable to do so. His lungs burned.

The thing began to levitate again and Mike swung again and this time he missed. He tried to reverse course with the big club but it was now too heavy to control. He made contact with the thing's body but because he had been unable to get any torque behind the swing, it didn't fall over. It didn't react at all.

He was out of time.

It was over.

His arms felt as wooden as the club.

He desperately reached back to swing again and the thing was upon him. It lifted him high into the air with one cold, dead hand on his neck and the other on his jacket. Then it flung him effortlessly away.

The death-smell was so much worse when the thing actually touched him that Mike gagged, he couldn't breathe, and then he was flying through the air on a short but violent trip. He crashed into the same tree that had impaled the monster a few short moments ago and fell in a heap on the ground.

Mike felt pain radiate through his body. His head snapped back and more pain exploded in his skull, and he felt warm blood running down the back of his neck. His knee was bent at an odd angle and practically useless.

He coughed weakly, spitting up blood, and sensed the spirit moving silently behind him to finish him off. It wouldn't take long.

He apologized in his mind to Sharon, the woman he had fallen in love with and the woman he had gotten killed.

Again the cold but inhumanly strong hand of the thing lifted him skyward. He wondered why the apparition wasn't ripping him apart and decided it must prefer to kill its victims first.

Small favors, Mike thought, as he felt his body being lifted into the air like a rag doll. He tensed for the final toss, the one that would undoubtedly shatter his neck or smash his head against a tree or break his spine and paralyze him.

For a long moment he hung suspended in the air, gagging from the smell and awaiting the inevitable. Then, to his amazement, the thing dropped him. He tumbled straight down from a distance of seven or eight feet, landing on the thick carpet of leaves and pine needles with a muted *thud.*

For a moment utter stillness reigned and the thought flashed through Mike's brain that maybe he was already dead and had somehow missed the particulars. Then the monster's stench began to fade, and Mike realized the thing was moving away from him.

He turned his head gingerly, thankful he had somehow avoided paralysis and was still alive and kicking, more or less. He watched the retreating body of the spirit, and then looked beyond it and his breath caught in his throat.

Thirty feet away, standing woozily where he had fallen moments before, was Professor Ken Dye. He was white as a ghost, an observation which struck Mike as strangely appropriate, all things considered, and he was once again standing upright with his arms spread in a gesture of supplication to the spirit.

Mike could see him shaking like a condemned man getting juiced in the electric chair, even from thirty feet away and lying on his side, but the professor was not running or in any way attempting to defend himself. He simply offered himself to the thing.

This was your big plan? Mike thought angrily.

The spirit reached the professor in seconds, and Mike heard the man whimper in abject terror. Still he stood motionless, inviting a certain and violent death. The monster lifted Ken up in one smooth motion and flung his body against the boulder, smashing it against the jagged surface.

For the second time in minutes Ken Dye left a splash of blood on the huge rock, this one much bigger than the first. The professor crumpled, and the thing lifted his motionless body again as Mike struggled to his feet. He still had his backup weapon, the one in his ankle holster. He could put the apparition down for a few seconds like he had done before, and then try to drag Professor Dye away from the monster while he figured out what to do next.

Mike's exhausted and aching body began to move, slowly and painfully. He took a single step forward and immediately went down as his right knee failed him.

He watched helplessly from the ground as the spirit lifted Ken Dye and in one sickening motion ripped his arm off his body. The wet sounds of ripping and rending continued, and Mike threw up on the forest floor. He lay on the ground on his hands and knees, head hanging, tiny tendrils of steam rising from the yellowish gunk that had come from his gut and was now splattered on ground, until the awful noises finally stopped.

Mike knew he would live this moment in his nightmares forever.

He lifted his head and peered through the trees at the boulder where he had last seen Professor Dye in his curious pose of submission and surrender. Blood covered the area. It appeared to have been sprayed in a fine mist from a fire hose. There seemed to be too much of blood, even to a man who had investigated plenty of accident scenes, some nearly as gruesome as this.

Mike knew he was next; that he was about to suffer the same

fate as Professor Dye. There was nothing in the short, violent history of this destructive apparition to make him believe he would be spared. The only reason he was even alive right now was because the professor had awakened and somehow managed to stagger to his feet and offer himself to the monster instead.

Mike wondered why he would do that instead of trying to get away. All he had accomplished with his foolish act was to reverse the order of death and destruction so that Mike got to live for a few extra moments while Ken Dye perished a little sooner. What the hell was the point?

Right then and there he resolved to somehow make the professor's death matter. The man who had been ridiculed and excommunicated from academia, who had been quiet and afraid but steadfast, had heroically given his life to save Mike's. Even if he only spared Mike for a few minutes, it was still a valiant act, and act most people would never have considered, much less acted on.

He reached for the backup weapon at his ankle, already formulating a plan. He would draw the thing as far away as possible while radioing the location of the cabin to his officers. While he lured the monster in the other direction, the officers could make their way to the cabin and with any luck find Sharon alive, rescuing her and salvaging something from this disaster.

As plans went, Mike knew it was pretty thin, but he had to try. He unsnapped the leather restraining strap on his ankle holster and lifted the pistol. He thought about calling for help now but decided to wait until he could at least get the monster moving away from the cabin. He gripped his weapon and looked toward the boulder at the blood and the devastation.

Pieces of the professor's body were scattered in a ragged circle around the figure of the Chief Court-thing. An arm, more or less intact, lay close to Mike on the ground, where the monster had tossed it. A lower leg, surrounded by blood and trailing muscles and tendons, lay in the same general vicinity. It had been ripped off at the knee along with a portion of the professor's trouser leg, the blue khaki pants torn as neatly as if they had been sliced with fabric shears.

Ken Dye's head was nowhere to be seen. Maybe the thing had thrown it behind the boulder. He thought about Harvey Crosker's head, tossed casually into a tree, and shuddered.

He forced himself to focus. Professor Dye was gone and wasn't coming back. He began to stand—his body fighting him, screaming in agonized protest—and prepared to start moving, to draw the monster away from the cabin and presumably away from Sharon. The apparition seemed entirely unaware of Mike's presence. It seemed preoccupied, if that was possible.

Mike took one shuffling step forward, favoring his right knee, the one that had let him down the last time he tried to move. Shooting pain ripped through his leg, radiating from the knee outward in both directions. His leg was on fire, a bright white agony blasting from ankle to hip. He bit his lip to keep from screaming and took another step, stumbling and catching himself on a tree bent nearly to the ground, perhaps beaten down by the storm.

Mike knew how it felt.

Sweat poured down his face even in the cold northern Maine woods. The pain was immense.

He gasped as he took another step, struggling to stay on his feet and almost falling again. The thing still hadn't paid the slightest attention to him.

He worked his way closer, and now the apparition began to move, but not in the manner Mike expected. As he watched in stunned surprise, the emaciated figure of the man who had once been Police Chief Wally Court and was now some demon from another world crumbled slowly and silently to the ground.

One moment the body was standing over the forest floor—hovering, actually, in its strange and eerie way—and the next it was dropping, seeming to fold up into itself and falling to the cold, wet surface of leaves and pine needles.

Mike watched in disbelief as the monster fell in the center of the wide swath of destruction and was still. The tattered remnants of Chief Court's clothing fluttered to the ground into a ragged pile not much bigger than the size of a basketball.

Mike waited and watched, leaning against a tree for support, horrified by the events of the last few minutes but also overcome by curiosity, needing to see what would happen next.

Nothing did. He kept his weapon trained on the inert pile of clothing lying on the ground, but nothing happened.

Minutes passed and still the body lay motionless where it had fallen. Mike wondered if it was a trick to get him to approach, but why would the thing attempt to trick him when he was injured and nearly defenseless?

The silence was absolute. Mike's knee throbbed and burned. The body lay unmoving.

He took a deep breath and struggled forward. Standing in the middle of the woods, injured and nearly immobile, with night falling and potential rescue still hours away, was no kind of a plan. It was time to figure out just what the hell was happening.

He limped and stumbled to the spot where the apparition had fallen and with the barrel of his gun, poked warily at the filthy, unmoving pile. Chief Court's body, broken and ruined beyond belief, lay inside the tattered clothing. The awful stench of death and rotting flesh rose off the corpse and Mike gagged, but the body didn't rise off the ground and hover.

It didn't do anything, in fact. It just lay on the cold ground inside the ruined mess of clothing.

Minutes more passed as Mike waited for something to happen, but he began to realize nothing was going to. For whatever reason, the spirit had departed. Where it had gone and whether it would return, Mike had no idea, but he decided he had better check the cabin for survivors while he had the opportunity.

The lonely log cabin seemed miles away. The sky had darkened to the point where Mike could barely see a vague suggestion of the home off in the distance through the trees.

He picked up the stout tree branch he had used as a club a few minutes and a lifetime before and examined it, deciding it would make a passable walking stick. He leaned heavily on his new cane and began moving toward the little house, wondering what horrifying revelations he would find when he entered.

Every few steps, he turned and checked the area around the big boulder, expecting at any moment to see the apparition gliding toward him again, preparing to kill him and tear his body apart. But with each glance he saw the same thing: the awful visual evidence of slaughter, but nothing else. No movement.

Finally, Mike had moved far enough from the area that he could no longer make out the pieces of Professor Dye lying scattered on the ground.

"Thank God for small favors," he muttered through clenched teeth to no one as a wave of pain radiated outward from his knee, momentarily stealing his breath and stopping him in his tracks.

When he reached the steps leading to the open-air porch, Mike grabbed the wooden railing with both hands and pulled his faltering body up to the front door. He had hoped his damaged leg would begin feeling better as it loosened up, but if anything it seemed to be getting worse, the pain exploding with each beat of his heart.

He paused at the entrance to the cabin, breathing hard, glancing one last time back into the thick forest, wondering why he had been spared and where the vengeful apparition had gone. He could see less than half the distance to the big boulder. Nightfall was nearly complete.

He took one deep breath and pushed open the cabin's heavy oak front door and stepped into a nightmare.

54

Sharon was thirsty. She was burning up. Her lips felt puffy and foreign, like they belonged to someone else. They were dry and cracked and bleeding.

She lay on the floor of the cabin wanting nothing more than for her suffering to be over. Blood oozed out her open mouth onto the dirty carpet, her face slick with it.

Unable to lift her head, she used her legs to push forward a few inches—ignoring the shrieking pain in her useless arms and her damaged ribs—until she was clear of the gooey mess. She immediately began drooling more blood onto her new location. It wasn't gushing out of her mouth but it had been oozing sluggishly for hours.

Sharon knew she should be worried but she was too tired to be worried. She had been fading in and out of consciousness for indeterminate periods, each time lingering in some fuzzy netherworld a little longer and sinking into it again a little faster.

Maybe this time when she closed her eyes it would be the last time. Maybe this time it would all be over, this crazy nightmare she had been thrust into with Mike McMahon. Strong, steady Mike, with whom she had shared her bed and her heart, with whom she had fallen in love.

That was the only real regret Sharon felt as she waited for the end. She had slept with plenty of men, starting at about age fourteen—or was it twelve? She couldn't remember for sure and that was so sad—when she perfected the art of exchanging sex for drugs or alcohol. Dozens of men, mostly during those four sick, insane years of high school when she had been out of control.

Not so many recently.

But during all those hookups, all the times she had awoken in strange places next to strange men, often much older than Sharon and whose faces she could often, frighteningly, not recognize, she never once felt a connection, a bond beyond the physical like that which she had experienced for such a short time with the new chief of police of Paskagankee, Maine.

She treasured that bond and didn't want it to end but at the same time was thankful she had been able to experience transcendence above the physical at least once before exiting the pain of this world into whatever the next one held, if even there was a next one.

The front door opened, squealing slightly on its hinges, and Sharon knew it was the Court–thing returning to its lair. She wondered if this would be the time it finished her off.

She raised her eyes toward the cabin's only entrance, trying to ignore the pain pounding through her body, and was surprised to see that the spirit no longer floated above the floor. It now moved with its feet on the soiled carpet.

Something was different, though. The thing wasn't walking as much as it was limping. Badly. It would rest its entire weight on its left leg, then hop/shuffle painfully on its right, before coming to rest again with the full weight of its body on its left side.

The thing was now dressed differently, too. Instead of the tattered red hunting jacket with its checkerboard pattern and the disgusting matted hair, the apparition now wore a Paskagankee Police uniform and looked…incredibly, impossibly, unbelievably… like Mike McMahon!

Sharon smiled, her bleeding lips screaming painfully at her to stop.

Then her eyes rolled up into her head and she was gone again.

55

Mike stepped into the cabin and almost had to retreat. The stench was overwhelming. From somewhere inside the darkened home wafted the smell of corruption, of decaying flesh, of death.

He gagged and moved a step or two into the open living area and waited for his eyes to adjust to a gloom even more complete than that of the thick forest.

Nothing leapt out at him.

Nothing attacked him.

Nothing even moved, as far as he could tell. Whatever horrors had taken place here had apparently been perpetrated by the single renegade spirit inhabiting Chief Court's body, and for some unknown reason that spirit had vanished. Mike wondered if it was gone for good, and if not, how much time he had before it returned.

A stealthy sliding/slithering sound interrupted Mike's train of thought, and he strained to see through the darkness. Something across the room moved almost imperceptibly on the floor, something that looked like a pile of clothing.

Someone was alive! He rushed as quickly as he could through the darkened room on his damaged knee and as he got closer his heart leaped into his throat.

It was Sharon Dupont, smiling up at him incongruously, surrounded on the floor by what looked like gallons of blood, barely able to move and in very bad shape, probably dying.

But she was alive right now, and to Mike McMahon, who had

seen more death and devastation in fifteen years as a law enforcement professional than he wanted to remember, it was nothing less than a miracle. He had been hoping against hope to find Sharon alive and now, here she was.

Alive.

He knelt beside her broken body, ignoring the pain in his knee, and took her hand, hoping to assess the extent of her injuries.

After that fleeting smile, she fell into unconsciousness, and Mike prayed it wasn't permanent. She was clearly very badly injured. Both arms bent at awkward angles, broken and/or fractured and obviously useless. Blood streaked her face, oozing from her mouth in a slow but steady trickle and forming a map on the carpet marking her slow progress across the floor as she attempted to keep her beautiful face clear of it.

She had lost so much blood Mike wondered how much longer she could hold on. He hoped fate would not be so cruel as to allow him to find Sharon alive, only to snatch her away while he watched helplessly, injured and awaiting rescue.

He leaned against the side wall, sitting in a sticky reservoir of Sharon's drying blood but not caring. Reached for his radio with his left hand, fumbling to remove it from its leather holster. He held both Sharon's hands, so tiny and frail, inside his big right hand and wasn't about to let them go.

Mike unclipped the radio.

Dropped it.

Picked it up, now slick with blood, and keyed up the Paskagankee Police frequency. He tried to remember exactly where the cabin was located and how he and Professor Dye had gotten to it, passing the information as quickly and succinctly as he could along to Gordie Rheaume in the dispatcher's office.

He knew how difficult it would be to find this cabin in the dark, especially given the near impassability of this ancient primeval forest, but he also knew that time was running out for Sharon Dupont. If a rescue wasn't affected tonight, it wouldn't matter how long it took afterward because she would be dead by morning. He knew she might die anyway, it seemed quite likely in fact, but he wasn't about to give up now that he had found her.

Dispatcher Rheaume asked for details. "What the hell went on up there?"

But Mike was too tired to pass along irrelevant information, and besides, he didn't really have a clue what had happened, did he? One moment he found himself dangling helplessly eight feet off the ground, held aloft by an angry three hundred-fifty-year-old spirit of a dead Native American girl, then the next moment he watched in horror as his friend Professor Dye was dismembered in front of his eyes. Then the thing disappeared into thin air, gone as thoroughly and completely as if it had never existed in the first place.

Mike shook his head in tired confusion, telling Gordie, "Just get those guys up here. Sharon's seriously injured and she needs immediate medical attention."

After terminating the radio call, Mike struggled to his feet, not wanting to let go of Sharon's hand but knowing he had to investigate the rest of the cabin. His stomach lurched as the awful stench of death penetrated his consciousness again. He had been so wrapped up in his discovery of Sharon and calling for help that everything else took a back seat, but now it came rushing back with a vengeance.

He tried to ignore the distracting odor and pulled out his Maglite. He shined the bright white beam around the living area, searching for a light switch. He finally located one in the corner of the room, next to an open doorway leading to the kitchen.

His knee pounded and throbbed, screaming out with angry insistence for attention. He ignored it and shuffled/hopped to the switch and then flicked it on. Nothing happened.

Mike chuckled. He must be more tired than he realized. Of course nothing happened. There was no electricity way out here in the middle of nowhere, so obviously Chief Court must have powered his home with a generator. The spirit inhabiting Court's body had been too busy wreaking havoc in and around Paskagankee to worry about anything as mundane as electricity, so it stood to reason that the generator would not be powered up.

In fact, depending upon how long ago Chief Court had lost himself to the powerful spirit, there may not be any fuel in the generator anyway. If the engine was running when the chief's body was taken over, then it likely would have continued indefinitely, chugging along until exhausting the fuel supply.

Recalling the only time he had met his predecessor, Mike remembered thinking something must have been bothering the man. He had appeared disheveled, with his tie askew and his uniform shirt buttoned improperly. His hair was relatively long and unkempt, and he had been sweating profusely, seemingly distracted and unable to sit still.

Mike chalked it up at the time to nervousness, to concern by Court about his pending retirement. Plus, he didn't know the man, and thought it possible he was just a slob. Later, as Mike got to know Sharon Dupont, and she related her admiration of Wally Court and all he had done for her as a teenager, it occurred to him that Sharon's recollections didn't mesh with what he had observed of the former chief with his own eyes.

Then everything went to hell in Paskagankee and he became far too busy trying to deal with the gruesome murder spree to worry about the personality quirks of the man whose job he had taken.

Mike wondered if things might have turned out differently had someone tumbled to the fact something was horribly wrong with Chief Court. He doubted it, but there was so much he didn't understand about the last few days that he just didn't know.

He shined his Maglite around the room, horrified by what it revealed. At one time this cabin had been a small but beautiful home, clearly crafted with care by a man who knew what he was doing. The hardwood floors still gleamed in spots, despite the general disrepair of the house. A chair rail ran the width of the room to protect the walls, and a beautiful patterned border encircled the living room wall at its junction with the ceiling.

Now all that remained was utter devastation. Dirt and mud covered the floor, smeared in places half an inch thick, dead grass and straw everywhere. Holes had been punched through the walls, in sizes anywhere from a couple of inches to several feet wide. Mike wondered what might have caused them and shuddered.

But far worse was the human wreckage. Body parts littered the room, some clothed and some not, all in varying stages of decomposition. A decapitated head lay on the floor, barely six feet from Sharon's prone body. Identification was impossible, but he assumed the head belonged either to Agent O'Bannon or his partner, Shaw, the men who had been so dismissive of Professor Dye and so anxious to leave Paskagankee behind.

The suffocating stench of corruption issued from these and the other human remains. Mike was aghast and his heart broke, not just for the victims, but for Sharon Dupont as well. He wondered what it must have been like lying in the middle of this horrifying scene, unable to move, knowing she would likely become the next victim.

He continued to play the beam of light around the room and froze as it fell upon what looked like a relatively undamaged human body. The figure was unmoving, lying face down in a corner of the room opposite Sharon, undoubtedly dead, but nevertheless still in one piece.

From the distance of twelve feet or so and in the heavy darkness crowding the room Mike couldn't be sure, but he thought he saw dark red hair. It looked familiar but he couldn't quite place where he'd seen it before in his exhausted and stressed condition.

He crossed the room, slowly and laboriously thanks to his injured knee, and winced from the pain as he reached the limp body and eased himself to the floor for a closer look.

It was a woman. He gently turned her head and found himself staring into the face of Melissa "the Maneater" Manheim, the Portland Journal reporter he assumed had left the bonfire last night in a huff following their confrontation.

Assessing the extent of Manheim's injuries was impossible, but the investigative reporter was breathing evenly. Mike felt for a pulse and found it strong and steady.

Despite—or perhaps because of—the gravity of the situation and the fact that both young women might still die before ever making it out of the forest, Mike couldn't help but marvel at how accurate Ken Dye had been. He was correct about everything, right down to his guess that the spirit would not intentionally harm women, but rather would save its wrath for males

Across the room Sharon groaned softly and stirred. Her eyes remained closed but she appeared to be regaining consciousness.

Mike limped into the kitchen, the pain in his knee constant and white-hot. He found a clean glass and filled it with water from a sealed jug, then struggled back to where Sharon lay on the living room floor, surrounded by human body parts and death and destruction.

His knee screamed as he knelt.

He ignored it.

He lifted her head gently in his hands and poured a small amount of water between her cracked lips. Most of it dribbled down her chin, mixing with the blood drooling out her mouth and staining her shirt. A small amount made its way into her mouth and she swallowed instinctively, her eyes fluttering open for just a moment.

Mike thought she showed a second's recognition and maybe even a faint smile before lapsing back into unconsciousness.

He sat on the floor next to her with his injured right leg splayed out to the side and cradled her head in his lap. He used his fingers to brush some of the matted blood out of her jet-black hair and began the long wait for rescue.

56

The hospital in Orono felt cool and comfortable to Mike, especially after the horrendous conditions inside Chief Court's house of horrors in the forest. He could hear the muted clop-clop-clop of visitors' shoes as they walked up and down the corridor outside looking for the rooms of family members and friends. The vinyl tile floor was freshly scrubbed and redolent of ammonia and disinfectant.

It smelled like life.

He sat perched on a tiny, uncomfortable plastic chair next to Sharon's hospital bed, his right leg encased in a cast from his toes nearly to his hip. Sharon was barely visible under the covers, impossibly small and frail.

She looked like an extra from "Night of the Living Dead." A bright white bandage covered her head, protecting the hole doctors had drilled into her skull to relieve the pressure caused by swelling of her brain, presumably the result of being tossed head-first into a tree by the spirit. Both her broken arms had been placed in casts and protruded more or less straight out to the side as she slept, making her look like she was beseeching Mike for help. Intravenous tubes ran into and out of her body in various places carrying various fluids, accomplishing various important tasks, Mike assumed, but what those tasks might be he did not know.

She looked like some high school kid's chemistry experiment gone horribly wrong.

She looked like the most beautiful thing he had ever seen.

Sharon had been drifting into and out of consciousness for two days. After examination by numerous specialists, the general consensus was that her condition would likely continue without any discernible change for weeks.

Or she might wake up completely lucid at any moment.

Or anything in between.

One thing the doctors all agreed upon was that she should eventually recover fully. She could expect a long, painful and frustrating rehabilitation, but ultimately a full recovery.

In addition to the swelling on her brain and her two broken arms, Sharon had suffered a pair of broken ribs, one of which had punctured a lung causing her to hemorrhage such a copious amount of blood internally that her doctors told Mike she would not have survived much more than another couple of hours in the condition she had been found.

He thought about their rescue and the trip out of the forest and marveled at how fortunate the rescue team had been to find the cabin at all. They'd traipsed through the thick forest in the middle of the night with only the vaguest notion of where they were going. It had taken more than four hours for the team to arrive, led by young Officer Pete Kendall, and when they reached the cabin they found Mike dozing fitfully on the floor next to Sharon, her head still cradled in his hands.

The hike out to civilization had been excruciating. Mike insisted on carrying one end of the litter holding Sharon's unconscious body, and even now he wasn't sure how he had managed to navigate the rough terrain, climbing over rocks and stumps and downed tree branches, wading through streams and around undergrowth so thick in places that it was practically impassable.

All of it he had done with torn ligaments in his right knee.

His men had continually offered to carry his end of the litter, and Mike knew he should have let them. His injury undoubtedly made a long and difficult hike even worse, but he had sworn that he was going to save Sharon if he was lucky enough to find her alive, and he wasn't about to quit with the mission nearly complete.

The small band of officers burst out of the forest and onto Route 28 at just after three o'clock in the morning. A trio of ambulances stood by on the side of the deserted county two-lane, their bright red strobes giving the night an eerie, pulsing glow that the men could see from several hundred yards away, even while still deep in the jungle-like woods.

One ambulance returned to base empty. Mike insisted on riding to the hospital in the second one with Sharon, after the first had rushed away carrying the semi-conscious Melissa Manheim. He refused to consider having his knee examined until he knew Sharon was safe and pulled rank on the poor EMT's trying their best to steer him to the back of the third vehicle.

The men finally shrugged their shoulders in defeat, and packed up their equipment and went home. Mike knew they must be pretty unhappy to have waited for hours in the middle of the night in the frigid cold of the northern Maine woods, only to be sent away with nothing to do.

He didn't care.

Sharon had been mostly unconscious and unresponsive during the hike, a fact for which Mike was extremely grateful. Had she been awake and alert, he suspected she would have suffered enormously, bouncing around on the litter, being lifted over rocks and trees and occasionally jarred seriously when one of the men lost their grip on the handles.

For one magical moment, as they were nearing the road, after several hours of hiking and with the cabin and its horrors well behind them, she had suddenly opened her eyes, seemingly completely lucid. She looked straight at Mike, focusing her bright, blue laser beam eyes on him and saying, "I think I love you."

He was so surprised he said nothing, staring back at her in stunned amazement. By the time he overcame his shock sufficiently to respond, she had slipped back into unconsciousness, and she stayed that way until long after her arrival at the hospital and her emergency brain surgery.

Doctors told Mike it was highly unlikely she would remember much of her ordeal when she awoke. In fact, they said, her unconscious mind would probably banish it to the far reaches of her brain if the situation had been as horrific as they had been led to believe.

Mike didn't buy that. He knew how tough she was and how

much she had overcome in her young life, and he felt certain she would approach the memories head-on, like she seemed to do with everything else. He believed her "Damn the torpedoes" attitude would make her much more successful in putting the whole thing behind her than the doctors seemed to think.

He glanced at Sharon's hospital bed, her prone figure looking so tiny and helpless, and did a double-take when he saw her staring back at him, her eyes clear and strong and shining like twin beacons of hope.

"I knew you'd come and get me," she said simply and quietly.

Mike knew he should alert someone immediately to the fact that she was conscious and talking but couldn't bring himself to leave her for even the few seconds it would take to go get a nurse. He was so surprised, the thought of pressing the call button at the side of the bed never even occurred to him.

"I'm glad one of us was sure," he answered.

She smiled weakly. "What happened to Chief Court? How did he get so sick? And you're going to think I'm crazy when I tell you this one," she said, "but I must have been even worse off in that cabin than I thought because I would have sworn he was floating in the air rather than walking, do you believe that?"

Mike nodded and said, "Yeah, Sharon, I do believe it because I saw it myself. You weren't imagining anything."

She tried to sit up in bed and groaned, abandoning the effort and slumping back against her pillows as she glared accusingly at her two useless arms. "What the hell's going on in this town?" she asked.

"You mean, 'what *was* going on in this town.' I'm pretty sure it's all over now," said Mike. "But as far as your question goes, I don't have a clue. This is without a doubt the strangest murder investigation I've ever been a part of or ever want to be a part of, for that matter.

"I'll fill you in on everything I know in time," he said, reaching for her hand and taking hold of it, "but for now I should let the doctors know you're awake. Then I think you probably need to get some rest."

"Maybe," she mumbled. "I do feel pretty tired."

She looked at Mike again. "Could you get me a mirror?"

"Listen," he said. "Don't worry about mirrors for now, alright?"

"Just hand it to me."

Sighing, recognizing defeat when it stared him in the face, Mike pulled a handheld mirror out of Sharon's travel bag, which he had hastily packed yesterday with everything he could imagine she might need when she woke up. He leaned forward to hand it to her and then realized she probably couldn't lift it to her face with her arms encased in twin sets of casts bent only about forty-five degrees at the elbows.

"Why don't you just wait a day or so…"

"Just do it," she ordered, and Mike shrugged. He lifted the mirror and held it up to her face.

She stared in silence for a long time at her reflection; so long, in fact, that Mike began to wonder if she had perhaps slipped back into unconsciousness. Vivid purple and green bruises colored both cheekbones under her eyes, one of which was partially swollen shut.

"Where's my hair?" she finally whispered.

"The doctors had to shave your head in order to do the surgery to relieve swelling in your brain."

"Don't sugarcoat it or anything," she said dryly.

"Sorry," Mike answered, embarrassed. "I just think you should know how close you came to dying out there in the woods and how lucky you are to still be alive. And by the way, for what it's worth, I think you look beautiful, with or without hair."

"But my hair," she said sadly. "It's just gone."

Mike put the mirror away and sat back down in the plastic torture device as Sharon drifted off to sleep, her features gradually relaxing as her breathing slowed and became smooth and rhythmic once again.

57

The wind gusted out of the northeast, driving sleet and freezing rain through the slate-gray sky and chilling Mike to the bone. He should have worn a heavy winter coat rather than the light jacket which was now flapping open unzipped as he struggled on his crutches up Professor Ken Dye's front walkway, but he hadn't realized how cold the day was going to be when he left his house.

He had finally been shooed out of Sharon Dupont's hospital room by the Orono Mercy Hospital nursing staff, all of whom seemed to agree a shower might be in order for the chief of police. After taking their not-so-subtle advice and cleaning up, Mike had called the police station and advised Gordie Rheaume he would be traveling to Professor Dye's home.

He wasn't sure what he expected to find but felt that walking through the house, which he and Sharon had visited for the first time barely more than a week ago, might provide some small clue as to exactly what had been happening in his little town.

The drive from Paskagankee to Orono had been an adventure, with Mike's right leg immobilized by a full cast. He stretched the offending leg across the front bench seat of the SUV and drove with his left foot to drive, an act that would have earned any normal citizen a driving-to-endanger citation but which to Mike represented one of the few perks of being a law enforcement professional.

The frigid, early-winter wind whistled and moaned as Mike balanced on his good leg at Ken Dye's front door picking through keys. Mike finally found the proper one and lumbered into the foyer, grateful to be out of the cold.

He stood for a moment soaking in the personality of the home. It already felt abandoned. It was cool but stuffy, filled with an air of sadness and finality that Mike couldn't shake.

He took his time walking through the small house and could see the man had been a meticulous housekeeper. His bed was made, crisp and fresh and wrinkle-free, the bedspread pulled tightly over the covers and squared away in a manner that would bring a nod of approval from Army drill instructor. No dirty dishes littered the sink or filled the dishwasher. A thin layer of dust covered the furniture, but aside from that, the house looked as though Ken Dye might walk through the front door at any moment.

Mike drew a glass of water and noticed a plain white sealed envelope placed squarely in the middle of the kitchen table. On the front was his name, CHIEF MIKE MCMAHON, spelled out in the professor's almost compulsively neat block letters.

He picked the envelope and turned it over curiously. Nothing else was written on either the front or the back.

He stared at his discovery for several long moments as if trying to absorb its contents through osmosis. He was tempted to open it right there at the table, but decided to wait and examine it at Mercy Hospital with Sharon. She had nearly given her life for the investigation, and he felt it was only fitting that they discover its contents together.

Mike slid the envelope securely into his jacket's interior breast pocket. He sat in the stillness of Ken Dye's kitchen and thought about Sharon's reaction to the discovery that her head had been shaved. He'd been surprised at how much it bothered her. After all, her hair would grow back quickly, and he didn't picture Sharon Dupont in any way, shape or form as a vain person.

He supposed she viewed her hair as one of the few ways she could maintain her femininity in the largely macho world of law enforcement.

Mike took a final look around the kitchen and decided he had nothing to gain by sitting here any longer. Ken Dye hadn't had any close relatives, he knew that much, and he wondered what would become of the professor's large collection of scholarly books and teaching materials now that he was gone.

He drained the last of his water, placed the glass in the sink—feeling slightly guilty as he did since the man had left his home in such tip-top shape—and limped on his crutches to the front door, turning to lock it behind him as he exited. The driving rain was beginning to freeze on the roads again, and Mike faced a slow, hazardous trip back to Paskagankee.

He still had a couple of errands to run and wanted to get back to Mercy Hospital and Sharon's bedside as soon as possible.

58

The hospital bed felt lumpy and uncomfortable, and on top of that, Sharon had to deal with a maddening itch. It attacked her left arm under the cast and about two-thirds of the way between her wrist and elbow.

If she could just escape her bed for a moment, she could grab a wire coat hanger from the little closet in the corner of the room, straighten it, and slide it under the cast. But of course she was hooked up to so many machines and tubes in this damned hospital that going anywhere at all represented nothing more than a frustrating daydream.

Plus, there was the small matter of the broken ribs, which made even breathing a painful exercise. Sharon reluctantly decided getting up might be more than she could handle right now.

Buzzing a nurse seemed the most obvious solution, but Sharon Dupont wasn't one to ask for help lightly. She'd grown up pretty much on her own and knew only self-reliance. The itch was wearing her down, however, and she was rapidly reaching the point where calling for assistance seemed like a reasonable option, even to her.

As she tried to make up her mind what to do, the door opened and in stumbled Mike McMahon. He was limping, with both crutches trapped under his right arm. His left hand clutched a huge bouquet of flowers adorned with a colorful balloon that demanded Sharon GET WELL SOON!

He somehow balanced two large cups of coffee precariously

between his elbow and his chest. He was swearing impressively and fighting a losing battle with the paper cups, which threatened at any moment to drop to the floor and splash hot coffee everywhere.

Sharon giggled in spite of herself, and Mike mock-scowled at her. He managed to set the flowers down on a small table and work both coffee cups into his hands without spilling a drop.

"You're supposed to be recovering. Shouldn't you be sleeping or something?" he asked gruffly.

The itch under her cast was forgotten as she admired the flowers, a dozen roses surrounded by yellow daisies with a spray of baby's breath.

"For your information, I've been trying to sleep," she said. "But I've just about had it with lying around doing nothing. It's boring as hell. What does a girl have to do to get a little excitement around here?"

Mike laughed and handed her the bouquet. "Please accept these as a small token of my appreciation to you for not croaking."

"You're such a romantic. They're for *me?*"

"Well, of course. Who else would they be for?"

"I don't know, I just assumed they were given to you by one of your many female admirers."

"Very funny," Mike said as he took off his blue Paskagankee Police baseball cap, revealing a freshly shaved head. The whiteness of the skin that had been covered by his thick head of hair contrasted sharply with the wind-chapped texture of his neck and face. His tan was fading with winter's approach, but it was still noticeable.

Sharon stared, her eyes filling with tears.

"What's the matter?" he asked, glancing upward as if he could see the top of his head. "Not a good look for me?"

A crooked smile lit up Sharon's face. "Why did you shave your head?"

Mike grinned. "Moral support. When I saw how much it bothered you that the doctors had to shave your head I decided to join you in the Chris Daughtry lookalike club. Plus, I figured this way we could have a little contest. We both start out with no hair and see whose grows back the fastest. I'm betting on me, but I have to tell you, this feels pretty liberating. I might never go back. It makes me look even sexier than usual, don't you agree?"

The tears ran down her cheeks.

"That was so sweet," she whispered. "Come here."

Mike approached the bed and she told him, "Bend down to me, I have something to tell you."

He leaned down and she lifted her head off the pillow to meet him, kissing him fiercely, their tongues dancing.

Finally she dropped her head back onto her pillow and said, "It's lucky for you I have all these tubes and wires holding me down, otherwise you might not make it out of this room alive."

"Threatening a law enforcement officer, huh? You had better be careful, Missy, we take that sort of thing pretty seriously around here. You could face severe punishment if you keep it up."

"Promises, promises," she said, looking up at Mike, her face still damp from her tears. "Thank you so much."

"Jeez, it's just a few flowers. If I had known you were going to be this excited, I would have pulled some out of old Annie Kramer's rose garden a long time ago."

"Those didn't come from Annie Kramer's garden. You wouldn't stand a chance against that old bird. Besides, I'm not talking about the flowers and you know it."

"Okay, I admit it, I bought them. Are you saying I could have saved all that money?"

Sharon laughed. "You're lucky I don't have my gun."

"Again with the threats," he said. "We're going to have to work on controlling that temper of yours."

Mike dragged his plastic chair next to the bed and reached into his jacket pocket. He fished out an envelope.

"I've been doing more than just figuring out how to sweep you off your feet," he told her. "I drove to Orono this morning to walk through Professor Dye's house. I don't even know why. I just felt like I needed to go there one last time, like we had unfinished business or something."

He took a deep breath. "Look what I found."

She glanced curiously from the envelope to Mike. "Is it from him?"

"Presumably," he answered. "I haven't opened it yet. I thought you might like to be here when I did."

"Absolutely!" she said enthusiastically. "That sounds way better than lying here trying to figure out how to aim a television remote when I can't bend my arms. Climb on up here with me so I can read it, too."

Mike looked dubiously at the frail-looking young woman surrounded by medical equipment and with tubes and wires and casts taking up space on the bed.

"I'm not sure I can manage that," he said doubtfully. "I don't want to take a chance of hurting you."

"Don't be such a wimp. Clear off some space and take a seat," Sharon demanded.

When he had carefully rearranged things as much as possible, he eased onto the bed, his right leg resting on the small bedside table. He sliced open the envelope and pulled out several sheets of paper.

"I'm surprised he didn't type it," Sharon said, looking at the pages filled with the man's carefully handwritten words.

"I think he wanted it to be a little more personal than a typed message," Mike answered. "That would be my guess, anyway."

Together they started reading:

Dear Chief McMahon,

I'm not sure exactly how to begin, the letter read, *so I'll start with a cliché. If you're reading this, I must be dead.*

That, of course, would be the bad news, especially for me. On the other hand, the good news would be that my hypothesis about what's happening in Paskagankee was correct, meaning I didn't waste most of my adult life and my entire professional career on a ridiculous fairy tale, as most of my colleagues have suspected (and some have come right out and informed me).

Small consolation, I suppose, now that I'm gone. But still, you should be aware that the knowledge that I was correct fortified me tremendously at the end.

Anyway, please allow me to explain some things you must be wondering about and some others you may have begun to suspect.

I believe you are aware that I was born in Great Britain and moved to the United States as a young man in order to study Native American folklore and customs. As a child in England I was able to trace my lineage back several hundred years, discovering in the process that one of my ancestors had been a missionary working with the natives in the late 1600's in the wilderness that would later become the United States.

Further research revealed that my long-dead ancestor had partici-pated in a tragic confrontation between his band of missionaries and a local Abenaqui tribe, a confrontation resulting in the slaughter of virtually every member of both sides.

The lone exception on the missionaries' side—the only European to survive—was my forebear, who suffered grave injuries but managed to escape the carnage with his life. Eventually he recovered sufficiently to return to England but did so having to live with the awful knowledge that he was responsible for the death of a young baby and her mother during the battle.

This long-forgotten family history formed the basis for my desire to learn all I could about Native Americans in general and the Abenaqui in particular. During the course of my research, I learned of a disturbing Abenaqui legend: that of a young mother slaughtered along with her infant child by a traveling missionary in such brutal fashion—the baby was nearly decapitated by a musket ball—that the distraught woman's spirit remained earthbound, unable to move beyond this world even in death while she awaited an opportunity to avenge her baby's horrible fate.

For years I refused to acknowledge my family's connection to this legend, but eventually I could no longer ignore the growing suspicion—the certainty, really—that my long-dead ancestor had committed the horrible act upon which this Native American legend was based.

But that is not the worst of it. The worst part involves the specifics of the Abenaqui curse. The legend states the spirit of the young mother must remain in the area immediately surrounding the location of her child's death. Lacking a human host, she would remain powerless, but should a person take up residence in that location, she would eventually manage to enter and gain control of the host's body.

Once having done so, she would begin to generate tremendous physical strength, which she would then use to terrorize the population, wreaking havoc as vengeance for her child's death.

I believe this to be the reason for the sudden relocation of the village of Paskagankee three hundred years ago. The buildings of the original town were constructed directly upon the site of the 1691 massacre, and I am convinced the spirit of that poor young woman was able to locate and inhabit a human host. Circumstances in the village eventually deteriorated to the point that the residents abandoned the entire town virtually overnight and reconstructed it several miles away in its current location.

I feel certain this tragic spirit has somehow found a new human host and is again wreaking havoc upon the surrounding population for the gruesome decapitation and loss of her baby so many centuries ago. All signs point to this being the case.

According to the Abenaqui legend, there is but one way to bring the killing to an end and allow the three-hundred-twenty-one-year-old spirit to rest forever: she must avenge her baby's death against a direct blood relative of the man who murdered her child.

Undoubtedly you have by now deduced where I am going with all of this. My bloodline descends directly from the misguided individual who—intentionally or not; I choose to believe it was unintentional but have no evidence upon which to base my opinion—caused the deaths of the young Native American woman and her infant child, and in such bloody fashion.

I am that descendant the legend dictates must be held accountable. Therefore, it is incumbent upon me to put an end to the bloodshed. It must be me and can only be me. No one else is capable of ending the horror.

Therefore, my plan, which I must assume was successful if you are now reading this letter, is to locate the spirit in whatever body she now inhabits and offer myself up as long-overdue retribution for her loss.

I am truly sorry for the pain and suffering my bloodline has caused, but am also truly thankful for the opportunity to bring this tragic chapter of Abenaqui history to a close.

Good luck to you in the future, Chief McMahon.

May God have mercy on me.

Sincerely,

Professor Ken Dye

Sharon and Mike remained silent for a long time after reading the letter.

"Now I get it," Mike muttered.

"He did exactly what he said he was going to do, didn't he?" asked Sharon.

Mike nodded. "I didn't understand why the spirit suddenly dropped me just as it was about to tear me to shreds, only to go after the professor when he revealed himself. Now it makes sense. Somehow the spirit knew Ken Dye was the one that would satisfy its centuries-old need for retribution. After it killed the professor, I assumed it was going to come back and finish me off. I was expecting it to do exactly that. Instead, I watched as it disappeared out of poor Chief Court's broken body. The chief's body just fell to the ground and was still. Now I understand why. The spirit's long quest was finally over."

"No one is going to believe this, you know," Sharon said, staring at the paper.

She noticed Mike's hands were shaking. "You're going to end up as much of an outcast as the professor was."

"I'm not the one conducting the investigation, remember? With the murders of O'Bannon and Shaw, the state isn't going to allow a hick-town police chief to investigate, especially since I was directly involved in everything. So, really, I don't have any say in how this thing ends up being presented to the outside world. All I can do is tell my story to the next set of investigators and wait to see how it all gets whitewashed."

Sharon shook her head, slowly and painfully. She was tiring and needed rest, but she needed to talk this out even more. "You really think they're going to gloss over everything that happened?"

"Maybe not intentionally," Mike answered, "but think about it. You were there, you saw things with your own eyes that defied conventional explanation. So did I. These incoming investigators, whoever they are, did not. There is absolutely no way they will accept that the spirit of a young woman killed in 1691 was dismembering people as retribution for the death of her baby, and that this aging professor, who most people viewed as a joke, brought it all to a close by sacrificing himself to that spirit. It's just not going to happen. I've spent my entire adult life as a member of the law enforcement community, and I can tell you that much conclusively."

"It just seems so unfair," she said. "He suffered for decades because of his research and now it turns out that he was right about everything, and nobody is going to know?"

"That's not the worst part," Mike answered.

"What could be worse than that?"

"Your friend, Chief Court, a man you described to me as the biggest positive influence in your life, is going to go down in history as a brutal serial killer when all he did was build a house out in the middle of nowhere. He was a victim in this as well, literally a man caught in the wrong place at the wrong time."

Sharon fell silent. She was struggling to stay awake and out of nowhere came a question. "Why the dog?"

"Dog? What dog?"

"You know, the dog," she insisted. "The call we investigated that got this whole ball of shit rolling. The dog that got torn apart up on Route 14. Why in the world would this wayward Native American spirit have done that? It's obvious the dog was killed by the same entity that killed all those people. My question is, why?"

Mike looked at her with a satisfied smile. "And the doctors told me you wouldn't remember anything," he said. "I knew they were wrong."

"Thanks," she answered. "But do you have any theories?"

"Well, I've been wondering about that, too. It doesn't fit with what we've learned from Professor Dye. Unfortunately we can't ask him about it, but my guess is this: Wally Court was a strong man with a strong code of moral conduct, would you say that's an accurate assessment?"

Sharon nodded her head and then grimaced from the pain.

"Absolutely," she said quietly when the discomfort had subsided.

"That's what I figured. My theory, then, is this: he must have known something was happening to him, although he couldn't begin to imagine what it was. He probably thought he was losing his mind, that he was literally going insane. I think he probably fought the possession as long as he could, but he couldn't hold out forever. When the apparition became too strong for Court to control, he went after the dog in one final, desperate attempt to avoid killing another human being. After that, I'm afraid the spirit became so powerful he couldn't fight it. Before long, I imagine the stress on Chief Court's body was so great it killed him. Toward the end he undoubtedly had no control at all over what the entity was forcing him to do."

As Mike spoke, tears began to run silently down Sharon's face. She couldn't stop them.

He wiped them gently away with his fingers and then climbed off the bed.

"You need to get some rest," he said. He took her hand and then leaned over and kissed her forehead.

"None of that," she whispered through her tears. "I want a real kiss."

Mike smiled and shook his head. "I'd never have the willpower to leave if I kissed you the way I want to."

"You say that like it's a bad thing."

He laughed. "It is when you've got serious recovering to do. You lie back and get some sleep, and I'll see you tomorrow morning, bright and early."

He lowered Sharon's hand to the bed, drained his coffee, and prepared to do battle with the crutches. She was asleep before he reached the door.

59

Mike wasted no time moving on to his next task after leaving Sharon asleep in her hospital bed.

He dodged doctors, nurses and visitors on the crutches he was already coming to hate, moving laboriously to Melissa Manheim's hospital room. He entered without knocking or waiting to be invited in. The payback felt better than it should have.

He spoke before the Portland Journal reporter could interrupt him. "How the hell did you wind up in that log cabin?"

Incredibly, Melissa "the Maneater" Manheim had suffered nothing more than a concussion and some bumps and bruises from her run-in with the homicidal spirit. Mike knew she would be the prime source of information for the State Police investigators—along with him, of course—and he was curious as to what, exactly, she may have seen and how much of it she would be willing to admit to.

She looked up at him from her hospital bed, where she was propped up on three plump pillows and surrounded by laptops, telephones, and what looked like some sort of portable fax machine that was busy beeping and spitting out a more or less steady stream of documentation. He pictured Sharon lying in her own bed a few rooms down the hall, nearly immobile and facing a long rehabilitation, and marveled at the unfairness of life.

"Well," she sniffed, "*you* weren't giving me anything I could print, so after you threw me aside at the Sprague bonfire, I marched right off toward the forest. I knew you had assigned your little girlfriend to patrol the bonfire, too, so I figured I would eventually run across her. When I did, I intended to find out if she felt differently than you obviously do regarding the freedom of the press."

"And by that you mean you intended to threaten her with public exposure for sleeping with me. You figured by blackmailing her, you would be able to get the information I wouldn't give you."

"I can't stop you if you choose to see it that way."

"It's not a matter of me seeing it that way, that's how it *is*. But in any event, it's obvious you never found her."

"Why do you say that?"

"You're still more or less in one piece. If you had tried to threaten Sharon Dupont, she would have kicked your ass. You'd have been begging for a serial killer to show up by the time she was done with you. She may look small, but she packs a punch."

"I know why you're here," she told him, interrupting as was her custom and apparently choosing to ignore Mike's comment. "You're on a fishing expedition. You want to know if I'm going to tell the investigators about the broken-down body of that poor man floating rather than walking and about him doing things that no human being could possibly do, especially an old man who—"

"So you saw quite a bit," Mike interrupted. He wondered how she liked it.

"I was knocked silly when that thing flung me into a tree and remained woozy until after you rescued me, which, by the way, seemed to take a lot longer than it should have for a *professional*."

Mike stayed silent, refusing to take the bait.

After a moment she continued. "Anyway, of course I saw quite a bit. I really wasn't injured that badly."

"I hope you're prepared for the investigators to label you a nutcase," he said.

"I've dealt with much tougher than the Maine State Police, believe me," she said dismissively, waving her hand like a petulant princess. "But in any event, no one will label me anything," she continued. Her face was a mask of innocence. "As far as they're going to know, I was unconscious the entire time. I didn't see a thing."

"Are you telling me you're going to withhold evidence from the police in a murder investigation?"

Melissa Manheim snickered. "Come now, Chief," she said. "This isn't your first time around the block, is it? You know as well as I do that if the evidence points toward a supernatural element or any sort of connection to Native American mysticism, it will all be whitewashed away like Tom Sawyer painting the fence. I'm sorry, but poor old Chief Wally Court is going to be the fall guy here, there's simply no way to avoid that."

"And you're comfortable with an innocent man being rail-roaded, even though he's dead? You don't want the truth to come out?"

"I didn't say that," she answered coyly. "There is definitely a bestseller in this, a book waiting to be written, and I hope you don't think I'm bragging when I say that I feel pretty confident I should be the one to write it."

Great, Mike thought. *I wonder what Ken Dye would have to say about this?* Then he decided the professor would probably applaud the idea, in spite of all that had happened to him and the beating his reputation had taken.

Mike shook his head at Melissa Manheim's obstinacy. "Well, I'm glad you're going to be all right," he said, leaning on his crutches and turning toward the door. "Good luck to you, and—"

"Wait," she said quietly. "Please."

He turned. "What is it?"

"I know what that college professor—"

"His name was Ken Dye," Mike interrupted.

"Yes, Ken Dye. I know what Professor Ken Dye did, how he was directly responsible for saving Officer Dupont and me, and I'll never forget it."

Mike listened in amazement and wondered, not for the first time, where she got her information.

"He was quite a guy," he said, not sure where she was going with this.

"Anyway, effective immediately, I am establishing a scholarship fund in Professor Dye's name, to support research into the field of Native American folklore that was so close to his heart. My newspaper will be contributing big bucks, too, you can mark my words on that one."

"I sort of think the University would just as soon Ken Dye

fade off into the sunset with as little fanfare as possible," Mike answered.

At that, Melissa Manheim laughed, the sound echoing off the walls and out into the hospital hallway. "Really, Chief McMahon, I'm starting to believe you actually *did* just fall off the turnip truck."

Mike could feel his ears start to burn as his face turned red.

"Once the money starts coming in, and I will personally ensure it flows like the Penobscot River, the school will do an about-face on the subject of Professor Ken Dye and his research. It'll happen faster than you can say 'ghosties and apparitions.'"

Mike stared at her in slack-jawed amazement. "*You're* going to help rehabilitate the man's legacy?"

"Don't sound so surprised," she answered with a smile. "Like I said, I'm well aware that I am alive right now solely because of his sacrifice. I consider it the least I can do, especially given how much money I expect to make off the book I have already begun writing. It won't hurt me to throw some of that cash the school's way."

"Wow," Mike muttered as he turned back toward the door. "Strange bedfellows."

"Indeed. Interested?" she asked, throwing open her bedcovers in invitation.

Mike didn't think he'd spoken loudly enough to be heard across the hospital room. Apparently, as with nearly everything else regarding Melissa Manheim, he'd been wrong.

"You know what I mean," he said, shaking his head and limping out into the hallway. He dodged a couple of kids streaking down the hall as he pulled the door closed behind him.

Then he leaned reluctantly on the crutches and made his way toward the hospital's parking garage, looking forward to getting back to his apartment. Mike McMahon was late for a hot date with a shower and about twenty hours of sleep.

Epilogue

The early-May sunshine beat down on Revere with an intensity that belied the date. It felt to Mike much more like mid-summer than spring, especially compared with the relative cool of Paskagankee, located so far to the north.

He held Sharon Dupont's hand tightly as they strolled together across the cemetery field, surrounded by centuries-old maples and oaks. In the distance Mike could hear the muted sound of highway traffic. He had almost forgotten the symphonic constancy of tires on pavement and realized he'd already grown to prefer Paskagankee's silence.

Sharon tossed her head to clear her black hair out of her eyes. It had grown back quickly and was now almost as long as it had been prior to last November's emergency brain surgery. Her grip was still weak, thanks to the two broken arms, but seemed to be improving daily with physical therapy.

When Mike had suggested the weekend trip down the seacoast to his old stomping grounds, he knew she suspected the reason. But he didn't say and she didn't ask.

Melissa Manheim's book on the Paskagankee killings was due out within a few weeks, and it would create a media firestorm. The investigation had gone exactly as Mike expected it would: the entire mess was pinned on Chief Walter Court's defenseless shoulders. He had gone mad for some unknown reason and executed six people, tearing their bodies apart in the most grisly fashion imaginable.

How he had managed to dismember six full-grown adults—with no tools, no help, and an arm so badly broken it was nearly falling off his body—was never addressed in the official report.

How he managed to keep coming when Mike McMahon pumped twelve slugs from a semi-automatic pistol into his body was never addressed in the official report, either.

Publication of Manheim's book would focus the world's attention on tiny Paskagankee, Maine, again for a time, just as it had been late last year. News crews would come and shoot their footage for reports that would cast doubt on the State Police investigation, townspeople would be interviewed, theories on the crime spree advanced, a few—but not many—of them even more outlandish than the truth.

Eventually, Mike hoped within a few days of the book's release, some other bizarre story would grab the public's interest and Paskagankee would become just another footnote in the unending news cycle. In the meantime, there was nothing to do but ride out the impending flurry of unwanted publicity and hope it was short-lived.

It was almost time to begin the drive back up I-95 to northernmost New England. Mike and Sharon had eaten an early dinner at one of Mike's favorite Italian restaurants in East Boston, and afterward he'd purchased a single exquisite long-stemmed yellow rose from a street vendor as they strolled the sidewalk back to Mike's truck.

Now the sun dropped toward the horizon in the unseasonable heat as the pair walked hand-in-hand across the cemetery. Mike walked with a sense of purpose that conveyed itself to Sharon.

"You've been here before, haven't you?" she asked.

"Many times," he said tightly, holding her hand the way a hungry man might clutch a slice of pizza.

They reached a small granite marker, tucked away in a remote corner of the field and decorated very simply with a carving of a baby angel winging her way to heaven. On the stone were written the words, "SARAH MELENDEZ, JANUARY 12, 2003 – JULY 16, 2010. REST IN PEACE."

Mike placed the flower on it, saying nothing.

Sharon looked at him closely. "What a beautiful stone."

PASKAGANKEE

"Thanks," Mike replied.

"You bought it?"

He nodded. "The grandparents had no money. They couldn't afford to memorialize her. I thought, under the circumstances, that it was the least I could do. Of course, they wouldn't accept anything from me—I can't say I blame them—so I purchased it and had it sent to them anonymously. I wanted that little girl to have a fitting memorial."

They stood silently, listening to the muted sounds of the late-afternoon Revere traffic, of commuters rushing home to their families and people frenziedly living their lives. It all seemed far away from this little wooded corner and the peace and quiet of the gravesite.

Finally, still without speaking, they turned as one and began walking back the way they had come. The grass was a carpet, intensely thick and green and lush, reborn after the long winter.

They held hands and moved in comfortable silence through the cemetery, ready to begin the long trip back to Paskagankee.

To be the first to learn about new releases, and for the opportunity to win free ebooks, signed copies of print books, and other swag, please take a moment to sign up for Allan Leverone's email newsletter at AllanLeverone.com.

Reader reviews are hugely important to authors looking to set their work apart from the competition. If you have a moment to spare, please consider taking a moment to leave a brief, honest review of *Paskagankee* at Amazon, Goodreads, or your favorite review site, and thank you!

Also from Allan Leverone

Thrillers

Parallax View: A Tracie Tanner Thriller
All Enemies: A Tracie Tanner Thriller
The Omega Connection: A Tracie Tanner Thriller
The Hitler Deception: A Tracie Tanner Thriller
The Kremlyov Infection: A Tracie Tanner Thriller
Final Vector
The Organization: A Jack Sheridan Pulp Thriller
Trigger Warning: A Jack Sheridan Pulp Thriller

Horror/Dark Thrillers

Mr. Midnight
After Midnight
Paskagankee
Revenant: A Paskagankee Novel Book Two
Wellspring: A Paskagankee Novel Book Three
Linger: Mark of the Beast (written with Edward Fallon)

Novellas

The Becoming

Flight 12: A Kristin Cunningham Thriller

Story Collections

Postcards from the Apocalypse
Uncle Brick and the Four Novelettes
Letters from the Asylum: Three Complete Novellas
The Tracie Tanner Collection: Three Complete Thriller Novels